Slob

Rex Miller was a teenage 'radio prodigy' who quit the broadcasting business at its highest level (he was a Chicago jock, and doing voice-overs for accounts like Dodge Cars and William Penn Cigars) to try his hand as a nostalgia entrepreneur. Today his mail-order business is one of the most successful of its kind. Rex Miller describes his life as a 'perpetual escapist daydream' shaped by the American dream merchants. The initial trilogy of Eichord novels reflect his obsession with the on-going, larger-than-life battle between good and evil.

Rex Miller

SLOB

Pan Books
London, Sydney and Auckland

First published in Great Britain 1988 by Pan Books Ltd,
Cavaye Place, London SW10 9PG
9 8 7 6 5 4 3 2
© Rex Miller 1987
ISBN 0 330 30438 0
Printed and bound in Great Britain by
Cox and Wyman Ltd, Reading, Berks

PROLOGUE

Her first awareness of him is a presence. Unseen. A stench. It comes around the corner before him, preceding his physical entrance, in a sickening downdraft that washes over her and she recoils from the smell which is a combination of rank body odor and sewage and sulfurous stink of rotten food, and it assails her nostrils with the foulness of evil. Then seeing him she flinches again, fighting to regain her composure, resolutely, politely, trained to serve the public, a smile fixing itself to her mouth as he approaches the counter in this awful, stinking swirl of poisonous air.

He grunts out a monosyllabic name, not his real one, and she mumbles something as she hands him his order and checks the amount. It is exactly forty dollars to the penny. She tells him and he produces the money. He hands her the exact amount in filthy, sweat-soaked, crumpled bills that she can barely stand to touch. She thanks him, ringing the order on the cash register and vowing to wash her hands immediately. He swoops up the large sack of food in a giant paw and lumbers away, leaving behind the stinging, terrible odor and the paralyzing, heart-hammering fear of some imagined and unspeakable threat. To her he will always be "forty dollars worth of egg rolls."

He is the one they called CHAINGANG in Viet-

nam. He was the one who they said back in Marion
had taken a human life for nearly every pound of his
weight, and he weighed nearly five hundred pounds.
He is death personified, demoniacal, unstoppable,
bloodthirsty, and very, very real. He wrenches open
the door of the stolen car and tosses the sack of food
into the passenger seat as he crashes down behind the
wheel, the springs groaning in protest. He thinks how
easily he could have killed the aloof woman behind
the counter in there. How pleasant it would have been
to sink a sharp object into her throat, ripping down
across the breasts and then the abdomen and then
gutting her and taking the parts he liked the best. And
the thought of this fills his head with a scarlet roar.

Ed and
Edie Lynch

She was one of those women who could look like eleven different people depending on what she felt like, what she was wearing, and when you saw her. At thirty-eight, Edith Emaline (rhymes with valentine) Lynch was the woman you see but can't quite describe five minutes after you leave the checkout lane of the Piggily Wiggily. She's the sort of vaguely good-looking one in the second row at PTA. The anonymous-featured Wednesday-night mother whose turn it is to drive the kids in to church. But catch her when the moon is right and her self-esteem is in overdrive, give her a few minutes to pull herself together, and another Edie steps out on those long, long, shapely legs that seem to just keep going. And you've got a knockout.

Knocked out was more like it at the moment. Stray wisps of hair loose around that wide, interesting although not precisely pretty face, she wasn't at her peak. She hadn't had a pang of loneliness for Ed hit her like that for weeks, and when she dusted the mirror frame in the hallway she had seen a sort of a shadow or something and she jumped halfway out of her skin and felt her heart nearly jump out of her chest. Christ! Oh, my God. For not more than a fraction of a second she thought she'd seen something, not in the mirror exactly but in the shadows and just a hint of movement and Lord have mercy she'd just had the feeling Weirdo was outside the window again watching.

Weirdo was a totally harmless but maddeningly incorrigible old handyman who had all the women in the neighborhood looking over their shoulders. He was a peeping Tom, as her mother's generation had said, a voyeur whose major thrill was to peer in windows. He had never done anything, and in spite of having been rousted by the police endlessly, locked up a few times for short periods, and having generated a sizable rap package at the local constabulary, he'd never actually committed any crime beyond being a public nuisance. His peeping misdemeanors paled in a big city where even the affluent yuppie suburbs had their fair share of raincoat flashers, hugger-muggers, dong danglers, and wienie waggers. Still. Who knew for *sure*? Maybe one day Weirdo would glimpse something that might turn him around and he wouldn't just look in the window, he'd COME in the window.

After having laughed with the coffee-crowd gals about the Weirdo stories, he'd paid her a social call—and it hadn't been all that funny. The first sign of him had been the tracks that they kept finding around the house from time to time. At last they figured out what it was. It was the wooden box Weirdo dragged around to carry his tools in. Suddenly the jokes about him doing "odd jobs" had come back to haunt her. He was coming around, presumably at night, peering in the windows, thinking God only knows what thoughts. Ed went crazy. Finally they called the police and the cops picked the old guy up.

He promised he wouldn't come around Edie's house. And since they'd never actually caught him looking in, the cops let him go with a tough warning. If anyone saw him anywhere NEAR the Lynch house again they'd throw away the key. He was his usual meek, apologetic, harmless old self. She knew he was still out there somewhere doing his thing and scaring housewives and kids half to death. He wasn't so harmless, Edie thought to herself, if he gave somebody a heart attack.

It was just at that second, with her thinking of her own pounding heart as she took the rag and squirted Windex on the mirror and started rubbing, that she thought about how it had been done to Ed and then she had just let it all come back flowing over her again and for just that moment she squinted her eyes shut as tightly as she could and pretended that the shadow had been Ed sneaking up behind her the way he liked to do, and she recalled the last time between them and how sweet it would always be to her.

He'd come home early and Lee Anne had been over at Jeanne's and they'd had most of the weekend to themselves. They were never great, imaginative lovers. Sex had been fine between them but no big thing. For a while she'd kind of worried about that but no matter what the other women said or what she read in those magazines she subscribed to and picked up at the grocery store, instinctively she knew it was all right between them. They just didn't go for anything kinky or far out. Just the plain old-fashioned way was plenty okay for Eddie. He was gentle but he never wasted a whole lot of time with it. It was something that he enjoyed, in other words, but it hadn't occupied a big part of their shared life.

She remembered how prosaic and boring the conversation had been. They'd talked about Lee coming down with flu, about the contract he'd picked up from Rathmusson Farms, how Sandi and Mike wanted them all to go to Gatlinburg again that year and split the cost, how the Jehovah's Witnesses had come by again that day and left a *Watchtower,* how you shouldn't pick up hitchhikers anymore, all kinds of typical, thrilling stuff that a married couple discusses. She remembered that dialogue as very special, though, since it was their last time together. She still recalled how he'd told her they needed new locks, that he'd seen something about those chains being worthless and the word *dead bolt* had lingered in her mind. The word echoed around in her mind now with its dark imagery. *Dead bolt.*

She thought of how vulnerable she was, alone in the big house with its windows everywhere and the shadows and how the neighborhood was so empty at this time of the day. She thought of a news story she'd read in last night's paper about a little boy being abducted not far from them. Somebody could grab Lee even in the few hundred feet between the school door and her car. God. It was all enough to make you scream. Nobody was safe anymore, she thought. But why *Ed*? He was such a good man.

"Ritualized," the detectives had said when they were describing the way he had been mutilated. Mike's folks had died like that in a way. Mike had been Eddie's best friend and his wife Sandi was Edie's best friend. It had made for such a great foursome because even the kids could play together, Edie's eight-year-old and Sandi's youngest. And Mike's mom and dad had won a trip to Japan and the plane had crashed into Mount Fuji and everyone had lost their lives and Mike had never recovered from it. There had been something almost ceremonial in the mass death. She could never quite explain it but that had somehow made it seem even more awful. And then to have someone do that to Ed.

The thoughts were all running together and she started to squirt cleaner on the mirror again and realized she'd been polishing the same circles over and over. It was squeaky bright. It was her eyes that were misting over. She gasped involuntarily and pulled out one of the dining-room chairs and let herself slump down in it momentarily, but then she snapped right out of it. Stop feeling sorry for yourself, missy. You've got to clean this house and go shopping and you've got a fine little eight-year-old darling of a daughter to care for. And none of this is going to get done with you sitting here wishing Ed back. And she jumped out of the chair and attacked the household chores.

With any luck Lee Anne would never see any of the

old newspaper headlines. The ones that said "MAN FOUND MUTILATED" were bad enough. But the tabloids had started calling the murderer "The Lonely Hearts Killer." It was a phrase that still hovered over Edie like a cloud full of acid rain. And now, two years later, the name was back in the papers again. He was still out there somewhere. That—that THING that had killed Ed and taken his heart.

Death

The mist thickens, solidifies, begins dripping, settling over him like a wet, clinging blanket. Dropping down over the trees like a vast, ominous shroud that drapes the triple canopy in moist blackness. The night noises intensify. The air is redolent with the smell of rotting fish and the presence of death. This is cadaver country.

The spooky killer's moon has all but vanished now, the yellow almost gone, and yet he sees HE SEES each blade of grass, each slime-covered twig, every veiny leaf and every drop of every bead of moisture rain mist dew dampness glistening clearly sparkling and dancing on the leaves. HE SEES. It is not just night vision. He sees without seeing. Sensing would perhaps be a better word. Sensing the atoms and molecules of the air and the matter and the nothingness of the dark. He owns the night now.

The presence of death stands and breathes slowly, deeply of his nightworld. He hears the trees whisper and laugh there in the wet blackness. It is the faraway tinkle and shatter of jagged vampire laughter and it makes Death smile his huge, radiant, dimpled smile. In his mind's eye he sees a coven of witches moving now, gliding through the jungle night like a breeze rustling through rice paper, and he slows wills slows his massive heartbeat almost to a standstill.

It is the lurking presence of black, oily death waiting there in the jungle scarcely breathing, unmoving, still, infinitely patient, unspeakably evil. It senses the movement that is coming down the worn hardball trail, out there in the night somewhere beyond the great triple-canopied jungle edge, across the fields and paddies and beyond the far treeline, coming down the hardball that is their nighttime four-lane blacktop, moving quietly through the darkness.

Tick . . . Tick . . .

But he is not in the jungle now he is driving in a stolen car, driving carefully if aimlessly, driving the darkened streets of a strange town, sensors purring, tuned, vigilant, concentrating on his surroundings. He is never lost, confused, he has his strong inner compass that always points him back on trail. His mind is a heat-seeking device that homes in on the warmth of a vulnerable human heartbeat. He likes it here, driving without purpose through these cozy suburbs. His smile is wide and dimpled. He beams with pleasure at the thought of the families inside those houses.

Death likes to drive through strange, darkened, suburban streets at night, sightseeing as you would take your loved ones to look at the Christmas lights on a chill and snowy December's eve, bundled up and filled with good cheer, your heart filling with joy at the sight of the brightly lit yards and homes bedecked in multi-colored displays and scenes of the Nativity. He warms at the sight of the golden lights, the *mystery* of the darkened homes full of loving families. He loves it.

For to Death a drive through the suburban tract homes of idle America is to take a sightseeing tour through the strange, wondrous, and exotic locale of some unknown country. The residential landscape at night is as alien to this creature as if it was a vision of a far distant planet. Who could live in that home with those twinkling, golden lights, he wonders in something approaching awe. What are they doing in there? In that expensive, neat, well-tended home over there he senses that there are human beings living their quiet lives behind those walls.

And in the foreign landscape he sees, senses, an endless smorgasbord of humanity there for the taking. An infinite variety of humans all happy and snug in their little, brightly lit shelters, safe from all harm behind their ridiculously thin walls and flimsy doors with their televisions sets and pets and toys, and as he imagines the boundless delights that await his pleasure that are his for the TAKING he can taste the thrill of it and if he doesn't stop the spreading heat of it that is coming over him he will pull up in one of these concrete driveways and go kick down a door and feed this rapacious, awesome appetite of his, and he lets it roar up into his head and it is the color of blood and it has the rich, red, bitingly cuprous smell and taste of life's fluid.

And now he is out of the car and moving toward humans again, moving through the darkness on those powerful treetrunk legs, faster than anyone alive has ever seen him move, and in his right hand he is holding a heavy coil of taped tractor-strength safety chain. In a few seconds he will see the little people coming down the hardball there in the blackness and he feels the strong human heartbeat nearby and he churns ahead into the pitch black where the human is.

The blunt, thick fingers shaped like huge, steel cigars lash out with the coil of chain and it cracks into something solid and there is a scream and his face beams with the joy of it using that thick, rock-hard wrist and forearm of bulging muscle with the fluid snapping motion that he's worked on until it is a part of him all smooth and automatic as he makes the lethal chain smash out, uncoiling and striking like a big snake whipping out and splitting the human head open snakewhipping into the man killing him in that one powerful smacking wet bloodsmear.

And the hot, red, rushing thing has set his brain on fire and Death has dropped the dripping links of chain and is slashing out with that big, razor-sharp bowie all wild and insane with his surging pressure cooker exploding as he rips the human open taking the fresh heart in a tearing, gutting, rending of flesh and offal and bloody organs and bone as the profluent river of Death floods the night and nothing stops a river.

Jack Eichord —Reformed Drunk

Even nine years later I could still taste the sharp and smoky bite of Tennessee sour-mash sippin' whiskey. I could remember just the way it looked all honey golden and amber there in the glass, the first Blackjack Rocks of the day, four fingers of Jack Daniel's black label sloshed into a big, serious drinking glass loaded with ice cubes. And the way that first sip tasted, the sharp kick of it as it burned down to warm your innards. God, how I loved to drink. And how I hated to stop.

I pulled my life together nine years ago. I remember it vividly even now. It was one of those suicidal Mondays when the pervasive mood was bleak, hopelessly dour, wintry, and downbeat. Another motel room. Another awful day full of depression, lots of scary surprises, hidden horror, coming confusion that would want to make you go back inside and pull the blinds shut. One of those cold, anxious, bone-chilling days you could still recall from the sixth grade, bundling up in a sweater and then some great, heavy coat topped with hat and muffler, on your way nowhere, facing the desolation of imponderable, countless weeks of nothingness before the next vacation when a kid could live again. It was like that and a hundred times worse. A killer hangover kicked on the door of my mind.

I was out east at the time, jobless and purposeless, a

bust-out drunk about ten cases away from a relief mission. Getting close. I sat in this cockroach motel drinking Black Jack at 8:25 A.M. Aimless and helpless. I didn't know why I was awake this early. Why I was in this motel. What had happened the day before. Or where I was going. I went out and got in my car, the interior of which smelled like a distillery, and that's when it began.

I still recall the feel of those cold seat covers and the way my hot breath fogged up the windshield as I sat there with the DTs—I'd had the shakes before but never like that. I felt like my whole body was going to come apart. I could hear my own nerve ends screaming in pain. And that's where it hit me, right there in the front seat of that old Chevy, it hit me that I had become an alcoholic. Because in a frightening moment of icy reality, I realized that I had forgotten who I was. I actually wasn't sure of who was inside my skin. I could remember my own name but nothing else. It was so monstrously disorienting that it scared me sober.

I remember I cranked down the window, head throbbing like a set of drums at a rock concert, and I poured my booze out onto the parking lot. That was the last time I ever took a serious drink. I'll still have a cold beer or two. Even three. But the booze is just a memory now. Beginning that very day I started pulling my life back into shape. Within a year I was totally off the sauce, back on the force in the Midwest, and married, with a pregnant wife.

A lot of people have wondered how I quit "so easy." I couldn't explain it to anybody else. Think of it this way. Do you smoke cigarettes? If so, imagine a doctor you really trust coming to you and saying, "Okay, pal, if you smoke ONE MORE CIGARETTE you will die. Instantly. That's it. Good-bye." Unless you are the exception, even the five-pack-a-day folks will probably stop lighting up. Fear is an amazing thing. Imagine if the Surgeon General could put on a pack of weeds IF YOU SMOKE THESE IT WILL KILL YOU. It would probably work a bit more effectively than the current pussyfoot disclaimer. There was never any thought of drinking for me. I was through with it.

But I still loved the thought of the booze. I really liked to drink. I could still enjoy just thinking about walking into some dark, salty bar about two-thirty in the afternoon and watching the bartender pour my first double or triple shot. Maybe it's something a drunk never gets out of his system. Perhaps your body chemistry never goes into remission or readjusts to doing without. And I never doubted that inside my middle-aged skin I was still every inch a drunk. As the saying went, the only difference between being an alcoholic and being a drunk was that a drunk didn't have to go to meetings. I guess I'm a drunk and not an alcoholic. I'd like to say *reformed* drunk but I've read enough of the literature to know you don't press your luck.

For insurance I still had a real clear picture of that day sitting in that refrigerator of a car, gasping for air as the sledgehammer-anvil chorus worked out on my head, smelling that car's stink and trying to remember exactly who and what I was and where I was headed.

I woke up alone as I often did, not getting off on hookers and not being the type who gets lucky with strangers that often, and didn't waste any time getting ready for work. Work was my whole life now. I had been alone so long that I'd wiped most of the memories of Joan out of my mind. Joanie had been gorgeous, seductive, and a rich preppie to boot. I blew it with her. First with the job, then with the booze, and then with the job again. Looking back on it, which I no longer bothered to do, we probably didn't have that much going beyond a fierce physical compatibility. She hated The Job. It dominated our lives, of course, and quite rightly she viewed it as her competition.

So Joanie would try a little harder to be sexier, and she started taking courses in gourmet cooking, and reading these self-improvement books, and every conversation started to be a kind of verbal duel. She'd wake up each morning trying to see who was ahead, and it would be The Job 31, Joan 14, and so she'd seduce me before I could get my first cup of coffee down, and even that wasn't such bad duty at first. It was only when she couldn't compete against the "other woman," the bitch that took me away in the night, that our thing started wearing thin. A call was enough to send her right up the wall. And one night the damn phone rang as she was serving up the latest in her great culinary experiments and she overheard me saying I was on my way—and that tore it.

It was kind of funny looking back on it. She picked up a piece of her mother's Havilland and walked up to me and broke it over my head, called me a sonofabitch, and stomped into the bedroom in a symphony of slammed doors. It doesn't sound like much. It didn't hurt much. I have a thick skull as many of my colleagues will readily testify. But our relationship shattered like the china from that moment. It just sort of shrugged its shoulders and disintegrated.

Now when I woke up I'd try to get out of my small apartment as soon as I could, and I was very seldom there before bedtime. I'd gone from alcoholic to workaholic and I was thriving on the regimen. And it hadn't hurt the career. I'd been lucky a couple of times and developed a reputation, partially undeserved, for being one of the nouveau experts in certain types of homicides, the so-called serial murders.

When Jack Eichord poured out his last Daniel's and threw himself into the business of crime solving he became something of a textbook classic. In a city where the way of life on The Job is the "pad" or "arm," a kind of acceptable blue-suit payola that evolved from stolen apples and freebie doughnuts up through complete wardrobes and home entertainment centers, and then into the natural progression of dope and dope money—Eichord was a glaring anachronism.

The police in his midwestern city had excused corruption and stealing for so many years that it was regarded as simply the way to play catch-up for the short salaries and the absence of hazard pay. Nobody talked about it. It was just the way things were done. It started at the top level and worked its way down through the deputy chiefs and the rest of the top brass and filtered down through the street-beat cops, traffic cops, and flat-footed detectives.

But Eichord kept his principles because he didn't care about anyone else's corruption, he was only interested in solving murders. And if there were as many thieves on the force as off it, that wasn't his worry. He didn't like it much but he knew he couldn't do anything about it and it didn't keep him awake nights. He'd take the little stuff so as not to call undue attention, the free cop meals that went with the territory, but the rest of the goodies he passed on. And nobody else cared. He wasn't a boat rocker. He was just a little weird.

He had what even the worst cops had to admit was a basic good Cop Attitude. He never saw himself as a white knight or a big-shot crime crusher. There was no elitist attitude, even after Jack got tagged for the elite squad McTuff, and he actually didn't feel that he was any better a cop than his co-workers so they all got along okay. That kind of an ego thing can be sensed intuitively by even the most desensitized and stupid police officer. And it wasn't there. He was just interested in getting the job done. He loved solving murders.

McTuff, as it was pronounced, was the force's work name for the commissioner's Major Crimes Task Force, MCTF, which had been formed to handle unusual major crimes of violence. The unit had special funding that took the whole thing somewhat out of the realm of local law enforcement, plugging the machine into a small but highly sophisticated network of similarly focused agencies around the nation. McTuff as symbolized by their version of the take-a-bite-out-of-crime dog in the trenchcoat, was partly theatrics, part image tap dance, and part computerized anticrime think tank. It would let somebody in, say Pittsburgh, tap in to areas like Threat Assessment and Counterterrorism, formerly sole domain of the feds, or plug the boys in Oklahoma City directly into the latest serial murders in Los Angeles. And all of these capabilities gave the unit at least the surface trappings of an elite squad.

But Eichord was no elitist. He was just another cop. He saw himself as one more cog in the big machine. And he lived for the work. He had an ego like anybody else, and a healthy ego is mandatory in The Job, but it got its strokes from accomplishment as opposed to accolades or honors. He could have cared less what somebody else thought about him. He wanted to be liked to a certain extent, but beyond an ordinary human desire to have his fellow man think well of him, he was into the work for its own rewards. And that made him something of an overachiever, when coupled with its proclivity for sixteen-hour workdays.

McTuff and its counterparts on the West Coast, out east, and across the country, had no century-old traditions of police work to enrich its heritage. Serial murders had seemed to spring out of the sixties like some kind of wartime anomaly or mutation caused by the poisonous karma of the Vietnam era. The Zodiac killings, the Manson Family kills; like all fads, the serial murders had swept the country from California eastward, leaving a wake of characters whose names would soon be a part of legend. Twenty-six bodies in Florida. Thirty-five more in Chicago. Two hundred here. Three to four hundred there. The serial murders got more and more bizarre. And the more raw, new data emerged, the greater the horror stories. Like the specter of terrorism itself, the concept of mass murderers was taking on a kind of spiritual glow. And we tried to understand the horrors of "Reverend" Jones and his mass suicide, and a clown killer of boys whose first two names were John Wayne. The whole thing was beginning to blur.

Cops around the country were staying up late burning lots of midnight and three A.M. oil trying to plug into it all. Working with the shrinks and the self-styled prognostics, fakes, clairvoyants, psychics, frauds, show-biz folk, anybody who might help them get a handle on this strange phenomenon that had the whole country terrorized. Was there a profile of a serial murderer? Who was he? Where did he come from? How could he be spotted early on? Computers whirred, and clicked, and billions of facts and opinions were stored, retrieved, and stored again. It was out of this milieu that Jack Eichord, professional crime solver, emerged as something of a new eighties celebrity. A genuine, dyed-in-the-wool semi-expert on that scary, hairy thing called the serial murderer.

It would be inaccurate to say that relatively few murders are solved. Relatively few *difficult* murders are solved. A surprisingly large number of killings go into the files to remain theoretically "open" but with the assailants running high-and-dry free. Most or at least many of the tough crimes go unsolved. Ma stabs Pa in the neighborhood bar fight. That one gets wrapped real fast. Bubba shoots Tyrone in front of eight witnesses. That one's off the books lickety-split. The unknown John Doe in the trunk of the abandoned car over on South Twenty-eighth—that one may end up in the files to gather cobwebs. Whatever else you want to say about a cop's balls, they're not crystal. And the old "run those fingerprints down to the lab" bit works on TV but not often in real life.

Eichord knew how you solved murders. Tough, long, boring hours of legwork and homework. A web of carefully cultivated, secret informants. Logic. The willingness to put in an eight-hour day. Take twenty minutes for a hamburger and coffee and back for the rest of the night. Waiting. Waiting by telephones that never rang or never stopped ringing. Waiting in cold, lonely plants, eyes burning from smoke or lack of sleep, trying to concentrate and not miss the subject under surveillance. Questions. A thousand questions asked over and over and over to 999 people who either didn't know, thought they knew and didn't, or knew and were stonewalling. And then maybe—just maybe—

you got lucky at a quarter to ten and one of the questions got answered and put you back on the path. Homicide.

It clearly wasn't for everybody. But Jack Eichord thrived on good, solid detective work. He loved it. It filled all the empty places inside him and he let it engulf him in the job and he breathed it and lived it every waking hour. He'd been in clothes for nine years. Half of that on the McTuff thing. He'd caught a homicide of a teenage girl a few years back and run with it. It was the third death in a run of what could be serial murders. He wallowed in it. Got down in the filth of it. Let it take him down. And when the next body was found he'd already exhausted a few of his theories and he was right on top of it. He got lucky. He was there in the office when the special phone number rang and it was a sick junkie informant looking to get well. He knew not to call with garbage. He had something. He'd worked to get something. He gave Eichord the killer.

It was a big thing locally. The murderer was a dentist. Young, good-looking guy. Turned out to be bisexual and into the leather scene. A real sicko who liked to hurt the girls when he took them off. It got miles of ink, Dr. Demented Captured!—film at eleven. Jack Eichord found out that he didn't like being a celebrity. He wouldn't give interviews. An absolute clam. That made it worse. You don't tell the press no on a hot story. They'll just make stuff up and you end up looking even weirder. They're *still* trying to interview Garbo for heaven's sake. He learned about the press the hard way.

The Lonely Hearts Murders in Chicago came to him because of all that undue ink and media spoonfeed. Chicago came reaching out for him through the McTuff chain of command, and one day his chief sent him packing off to the Windy, his old stamping grounds, My Kinda Town, Chicago Is. He felt like an idiot, winging in on a first-class ticket from the CPD as Mr. Crime Crusher to the rescue. Too ridiculous. He was just another flatfoot. Why me, Lord, he asked silently, as the big jet dropped down over the luckless folks who had bought real estate dead bang in the O'Hare flight path.

Chicago, in the hands of a lesser cop, could have been a horror story all its own. In the hands, that is to say, of a less-controlled ego the first day on could have been a disaster of a downhill slide. He came in the way he always did, all self-effacing and colorless, just friendly enough and sincere enough to win over the ones that hadn't decided, and oblivious enough to the others that his coming was an easy transition. Inside the first week they were asking him to their homes for dinner and the honcho in charge of the Lonely Hearts cop shop had Jack calling him by his nickname "Lou."

Eichord was on the street most of the time. Renewing old acquaintances, making new ones everywhere he went, asking questions, and listening hard to those answers. He was a helluva listener. All the time letting Chicagoland come back to him like a lake where you swam as a youngster. Letting the current move him like the wind on the lakefront. Listening. Moving into the guts of the city. Getting to know her again. Hearing her pulse beat. Waiting.

Sylvia
Kasikoff

Does it matter a whit how a person dies? Do you care whether you die in bed asleep, dreaming of verdant fields in Scotland, or plunged deep into the wetness of hot, full-tilt sex? If the coronary is relatively painless, what does it matter? Death takes you and you are a memory. Death has a way of sandpapering the circumstances of the death and the status of the decedent. If you die by being shot by an unknown perp who takes your heart there in a dark alley near West Erie and leaves your blood-drenched, mutilated corpse for the snapshot scrapbook of a crime photographer, is that somehow a worse death than a president succumbing to gunshot wounds while comatose on a blood-soaked emergency-ward gurney? The only difference is the latter pictures may get a wider circulation.

And what of the assassin or assassins unknown? You are scoped, with a Mannlicher-Carcano, a ridiculous mail-order carbine, a piece of dreck, and—just for argument's sake, let's say a second weapon. Cross fire. You're a dead man. Is this appropriately presidential, somehow, as opposed to the decedent with the missing organ? Probably not. We die a death. It doesn't seem to matter much how, or what, or why, or where—or even who. You can hope for a minimum of pain, a modicum of dignity, a maximum of privacy, and that's about the best you can do.

But then on the other hand, there are some deaths so ignominious and awful that we shudder at the nightmare suggestion of such an end. Some deaths seem designed to kill you again and again, taking you by inches, letting you contemplate the moment when life's flame winks out as you cringe in screaming, fearful terror. The woman in the field was about to die one of those deaths. Not the worst imaginable by any means, but a brutalizing shocker to someone pampered and protected and—like most of us—isolated from the cruelties and depredations of the street life.

At first it appeared that he had no dick, she thought to herself, irrationally, in the frightening perplexity of the moment. She thought "thing" not dick, but all the same. It wasn't enough that she was about to be raped and murdered and perhaps even tortured brutally by this hideous, waddling mastadon of a madman, this fat, stinking horror that had suddenly overturned her life, but to be assaulted by some prickless FREAK only added to her overwhelming nausea, terror, and discombobulation.

The good-looking, youngish brunette, nude, flat on her back, terrorized to the point of paralysis, stared wide-eyed at the huge, gross figure that hovered above her as she lay there helpless on the rough blanket. He was enormously fat, a moving mound of flesh, and as he stood there slobbering over her, he did indeed appear to have no penis. He was the one they had built that Vietnam spike team around, the one called CHAINGANG.

Actually Daniel Bunkowski's genitalia was normal, perhaps even slightly larger than average, but his sex was covered by cascading rolls of fat that encircled his gut like ugly, rubbery truck tires.

"On your knees," he mumbled as he dug around in the lower of the fat rolls and produced the wet end of a pink cock which he held daintily between two fingers the size of big, steel cigars. "Suck that, bitch," he commanded.

She started to run from him, instinctively, just as she remembered that one of her hands was handcuffed to a device that was wired to a large tree nearby. They were near some farmer's fence row, on an army blanket that he'd thrown over some weeds at the edge of a wooded area near the road where she was now parked. If only she could somehow manage to get loose and make a run for it.

It had all happened in a heartbeat of nightmare reality. She came over the crest of hill on her way home from grocery shopping, doing maybe forty or forty-five in the Datsun, and the man was standing right there in the middle of the road all of a sudden, a great big man waving his arms, and she almost ran him down before she could get her vehicle to brake to a stop.

She smashed one of her expensively shod feet, almost standing on the brake pedal, the Datsun fishtailing along the gravel to a rubber-peeling stop. She was so angry at first. He hadn't moved except to wave his arms, and she was running late anyway, and he had this look of great concern on his face as he kept yelling something she couldn't hear. Why doesn't he come around to the side? she thought.

"What?" She mouthed through the windshield. He appeared friendly somehow, and certainly not menacing despite his huge, ursiform appearance, and in fact stayed around in front of the vehicle as he continued to yell something to her, doing his usual complete and flawless little mini-job of method acting.

She had the window almost all the way down, still unable to hear what he was saying and she asked him loudly, "What? I still can't hear you."

"I'm sure sorry, ma'am," he was saying politely as he came waddling around by her side of the Datsun, "we've had a problem on down by the [something, it sounded like France Place] there." He spoke quickly, that deceptive look of great concern on his face, talking very fast as he came around the side and leaned down, and she was wondering if that road had washed out again when, as he was laying down his bland camouflage of conversation, speaking some gibberish to her, she felt herself immobilized as this hulking, giant *presence* froze her to the seat, reaching in and taking the ignition keys, switching off the engine as he did so, pressing her back, pulling on the hand brake, opening the door all in a smooth, practiced series of rapid hand movements.

"Listen," he rumbled as he reached for the seat adjustment below. "Listen to me very carefully and you won't be hurt or molested in any way. Listen—now," he admonished in a deep, rumbling, basso profundo, "don't scream or try to attract attention or I will hurt you. I do not wish to harm you or bother you in any way. Do you understand what I'm saying? Nod if you understand me." She nods like a trained Shetland.

"You must obey me or I will hurt you. Neither of us want this. First, I want you to push the seat back to the farthest position it will go. Now *do it!*" She is shaking so badly she can barely find the release and she jumps as she grabs his hand, which is covering it. He roughly shoves the seat back, slamming her with the impact like car-crash whiplash. Obviously he is just teaching her to obey his orders. "Very good. Now you will come with me and do exactly as I say. Follow me? Nod." She nods about twelve times.

In the few seconds it takes for him to look up and down the road and double-check the field beside the road he gives her a rumbling, terse set of instructions about following orders, not making a scene, all the usual things he says to a potential victim as they lock with fright. She is now nearing that fear-paralysis stage and he has other ideas for her so he snaps her out of it.

A paw closes about her thin wrist and encircles it like the jaws of a mighty, steel workbench vise. She is unceremoniously jerked out of the car and feels herself being transported through the air, dragged over into the road ditch where he retrieves a huge duffel bag. The bag, one you or I couldn't even get off the ground, is lifted as you'd pick up a small stack of books. He grabs a blanket off the top of the duffel and hurls the big bag back into the ditch, and they are heading out across the nearby field, he is carrying her really, and her high heels touch ground only every fifth or sixth step.

"Smile," he commands her, and before it can register on her dazed brain she is snapped through the air like a helpless puppet. *"Smile!"* She plasters a ludicrous grimace across her face in compliance and they reach the near fence row.

"Now. You must listen to me *very* carefully if you want to survive this day." He is snapping a pair of steel and teflon handcuffs on her and fixing some sort of chain to a nearby tree trunk as he speaks. "I will not hurt you badly unless you resist me, scream, try to attract attention, or otherwise irritate me in any way. If you do exactly as I say, you'll be allowed to go home soon. Nod your head and tell me if you understand."

She nods again as a trained pony would paw the ground, with careful, methodical movements, and says in a dry hoarseness, "I—uh—understand."

"Good. Now you're starting to cry. I do *not* want you crying. Stop." She cannot stem the flood and bursts into tears.

WWWHHHHAAAAAPPPPP! She is slapped harder than she has ever been struck in her life. Smacked by a hand like a steel frying pan. It smashes her down to the ground and all but knocks her unconscious. She sees bright blue stars for an instant and then a shock wave of pain brings her back fully alert. She is crying openly now so he takes it down a peg and gentles her a bit.

"I'm very sorry I had to do that but you have to act normally. I do not like crying. If you start crying again now, I'm going to hit you again and it will hurt you.

You are crying now. You must stop, do you understand?"

"Eh—I—uh—I'm sor—sorry."

"Stop!" She wills herself to shut off the tears in a snuffling, sniffing back of the flow. She tries to breathe deeply and concentrate.

"Do you know what I want you to do next?" He is peeling off his shirt and dropping his pants, which are as big as a large flag. She shakes her head no.

"Get over here and suck it. Do it now." She tries to obey, trying to take the hideous thing in her mouth, begins to gag, and draws back instinctively, involuntarily, and she is in lots of pain again. He has those steel fingers in her long hair, which is knotted into a ball, and he pulls her forward onto him. He is stiffening and growing as he gets rougher with her and she can barely take him in her mouth fully.

He rams his erect member back into her throat and she chokes on it but she can't get her head away to breathe and before she can stop her own actions she bites down reflexively.

"You bit me!" He screams. Holding her hair in that left-handed vise, he pulls his dick out to its fullest length with his right hand, pushing back his lower fat roll as he does so and trying to see if she has done any visible damage to his already-shrinking penis.

For a beat he is inert. Lifeless. Then his other persona emerges, springing like Frankenstein from out of whatever abiogenetic origin spawns living matter from nothingness. A backfist like a shotput rips through the air slamming into her face with the loud, resounding crack that is unmistakably bone. Her neck snaps from the mighty blow. He continues to twist her hair with·his left hand as he begins masturbating into her inert, now-lifeless face.

He jacks his shrunken penis back into a semblance of an erection and finally is able to pound off, shooting his semen into her face. He wipes himself off on the army blanket, then wraps her body in it, and stomps the package down into a slight declivitous spot in a bed of poison oak. He does this out of habit more than anything else as he could care less when or if the body is found.

Making sure nobody is coming, he limps back down to the side of the road and retrieves his duffel bag from the ditch. He is slightly disgusted by what he considers poor behavior. He notices he has been acting more and more like a basket case lately. Allowing himself to run out of control uncharacteristically.

A Ford pickup truck comes over the top of the hill, and full of his rage and waddling around with a sore penis, he hurls his duffel into the back of the Datsun and flags down the truck.

"Say, friend, could you tell me where I can find the Frannis Scrace?" This is a slurred double-talk utterance, one of dozens he has mastered that produces the desired time lag.

"Find what place?" a tough-looking, hirsute individual asks, somewhat warily. Bunkowski smiles his disarming, dimpled smile.

"Sorry. What I said was, I was wondering if you can tell me how to find—" but by then he has the steel cable looped over the man's head and his massive hands are holding the crossed PVC-covered rings which he pulls out and down by the side of the truck's door on the driver's side, the driver's head coming out through the window, a circle of blood welling out through the beard and onto the truck driver's fingers as he claws at the strangling wire which is biting deeply into the man's neck.

He is oblivious to the man's wild struggles, but keeps a keen eye on the road, looking for more traffic. When he has held the wires for another thirty-count he lets some of his hot tide of rage subside, and begins quickly working the wire loose where it has bitten deeply into the man's throat. He wipes the garrote on the man's shirt.

Bunkowski opens the door and pushes the bearded man over into a kind of slump, ripping his pants pockets off and searching for a wallet. He examines a watch and rings which he deems of little value. He finds a money clip in the man's front pants pocket and is surprised at the hundred-dollar bills on the outside of the roll. At least $400 in the clip, which is a big haul for Daniel. He almost never finds any real sizable money on his victims, but then of course he kills for money only when necessary. Most of his kills are done for the sheer pleasure of taking life.

He is an astute observer, and he notices that he took no pleasure in either of these kills. This is not one of his better days, he thinks. He shoves the body over farther with some effort and squeezes himself up into the cab of the truck, grinding the ignition into life and pulling the vehicle up ahead of the Datsun and off the road into a nearby turn-row at the edge of the field.

He rolls up the windows and locks the doors of the Ford, wiping his paw prints automatically, and double-checking the glove compartment for goodies. He finds a small baggie of weed and pitches it back in. He doesn't smoke. He locks the truck and leaves, not even bothering to wipe his footprints out as he limps back to the other set of wheels. His mood is sullen and dark.

With a grunt he hurls his massive bulk into the Datsun, kicking it into life. He empties out the contents of her groceries, pouring everything out into the seat, and brightens slightly at the find of a group of candy bars. He rips the paper off a Mounds bar and inhales the candy at a gulp. It has melted and he eats a bit of paper with the chocolate. He opens the warm half gallon of milk to wash it down but it is already too hot to enjoy and he pitches the milk out into the ditch leaving a nice fat print or two on the plastic jug.

He sits sulking for a few moments, again not like him, then gets out of the vehicle with great effort and retrieves the milk jug, which he empties and tosses onto the floorboard of the backseat. Rummaging quickly through her purse, the glove box, the ashtray, feeling up under the dash, he takes an item or two of interest and dumps the rest of the contents into the empty grocery sack. He slips the brake off and trods heavily on the gas pedal.

The name that would appear on his Motor Vehicle license if he had one is Daniel Edward Flowers Bunkowski, and even that would not be quite precise. He has killed more than any other living person, "as many as 450 humans" he once estimated when he was sedated during one of his many periods of institution-alization.

At the moment he weighs 469 pounds, and stands six feet, seven inches tall. He was originally "discov-ered" in the hole in The Max at Marion Federal Peni-tentiary, which means in solitary confinement in the maximum-security section. He was diagnosed as a unique blend of seemingly retarded psycho and genius-IQ-level killer. He had been the core for a govern-ment project. An experiment in the field, so to speak.

In Vietnam he had earned the nickname "Chain-gang," hunting freely as a self-contained hunter-killer unit. He had foreseen danger to himself with the spike team during its covert operation, somehow sensing the betrayal that doomed the rest of his team members to destruction up in Quang Tri province, and he had deserted the unit shortly before it was destroyed by friendly fire.

For a time he had prowled the lowlands of Quang Tri's Echo Sector, growing less sane as he began to cannibalize his freshly slaughtered targets. Finally, at the breaking point, he'd summoned powerful inner reserves and managed to pull himself back.

He had been able to keep his grasp on whatever semblance of sanity remained and forced himself to begin the long and arduous return to the more civi-lized world. Eventually, through a brilliantly executed escape plan, he had been able to return, making his way first to Hawaii, finally back to the North American mainland.

He'd begun killing again shortly after his return to the urban landscape, although nowhere near the scale of his Southeast Asian activities, and he sometimes longed for the good old days, back when victims were a dime a dozen.

Everything about him, from his appetite for food to his proclivity for violence, was irregular and extreme. His body was a storehouse of odd tolerances and unusual metabolism. He warped every curve, deviated from every chart. Mentally abnormal, emotionally anomalous, he was that rare human called the *physical precognitive,* regularly experiencing biochemical phenomena that transcended the mechanistic laws of kinesiology and kinetics. Stir that in with his psychological imbalance and gigantic size and strength, and you had a human killing machine without equal.

Edith
Emaline
Lynch

Evening was the end of a day of physical catharsis. Lee Anne with hands washed, sitting at the table rather studiously avoiding her veggies and making neat, geometric segments of dinner in preparation for the evening meal.

Edie remembered how absurdly prosaic it seemed, whenever she thought of Ed, how he hated food that wasn't neatly divided on the plate. Some overreaction to military chow, she supposed. Ed even ate in little sculpted layers and she could still visualize him scraping each edge of the ice cream or the mashed potatoes in meticulous, draftsman perfect lines.

It had been a Saturday that would not go down in history as far as she was concerned. A day of hard work done with a vengeance, a day of heavy clouds of depression and sorrow that followed her every move, refusing to go away even as she attacked tiny footprints, waxy build-up, and the assorted detritus that littered the kitchen floor, just Edith and her old pal Mr. Clean. A long Saturday that still wasn't over.

"Let's eat!" Lee Anne was ready to pounce on dinner.

"Would you like to say grace tonight?"

"God is good god is great thank you [mumble] on this plate. Amen."

"Dear Heavenly Father," Edie said, taking a deep breath and feeling the return of a killer headache, "thanks for giving us this food. Many will go hungry tonight.

"Lord, thank you for letting us have each other to love. Even though we are sad for those we miss, we know our loved ones are with you and are at peace now, Heavenly Father, and many will be lonely tonight. We have much to be thankful for.

"Heavenly Father, we thank you for the gift of life, and we ask you to guide us and be with us always, and help us to do more Thy way. We ask these things in Jesus's name. Amen."

"Amen let's eat."

"Amen."

"Mom, why isn't there any blue food?" Lee Anne asked, attacking her hot dog.

"Well, perhaps when the Lord made blueberries and blue potatoes, He decided that was enough blue food. And he thought it would be nice to have something green and yellow and orange, which is why you have those mixed vegetables on your plate that you're going to enjoy so much."

A mouth full of hot dog and bun said, "Yuk, I hate mixed vegetables. Are there really blue potatoes?"

"By coincidence that's what we're having for dessert tonight." Lee Anne laughed impishly, showing her missing front tooth space. Edie smiled and took a bite of food, chewing slowly, tasting nothing.

She'd thrown herself into a paroxysm of premature spring cleaning, after having woken up filled with some nagging paranoia in a bed that she could never quite get used to, and spent an hour dawdling over coffee and a piece of toast. She had read everything on the cereal box as if it had been written by Dostoevsky and by the time she forced herself into action she had memorized the entire nutritional contents of a dubious breakfast concoction that promised "all the essential vitamins and minerals," and the recipe for a highly suspect party mix that would allow one to consume even more of the product.

It was an exorcism. A physical cleansing in more ways than one. Ed's old ties had slipped down into a dark pile where they gathered dust, twisted together like snakes. An errant slipper. A hat lodged in the blackest, far corner of a closet, anything of his she'd overlooked or couldn't stand to touch in her initial, grief-stricken whirlwind of reminders gathered up for Goodwill. She emptied bottom drawers, too-tall shelves, catchalls and hideaways and rat-pack caches long forgotten.

A heartbreaking comb with its teeth still holding strands of a dead loved one's hair, a lost cuff link, a dog-eared family Bible—each of these memory triggers inspired ten minutes of wordless fantasy conversation with her deceased mother, husband, and a favorite aunt, as she sat mesmerized by a framed bevy of family photographs, absentmindedly brushing her own hair with one of Ed's brushes.

She was proud of her long hair, a luxurious abundance that he'd called her mane, and at thirty-eight it was still naturally dark and lustrous. Her skin was fair, with a light freckling, her eyes wide set and beautiful. They were darkly brown and hazel by turns, changing mysteriously in each light source. She had smile lines of wrinkling crow's feet at the corners of her eyes, and just the beginnings of lines at each corner of her mouth. Her nose was rather large, not straight, and in the center of another face it might have been unattractive.

She had never been pretty in the classic sense. She hadn't been an attractive child, but she was maturing into one of those interesting if somewhat forgettable-looking women that other women describe as "poised" and "self-assured," and that men are sometimes drawn to partially because they seem so unapproachable. She was not the snow queen she appeared to be.

In bed there was a natural lustiness and she had always secretly known that she was much the more—

what's the word? Not carnal. But perhaps the more elemental of the two of them. She was closer to her genuine feelings. Edie was one of those rare creatures who didn't have an insincere or mean or malicious or selfish bone in her body. And she had given herself to the man in her life the same way she did everything else. Wholeheartedly. Honestly. With kindness and with the attitude that the real pleasure was in what you could give.

Sex had been pleasurable for her but not a wildly exciting or all-consuming thing the way it had been with so many of the kids she'd gone to school with. Edie had seen marriage after marriage crash against the rocks of divorce and sink. And many of those marriages were those in which the female had confided to the girls about the hot, burning flames of sex that kept the relationship with their spouse a thing of explosive, emotional extremes.

She had been born into a devoutly Christian home, but as she grew older and left her home in a West Virginia town that she joked was so impoverished that "it made *Coal Miner's Daughter* look like it'd been shot in Beverly Hills," she had drifted away from the church. It was a thing that just happened. She'd blamed it on work schedules, illness, any number of convenient excuses. But the need for Jesus in her life had left an emptiness inside her.

Not long after she'd gone to work as a secretary for Chicago Carburetor she'd met a salesman named Ed Lynch and they had some dates. Ed was gentle, funny, and he was a good man with a strong religious faith. Now she started letting Ed lead her back and found herself looking forward to going with him. At first on Sundays. He'd pick her up and they'd go to church, and then around eleven-thirty or twelve head for a little place where they liked to eat lunch.

Soon she was going back on Sunday nights with him, and then they'd go to the Wednesday-night Bible studies, and before long they were regulars at the church socials, picnics, pot-luck suppers, fellowship classes, and she had given herself over to the Lord again. After a few months she got up in front of the congregation and confessed that she'd sinned and she asked the Lord to allow her to rededicate herself to Jesus. That evening Ed had proposed to her.

What Ed lacked in imagination he made up for in intensity. Sex with Ed was what she was sure God had meant for it to be, a warm and honest coupling between marriage partners. She appreciated the biological beauty of the act as a release but neither she nor her husband had been particularly preoccupied with it. Physiologically, it had assumed no more import in their lives than any other bodily function.

Once he had told her, "You know what I like about our love life?"

"Everything, I hope," she'd murmured to him with a smile.

"That's right. Everything. But what I like about it most is *you*. Doing this with somebody else"—he shook his head—"it just wouldn't *matter*."

"I feel like that too about you," she'd said, kissing him. Ed had made her a hot, loving, and complete woman. But now she had closed the door on that part of her life.

She found some old cologne in an unfamiliar bottle and tipped it to a finger, sniffing and saying aloud, "Arpège," to the mirror. She had cleaned out the freezer, gifting a next door neighbor with all manner of perfectly edible garden goodies, catfish Ed had cleaned, some unknown tinfoil-wrapped and unmarked leftover surprises, all of which the lady surreptitiously dumped in the garbage. She headed for the silver, then changed her mind and broke out the Easy-Off and cleaned the oven until it sparkled.

She made a shopping list, cut coupons, prepared a cup of decaffeinated coffee, and drank a third of it. Wrote a month-overdue thank-you note to someone she didn't know, took a long, hot bath, put on her best underwear, a long, suede skirt with high-heeled, leather boots, a blouse with a suede vest, and golden hoop

earrings. Looked at herself, undressed, put on a rag-
ged sweatshirt and her oldest blue jeans, threw out a
piece of bric-a-brac that she was tired of dusting, retrieved it in a small rush of guilt, and decided she was
spinning her wheels and quit for the day.

She chewed something, grateful for the sound of
eight-year-old chatter nearby, a lovely thing to hear,
now audible only subconsciously like the sonorous murmur from the TV set with the volume turned not quite
all the way down in the living room, and she struggled
inwardly to keep from thinking any depressing thoughts.
None of this feeling sorry for yourself, missy, she
thought, as she remembered thinking while she cooked
dinner tonight that her life's wholeness had somehow
drained like the liquid from a broken glass.

Daniel
Edward
Flowers
Bunkowksi

He has had extremely violent sexual fantasies for as long as he has memory. Because of his unique childhood they predate puberty. He fantasized in pitch-black, locked closets, inside a stifling metal box, chained under a filthy homemade bed, in a cell called the hole, in a thousand places, on death row in The Max, in The Nam on a hundred night patrols, on his lonely, wonderful one-man ambushes, on foot, in cars, in countless hiding places. He has the gifts of patience and stillness, and in his long, still waiting times he fantasizes unspeakable things.

The tape deck in the stolen car is blasting the bridge from Manhattan Transfer's "Route 66" and he does not bother to turn it down. Smiling broadly, he thinks how unusual and enjoyable it might be to rape and kill an entire group. Pondering the difficulties as a theoretical challenge, he diagrams the acquisition of the necessary intelligence, thinking how easy it would be for him to insert himself into their lives just long enough to take them.

He is capable of monstrous acts. He kills easily, effortlessly, with total pleasure. The place he is cruising through is on the outskirts of a small town in southern Illinois, "downstate" as they say there. The place is called Bluetown, a commercial error in judgment dating back to the post-Korean-fifties, when a group of desperate merchants who were watching their business desert a crumbling downtown and head toward the shopping malls, grasped at an all-blue theme as a cheap gamble. They had painted all their buildings blue and built their last-ditch hopes around an all-blue ad blitz, renaming their tiny community Bluetown, Illinois, and saturating media with blue bargains that were swept away by the onrushing tide of urban renewal and 1950s change.

Now the CHEAP!! USED FURNITURE!! signs hang from the fading blue walls of empty storefronts in the ghostly predawn as this monster of a man, squeezed behind the wheel of a stolen Mercury Cougar, drives through the place called Bluetown. He has a sore, throbbing ankle and his gall bladder is acting up again. He weighs close to five hundred pounds and he has taken three human lives in the last forty-eight hours. The steering wheel is digging into his gut as he drives gripping the wheel in those steel fingers, thinking about how he could easily find out where Janice Siegel lives. It is nothing personal with him, just a way of passing the time. But sometimes he will allow himself to take a fantasy daydream over the line and his head will feel funny and in the bloodroar he will do bad things.

A sixth sense tells him to control himself and concentrate and he jams a powerful index finger into the tape player's stop/eject switch spitting the cassette out. He kills the audio. He listens intently, hearing the Cougar's tires sing on the wet pavement, and the sixth sense nudges him again. Quickly, with surprisingly fast movements for such an enormous hulk, he reacts to the nudge and wheels the car into a dark parking lot next to a store, braking, killing the engine and lights, scrunching down out of sight on the passenger side, driving down the street one moment, now hiding in the shadows the next, operating on those unerring vibes.

He waits. Listening to the motor cool. Listening for what? A passing prowl car perhaps. He waits there in the dark shadows of a Bluetown parking lot. He waits for a long time listening and absorbing. Waiting. He shifts his weight and with a groan of springs sits up again and starts the car, pulling back out into the streets of Bluetown.

Out on his spooky, one-man night patrols in The Nam he would concentrate fiercely on preparation. He, the one they called CHAINGANG, was never caught unprepared. He believed in the Soviet dictum "plan hard, fight easy." Except that he planned hard and fought hard and by God if he fought you at all, this mountain of kill fury, you were going to have to—as the saying went—gut up and buckle for your dust. When he focused on a target with his special brand of laser-keen concentration and meticulous preparation, he was a remarkable adversary.

Each time he went out beyond the perimeter, whatever that might be, sprawling firebase or ragtag NDP, he itemized everything in his enormous ruck mentally. He carried a backbreaking storehouse neither you nor I could budge, in which would be packed an orderly array of every life-sustaining necessity from det cord to his precious freeze-dried "long rats," the goodies that let him have the slack to run free, untethered to Resupply and the idiots and amateurs who knew nothing of killing. And each time out he would painstakingly itemize each item. Not one to make mistakes, back then.

Now, calming himself, becoming more controlled as he winds through the ghost of some long-lost businessman's folly with the funky and meaningless name Bluetown, squeezed behind the wheel of a hot Merc Cougar, he begins acting more in character. Itemizing automatically, he remembers the plates that he took last night in the suburbs when he dumped the woman's tiresome Datsun. He decides which pair he will change to as he smiles over the kill last night, his thoroughly enjoyable suffocation of the salesman whose vehicle he now drives.

Wrenching his mind back to the current problem at

hand, he brakes, pulling the Cougar over to the curb beside an abandoned gypsy storefront with the peeling legend USED RNITURE, and reconsidering, coasts into a narrow alley between the stores. With great effort he propels his bulk out from behind the wheel, and getting out of the car with a massive creaking of springs, he takes a small oil can and tool bag from his duffel and heads to the rear of the Merc.

He selects the most appropriate of the plates (he has memorized the current plate prefix and number code for all fifty states), gives the oil can a few squirts, and with bolts soaking briefly contemplates his current options. He then begins to unscrew the woman's rusted license plate bolts from out of the plates, and he substitutes a fresh tag.

Completing that task, he then bends the plates into an unrecognizable metal accordion and locks them back in the trunk to be pitched into the next creek he crosses. He will repaint the vehicle tomorrow if circumstances permit, and the words MASKING TAPE, and NEWSPAPERS, are mentally added to a subconscious list of want items he has filed away, his shopping list. He slams his humongous body behind the wheel again and takes off, leaving the desolate streets as he found them, dead and blue.

Out on the highway again he drives carefully, but with the rapid flow of dawn highway traffic, keeping it as close to sixty as the rest of the rapidly speeding cars and trucks will permit, trying to stay within a string of vehicles as much as he can without going to extremes of speed. At this hour a car moving at the legal fifty-five would probably be as conspicuous as one doing ninety, so he lets his heavy foot press the accelerator a little closer to the floor.

Driving on one level, planning on another, lucid, coolly introspective, he methodically dissects, probes, examines—all with a cold objectivity unusual in even the extreme precognates. Rocking down the highway, crammed into his borrowed wheels, listening to the endless hum of the white line, the hypnotic white that never ends, humming between the wheels as he excogitates.

He knows, just as he always knew in Vietnam, in prisons of one kind or another, exactly the degree of danger to which he's exposed himself. Analyzing his recent carelessness and general ineptitude, he intuitively can feel himself being pulled down into a viscid pit of jeopardy that is taking him under like quicksand.

Three hours and ten minutes later he's whipping the Mercury down off a blacktopped levee access and beside an old, railless wooden bridge over an apparently deep drainage ditch, crashing through the chained gate that sports a rusty, CLOSED—DO NOT ENTER warning sign, and slamming to a stop in a cloud of sandy dust. Large, prominently placed admonitions nailed to ancient oaks and cottonwoods advise NO TRESPASSING, as they oxidize in the moist, cool shadows.

He limps back to the demolished gate, covering his tracks with a leafy tree limb, and with hard-eyed concentration does his best to right the gate again, restoring it to some semblance of its original state of disrepair. The broken chain and padlock lie in the nearby grass and he hefts the chain, liking the weight of it, thinking how easily he could put a human to sleep with it, but he repositions the chain back on the broken gate, the lock still attached and dangling from one end.

He fastens the whole thing to the gate with a couple of lengths of rusting fence wire and returns to the car. Years of experience have taken over and he moves now as he did on night jungle stalks, giving himself to animal instinct, each decision viscerally made, choices assessed and arrived at instinctively, deeply controlled, as he operates on some alien wavelength, responding to vibes, following the silent drum of the hunter and hunted.

The Mercury bounces along the overgrown pathway that now is beginning to buffet the underside of the chassis with hard stubble that feels as tough as corn stalks. He perseveres, roaring on undaunted through the tall, wet weeds, being forced to slow finally as the pathway becomes more and more difficult to follow as it winds its way down around the levee and heads toward the nearby river.

Now running parallel to the riverbank the path such as it was all but disappears, and the stolen car is splashing through even taller wet weeds, and then actually running in water, almost to the floorboards in the lower spots, and still he keeps going. He is driving through very deep water now, driving as he always does by following a secret magnetic pole, some inner compass, going with the flow, barely moving as water sloshes back over the chrome grillwork and threatens to drown out the motor.

Yet Daniel Bunkowski keeps on straight ahead, keeps pushing it, keeps moving, driving without apprehension, quite calm in fact, oblivious to the rising water. And then, sure enough, the vehicle is back on higher ground and the windshield-high weeds part as he drives up beside a trio of dilapidated summer cottages that sit waterlogged alongside the riverbank in an overgrown fringe of tall watergrass.

He senses that he is alone here, and his ability to detect the presence of other human life is quite uncanny, having kept him alive in Southeast Asia time and time again. He stops the vehicle and quickly prepares a crude camouflage of weeds and the huge, folded cammie-cover he carries in his ever-present duffel bag. He is deciding how he will set his people traps, and at this he has no equal. He is the absolute master of the final surprise.

He imagines, reasons, PRECOGNATES how they will come as he looks down the trail toward the winding levee road and the wooden bridge. He makes the estimates in his computerlike mind. How long he has before they find him. Not long. How many will come. Many. How they will make their play. Several clear options. He is in harmony with his physical being, and at one with the terrain as he meticulously rigs the traps that begin alongside the camouflaged Mercury Cougar.

One of the elements that makes Bunkowski such an

inordinately dangerous killer species is his automatic pilot light. It is on again now, and as he finishes rigging his people traps he automatically and subconsciously begins retracing his route of the past twenty-four hours, stealing the plates, the exit out of the blue ghost town, the squirting of the oil on the bolts that held the license plates, the manner in which he scanned the street, positions of dead bodies, finger- and footprints, residue of skin under fingernails, microscopic traces of fabric, the most minute forensics feed into his on-line terminal.

Each minute detail is viewed under the magnifier of his trenchant analysis: credit cards, blood trails, parking spaces, it all floods back across his mental viewscreen as he sets his booby traps. In his mind he is also killing again, coldly now, on automatic pilot, taking each one down as he feels the snap and crunch of bone, the gasps of asphyxiation, the final signs of ebbing life. He is driving again, mentally winding down the hillside, breaking the gate, wiring it back together, retracing each moment of the past day and night, relentlessly probing, dissecting, looking for the forgotten mistakes, the tiny flaws, the hidden tripwires.

He finishes and selects one of the cabins where he will make his hideout. He is light on his feet like a fat man dancing, a five-hundred-pound ballet star, easing toward the steps with grace and agility, an incongruous daintiness—if that's the word—to his precise movements as he cautiously negotiates the rotting steps leading up to one of the tar-paper shanties. Watching him you might see him as an oafish, dancing grizzly, smiling blimp of a man, grinning clown daintily stepping on the rotten boards.

The decrepit cabins stand, somewhat precariously, on a random system of stiltlike creosoted poles sunk into concrete and mired in the muddy silt. The support poles are fairly sound but the cabins are falling apart and he must remember to be very careful where he walks. He goes up the side of the steps, with that intensity of concentration that so often marks his actions, missing nothing, sensors on full scan, alert for any noise, scent, or movement.

He pops the lock with no effort and opens the swollen screen door, then jimmies open the wooden front door and is hit by an incredible foulness of rotting fish smell and stuffiness. The odor is palpable and vomitous. He hurriedly snaps the locks on all the shutters and props them open with the poles he finds scattered about the cabin. The dead fish aroma is overpowering, but it triggers a memory of a kill in Vietnam and he finds himself grinning from ear to ear remembering one night's work with nostalgic pleasure. He loved killing the little people. He smiles at the pleasant memory of the little man he bled dry that night.

With all the shutters up and a gentle breeze blowing through the cabin the stuffiness airs out sufficiently so that he can stand to finally come back inside, and he reenters the cabin, a small, crude affair of three simple rooms. A sleeping area which is closed off by a filthy curtain, and a larger main room with a table and a few chairs, adjoined by a kitchenette of sorts. The tiny cooking area contains only a sink with a hand pump, and an empty icebox that stands under some shelves.

He sets his big sack and duffel down and begins lining up his goodies on the shelf. His milk jug filled with fresh water. A sack of apples. Canned meats, chile, beef stew, canned vegetables, Spam, a quart of Wild Turkey which he will drink a little later. He will take it straight and at room temperature, polishing it off in an hour or so, in order to go to sleep with just the suggestion of a buzz. He can and does drink phenomenal amounts of booze without becoming intoxicated.

He opens up a can of Vienna Sausages and eats a handful in a single bite, washing them down with a couple of quarts of water. He makes the only noise or sound he has made since arriving, a huge, expansive, resounding, thunderclap of a belch that shatters the silence like the rumbling blast of a foghorn.

"BBBBAAAAAAAAAAAAAAAAAAGGGGGGG-HHHHHHHH!" Followed by a contented "Ahhhhh," and an expulsion of halitotic air.

The cabin's interior is that of a typical deserted fishing shack. A bed, a table, three small chairs, a folding cot, a folding chair, a coal-oil lantern that is about empty, a couple of fishing poles, and a cheap rod and reel, nothing much of interest. A banged-up tackle box sits in one corner with a small boat paddle made from a broken oar. There are a few grimy paperbacks and newspapers scattered around the place. No blankets, towels, nothing of a homey nature, indicating the cabin had not seen any use for some time.

He thinks the place smells as if it had not been opened for several months. The fish smell is still extremely strong and he pours a large glass full of whiskey and drinks it down in two gulps, shuddering as he swallows each time. He doesn't like the taste of whiskey, only the way it warms him inside when it hits. He wishes for ice. He wishes he could wash.

Later he will take a pan and go out and get some river water and try to prime the hand pump. But right now all he wants to do is get off his feet and rest his swollen ankle. He sits down hard on one of the chairs and it groans, threatening to collapse under his weight. He props his aching foot up on the table and begins drinking from the quart of whiskey as he lets himself imagine how much fun he could have if the family who owns this cabin would suddenly arrive for a vacation visit. What a nice surprise he could give them all; Mommy, Daddy, and little Brother and Sister. He'd let the kids and Daddy watch him give a big surprise to Mommy—and that's what he thinks about, sitting in the dark of a stinking river rat hole, smelling dead fish, swilling booze, and thinking about taking folks down.

He knows that if he remains static he is finished. They will be coming for him soon. His trail is wide and clear. A giant, pregnant bear of a fat man in a stolen Mercury, hotter than hell's hinges, silver with a vinyl top—all it needs are fluorescent signs on the doors saying HEY, LOOK AT ME! His first problem is he must lose the car. Then he must lose himself. He has been doing something that he never does. He has been making mistakes. Lots of them. He knows the cost of carelessness. Unless he mends his ways immediately they will get him.

He drags the heavy duffel over to him and begins removing items until he comes to the large, blue ledger. It is a well-worn Boorum and Pease accounts-receivable book; 439 of the five hundred pages are filled with meticulously rendered artwork and carefully researched data. The heading at the top of the first page is

UTILITY
ESCAPES

printed in neat, firm capital letters. This is Chaingang's Bible.

He takes a long pull at the Wild Turkey, shuddering slightly as it burns its way down, and he turns to page 106 and begins plotting out his first move. This is the book of plans that will allow him to remain free under their very noses. He will go back to Chicago and take human lives for his pleasure. Many, many of them.

Lee Anne Lynch

"Come on, young lady, you know what we said about bedtime."

"I know," Lee Anne replied, marching off to the bathroom to brush her teeth. Edie was grateful she had a good kid. Not much of a whiner. You laid down the law and usually that did it. It was a lot tougher without Ed, though, even with a good one like Lee. At age eight there has to be a firm disciplinarian around. Fifty inches of potential trouble.

She came out of the bathroom rosy-cheeked and naked, still marching with knees high to some unheard parade drum no doubt, slick as a baby seal across her flat chest and abdomen where she was starting to get a little tummy from too many sweets. Edie was going to start watching both of their diets real close for a while. It wouldn't be a problem.

"Mom," came softly from out of the bedroom and she went in to tuck her little treasure into bed.

"Mom, tell me about Icky and Boo-Boo," she said sleepily, starting to suck her thumb and then remembering she was years beyond such childish activities and cuddling her favorite teddy bear, a talking panda she'd named George, and had cuddled so hard and so often that its synthetic coat was worn slick, and snuggling down into the pillows. Icky and Boo-Boo were an Eskimo and caribou invented or remembered from childhood by her father.

"Okay, but say your prayers first, pumpkin."

"Now I lay me down to sleep. I pray the Lord my soul to keep. If I should die before I wake, I pray the Lord my soul to take."

"Amen."

"Amen."

"Once upon a time, there was a little Eskimo boy named Icky—"

"A girl, Mom," she corrected as Edie took a deep breath.

"Once upon a time there was this cranky little Eskimo girl named—"

"Cranky? Come on, Mom!"

"I'm sorry. Okay. Now close your eyes and I'll start over. Once upon a time, way up north, there was this little Eskimo named Icky and she had this beautiful baby reindeer named Caribou. It had always wanted to be one of Santa's reindeer, but it was a caribou, so Icky named it Caribou so that it would know what kind of animal it was. But she couldn't pronounce the word caribou because Icky was just a little Eskimo girl and so she could only say Boo-boo and that was the reindeer's name." She thought to herself, Is it a reindeer that wants to be a caribou or the other way around. I've forgotten how Ed used to tell this.

"And Boo-boo went to Santa Claus's workshop to apply to be a Christmas reindeer. But Mr. and Mrs. Claus were out, so he asked to speak to Rudolph"—and Lee Anne was already breathing deeply, thank the Lord, because she had no idea what she was saying at this point.

She got off the bed as soundlessly as she could and tiptoed over to the light switch. She put the room in darkness and started easing the door closed and a little voice came out softly, muffled by the covers and sleepiness.

"Mom, you get that story all messed up. Boo-boo's a caribou not a reindeer."

"Okay. You can tell me about it tomorrow. 'Night angel."

"G'night, Mom. I love you thiiiissssss much."

"I love you this much too, sweetheart," she said, shutting the door softly.

Jack Eichord
—the Cop

"You know how to get a nigger out of a tree in Mississippi?"

"How's that?" Eichord dutifully responded to the big cop standing next to him in Curley's, the cop bar where everybody in the 18th Division hung out. The guys off the four-to-midnight tour were coming in, all raunchy and thirsty, and Jack was nursing a Stroh's Light in between two guys from Property Crimes, longtime partners, standing on either side of him. The big one in the leather coat had a silk shirt on that must have cost seventy-five dollars, big, bad Fu Manchu, gold chains, ID bracelets, a miniature Mr. T, and the black one built like a fireplug, another open shirt and lots of chains, the white cop looking at Jack but *talking* to his partner, jiving around with him like they always did.

"You get a goddamn knife and CUT him down." Everybody at the bar laughed, Eichord laughing politely as he felt a tap on his right arm and turned.

"You know how to tell a plane in the Polack air force?"

"Shit, you dumb cacknacker don't you even know how to tell a joke fer' Chrissakes, it's how do you tell a Polish airplane not how do you tell a plane in the

Polack fuckin' air force you wooly-headed Watusi midget."

"Listen, ya' big, smelly chuck piece of dog shit, if it's good enough for ya' *Mammy* it's good enough for you. Anyway, ya' know how to tell a Polack airplane?" Eichord's smile muscles are still bunched up and he shakes his head in the negative. "It's the one with the *hair* under its wings!" The black cop just about gets a hernia laughing. Eichord has heard all this stuff a hundred times.

"Ya' know what you call six niggers in a Volkswagen?" the big cop asks the bar.

"A *stinkbug!*" Everybody roars.

"You know why it takes a hundred lawyers to change a light bulb?" Curley, the bartender, interjects.

"It takes one to put in the bulb, and the other ninety-nine to make sure it gets SCREWED!"

When he first quit drinking Jack wouldn't even walk by a saloon but after he'd stayed off the sauce a few months he realized that was a little absurd. You were either under control or you weren't. It was just that simple. If you could walk into a package store and stare all that Daniel's and I. W. Harper and Seagram's right in the face and walk out with a six-pack, you could do the same thing in a noisy, smoke-filled tavern. The kind of work he was in you had to go into bars frequently, and if you didn't you could miss something here and there. Also, he knew how important it was to appear sociable. And he could go into the drunkest joint in town, sip a couple of Oly Lights or whatever, and enjoy himself, go home and maybe top the night off with a strong cup of instant and hit the sack.

Curley's was typically dark, salty, and noisy. A little heavy on the groupie action, more than he was used to anyway, and the fact that these guys he didn't know from up in Prop Crimes asked him along was an okay sign, the word was getting out that he was all right. He was waiting because Bill Joyce, one of the homicide

detectives who'd drawn Sylvia Kasikoff, was going to
stop by and have a drink with him.

The 18th Division, they didn't call them precincts in
the windy, was a fairly high-crime division that em-
braced a good part of the downtown Chicago area.
The vast Chicagoland Megaplex was divided into areas,
those then subdivided into divisions which were led,
on paper, by division commanders. Eichord was on
loan to the homicide unit in the 18th, a division that
shared most of the town with the First. They had
explained to him where all the jurisdictional lines were
but after so many "Eleventh and State's" shot back
and forth like ping-pong balls he tuned out on all of
it. He was just starting to remember his way around
after a lot of years. The main thing he knew was, it
was a lot of city to get lost in.

"Walk south till yer hat floats," the white cop was
saying and everybody was laughing at a cop story.
Eichord smiled and tried not to look over at the clock.

The Property Crimes dude in the leather coat was in
the middle of a slightly loud and rather embarrassing
recounting of an amorous adventure in which he'd
starred when Bill Joyce came in and motioned toward
Jack Eichord. Eichord whispered see-yà'-laters, patted
both his drinking partners on their backs, and left a
couple of bills and change on the wet bar.

"What's up?"

"Come on." He followed Joyce out to the car. Joyce
had the light bar going but no siren. "They caught
another one. Over in the First this time."

"Four Ocean Six," the police radio crackled.

"Four Ocean Six responding, over."

"Four Ocean Six, please switch to Tac-two, over."

"Four Ocean Six, switching to Tac-two." He reached
over automatically, turning the scanner and switching
the setting to Tactical/two for a personal. This would
enable the car to transmit and receive a message that
you could not monitor on the open channel. He
squeezed the handset.

"Four Ocean Six in service, over."

"Jack, is that you over?"

"That's Gomez," Joyce said.

"That's a rog."

"They caught a bad one over here. Same MO as Sylvia Kasikoff and the others. Female Cauc, mid thirties, ME's just pulling in, gotta' go. Out."

A minute or so passed as they navigated the Chicago streets. The radio spat again.

"Four Ocean Six, what's your twenty over?"

"I'll get it," Bill Joyce said, taking the handset. "Hey, Gomer, we'll be there in about five, six minutes." He gave him the location. "Is Lou there yet?" he got an affirm and signed off saying, "We'll see ya' in a couple of minutes kay." They were there and Eichord found himself getting out at the crime scene, following Bill Joyce and a feeling of troubling premonitions that hit him the moment they got out of the car.

Sylvia Kasikoff was what they called the whole serial murder package but Sylvia Kasikoff herself had been a young, good-looking housewife from Downer's Grove, found on one of the few fields left within a short drive of where they were right now. She'd been found rolled up in a blanket and the killer had not taken the heart. She'd been tied to the others by the semen traces in her mouth. One of the other heart murders had been a matchup on the semen in the mouth, vaginal, and anal orifices, and that victim had also been found with neck broken. It looked like the perpetrator was on a roll now and back in business.

Eichord could feel or imagined he could feel the presence of death before they walked through the police line and around to the back. Joyce spoke to a couple of uniformed patrol officers who told them where Arlen was. A crime scene will sometimes give off a strong aura, particularly a type of homicide or messy suicide. Or perhaps you're only expecting the hideous and the frightening and all the lights and grim faces and black humor just creates an atmosphere conducive to those kinds of thoughts and feelings.

But real or imagined, Jack sensed or felt something strong.

"Hey, amigos," Vernon Arlen said.

"Lou."

"Got a Jane Doe," the lieutenant told them, gesturing at a metal container where a photographer was popping flashes; "maybe thirty-five, nude, mutilated, heart missing. Bag lady found the body when she was going through the trash dumpster. ME says semen, and all the rest of it. Slashed down the front the usual way. Blood all over inside the box but none outside. Perp might have killed her somewhere and wrapped her in plastic or a rug or whatever and dumped her in and taken the heart inside, which would explain the blood there and nowhere else." He opened a plastic-encased map of the downtown area and pointed as Bill Joyce moved in closer.

"We're about here—and we'll all work out in a straight line. Bill, you and Jack can take the alley on down that way if you will and just take it on straight out that way when we get done here. Probably won't find anything but we'll give it a shot and then meet back at the office." They were walking over to the dumpster.

"Anything from the bag lady?" Eichord saw an old, disheveled-looking woman slumped over by one of the units.

"Zip. Forget it. Worthless," he said, turning to Eichord. "Have a go but she's just a schizzy old whackadoo. You won't get much."

"Right."

"Showtime, folks," the lieutenant said, and they looked down into the horror of the dumpster.

"Jesus Christ."

"You get something like this, man, it can just paralyze a town. I've seen it happen once before here, like Atlanta, L.A., Boston, New York—it just terrorizes everybody. I want to make damn sure the papers and the TV don't turn this thing into another Jack the Ripper. Missing hearts, they get anything to run with, it'll be worse than fuckin' Dracula." He nodded agreement and looked at the mutilated Jane Doe.

The old bag woman was moaning now and Jack Eichord was tired of looking into the dumpster and he started walking over to where she was slumped up against one of the radio units, realizing he'd been holding his breath and taking in a big gulp of oxygen.

One of the young patrol cops was looking like he was just about to lose it and Eichord said quietly, "How you makin' it, pardner?"

"Awright," the young uniform cop mumbled and turned and heaved up nothing into the weeds. Eichord fought to pull his mind back to the matters at hand, as there wasn't much that could make him sick but one of the exceptions was listening to somebody else tossing their dinner.

He concentrated on what to ask the bag lady as he came up and said softly, "Ma'am?"

She turned and said something that sounded like, "Govayesell."

"Ma'am, ya' doing okay?" he repeated.

"Go for yourself." Then he realized she was saying go fuck yourself.

"I'm sorry. I know this must have been—"

"Ummmmmmmmmmmmmm." A sharp keening noise was coming out of her. He reached over instinctively and patted her gently and she twisted around and looked at him, but she stopped making the keening noise.

"You gonna' be okay, ma'am?"

"God chose me to be a beekeeper." Or at least that's what it sounded like. He asked her to repeat it and she said something else.

"People don't know what it's like. He sends me all the signals and I have to deal with it handle it some things some time some time some people and then and then and I and some sometimes some people and it gets and it is—"

She sagged a little and very gently he said, "God speaks through you, does he?"

"Yes, that's correct Mr. Police Person Man. God speaks through me does her yes that's is one hundred percent." She looked at him more closely, perhaps to see if he was making fun of her or teasing in some way.

"I've heard about that," he said, "it must be a big responsibility to carry around with you." She said nothing. Lowered her head again. "When someone does this kind of thing," he went on softly, "we want to find out who did it and stop them before they hurt someone else. That's why I need to know if you saw anything before—"

"I have eels and snakes in my hair and electrical energy voltage that runs up and down my arms and back into here and then that's we that's the that's how someway you see that they are here and that's and then and so I and can and what happens is you get it all mixed up and backward."

"Yes." He nodded at what she had just said as if it made perfect sense. "I know what you mean. And then when somebody does something awful the police have to stop them. You know?"

"Uh-huh. I know." She nodded sagely. They were having a real good discussion. She cocked her head at Eichord.

"I haven't seen you around here before. Do you live here?"

"No. I live a long ways away."

"I live a long ways away too. I live on a planet beyond the moon and on the other side of the stars and God speaks his wisdom through my electric tongue and I know you don't live around here because I have never seen you before and I know how to remember who I have seen before and who I have not and you I have not and so that is how I know you have not. So, there, and there, and—" He interrupted her with his soft, soothing tones and all the while gentling her, calming her down. "So you knew you hadn't seen me

around before. You knew I was a stranger around
here, didn't you?"

"Yes, that's right." She smiled, revealing blood in
her mouth.

"Ma'am, you've got some blood there in your mouth,
did you cut yourself?" he asked solicitously.

"Huh?"

"Your mouth. Have you hurt your mouth?"

"Uh. I—" She dabbed a filthy rag at her mouth.
saw blood on it and laughed and said, "I have bad
gums. My teeth are real good, it's my *gums* that are
bad and sometimes I hurt there and uh—so—" She
trailed off.

"You knew I was a stranger around here. You must
know everybody around here."

"I know everybody around here."

"If somebody was messing around over there"—he
pointed toward the dumpster where a team were working with a body bag—"and you'd never seen them
around here before you'd know it, wouldn't you?"

"Uh-huh."

"And I'll bet you could even describe them," he
whispered to her softly.

"I can describe them easy, and I speak in the many
tongues so that he can fast know the way that what
can come of being in the part where I can see something and then they come and take it back and I don't
and I will never can be able to see that I wasn't
and—"

"It's okay," he said, realizing he was going to get
nothing from the poor old lady, and he took a small
card out and a pen and began writing numbers on it as
he spoke to her. "I'd like to give you something, and I
want you to do something for me if you will."

"You want to give me a present?" She brightened.

"This card has my telephone number at work and at
home. Please keep this. It is very important"—he was
speaking very slowly and carefully, hoping he could
hold her attention—"that you call me if you remember
seeing anyone around here tonight you have never

seen before. Someone who might have done the bad thing to that woman. Someone strong. Will you think about that for me?"

"I have electrical energy currents that plug into my eyes and it hurts so I cannot receive signals from the moon unless they are sent where that I can and so you will see and come up and come around and come out and—" She rocked back and forth and held the card he had handed her. He had to leave with Joyce who was finishing a conversation with the lieutenant, and he thanked the old woman who didn't look up. But as he was walking away she said something that sounded like "You" or "Yoo-hoo" and he turned and she said, "Good-bye Mr. Police Boy." And he smiled and waved at her.

He and Joyce started working their way up the alley or down the alley, whichever it was, and he saw about a dozen others fanning out in teams, patrol guys, half a dozen clothes including two homicide dicks from the 18th, Gomez and Riordan, whom he'd met. Eichord could hear somebody, maybe the young uniform cop, with the dry heaves and he could feel his stomach rumble in spite of himself and he fought to keep the bile from coming up in his throat. He swallowed and concentrated on the make-work at hand.

Someone was both sick and very powerful. To be able to rip human beings apart like that. There'd been a couple with the rib cages totally torn loose. And he remembered the dead farmer they'd found in the pickup across the road from where they'd found the body of the Kasikoff woman. He was a huge, muscular brawler, had a rap sheet even, former bouncer, ex-marine, had a rep for liking to throw a few hands. The killer had taken him effortlessly. Perhaps he'd been an eyewitness to the Sylvia Kasikoff murder and the killer had wasted him to protect himself. But who had he killed first, the woman or the man in the pickup. And why the two together. And were the two of them, the farmer, who was named Avery Johnson he remembered, and the woman—were they connected in some fashion? A boyfriend of the married woman perhaps? All kinds of possibilities to exhaust.

After giving up a couple of hours later and they were dragging back through the alley toward their vehicle, something moved in the shadows against the wall and Joyce tapped Eichord and pointed as the bag lady came out of the shadows, moving toward Eichord out of the darkness, the wheels of her cart rattling toward him.

For just a second or so he imagined she was coming up to him to tell him she remembered seeing a big strong weight-lifter or bodybuilder type and he was going to solve this just like on TV and she came up to him in the light where he and Joyce were standing and smiled pleasantly and confided to him in a conspiratorial whisper.

"Marjorie has snakes and eels nesting in her hair and the current and electricity from the hair comes down and shoots through her hair and into her body and she cannot see what they want because so much planning and decisions all at once and then you don't know where to do or go to next because there is so much happening inside and how can you explain or understand that so much is coming through the air from the moon at night or when energy signals and they never stop so you forget sometimes."

Chaingang

Like some huge, vast, beached whale, the enormous figure lies sprawled across the tarp that covers the filthy bed. Flat on his back. Snoring slightly, a great rising, falling, ludicrous mound, clown man, dreaming, smiling sometimes as he dreams, his face contorting, pinching into a huge smile there in the darkness and stench.

He dreams he is still driving at this microsecond and in his sleep he hears the steady hum of the white line as he roars through the night toward another kill. He listens to its monotonous, comforting song and becomes one with it.

And the white line hums beneath him, steadily, hypnotically, and Little Baby Danny, the tiny boy who was abused and tortured and molested as a baby, then abandoned later, this other persona of Danny emerges from within, deep inside his dark hiding place where he whimpers from where he has been whipped with the electrical cord.

And Little Danny is hypnotized by the humming white line the long unbroken ceaseless never-ending song of the road humming beneath his moving wheels and his mind is a vision of all white. Virgin white and pure and blemishless and smooth. Hot. A burning, white fire. An incandescence of white heat that scorches the raw edges of his tortured mind.

It comes in a sphere of perfect and infinite roundness, and it burns, burns, burns. It burns with a familiar white fire and if Danny looks at it closely it resembles a white ball as the line continues to sing to him, reassure him, hmmmmmmmmmmm, and he can puncture it with the sharpness of his imagination pricking the white balloon and allowing the blackness of his dark hiding place to fill the sphere, cooling it with its inky liquid and feeling good where the cord has left its fiery stinging marks.

The stream of black fills the round white ball like the ebb of black water rising in a dish of perfect, pure white, rising as the white heat cools in the black water, and the curve of the white dish is a black curve now as the water overflows and fills the dish and the rounding of the black curve that he sees so vividly becomes their gleaming, round piano top that Mommy was so proud of and on the top of her baby grand sits a ticking metronome, his mother's metronome, and Daniel Edward Flowers Bunkowski-Zandt breathes in the essence of the black and stills his beating heart with the ticking of the metronome.

"Tick . . . Tick . . . Tick . . . Tick . . ."

And subtly, the imperceptible and inexplicable containment begins. Slower, with the slow, measured ticks of the ceaseless ticking pyramid, with every thu-bump, thu-bump, beat of his strong heart he slows wills slows wills slows his heartbeat down slightly, as he dreams he is driving listening to the hypnotic hmmmmmmmm-mmmmm of the white line roaring through the dark envelope of night piercing the darkness with his twin lasers zooming toward a kill as the white line comforts him and stills his heartbeat with the measured tick of Mommy's piano-top metronome slowing willing slo-ooowwwwiiinnnggg

"Tick . . . Tick . . . Tick . . ."

And at first he dreams of a time when he was afraid. Yes, even he is sometimes afraid. He is getting on a bird and he hates them because it hurts his ankle when he drops out of them and then he must walk a long ways and it is not good. He is also afraid of the edge there where he must sometimes sit and he cannot look down or the bloodrush will take him and he will pitch forward and fall thousands of feet and die there in the jungle and he is afraid when he walks under the whirling blade and he is afraid when the noise is so great and there is screaming and he knows that he can shift his weight quickly in a certain way and cause a bird to pitch over and kill everyone in it and it pleases him to think about that when the crew chiefs work to counter his bulk and the only reason he doesn't kill them is that he might hurt himself when the bird tipped over and he is always glad when he feels them lift from him in a whirl of rocks and dust and limbs and stinging things and he often thinks of pitching a frag up into the birds when they lift off and how much fun it would be to see the bird explode in a ball of orange flame and how pleasant it would be to kill the smiling occupants.

But he is a realist and a detail man and he must dream the dream in sequence or he cannot get to the lovely moment when he is there in the jungles killing the humans and taking the parts of them that satisfy his awful hunger and so he must think first of the time when he is still on the bird because that is the way that dream begins:

It is 0230 and he is standing with a fireteam on the pierced steel planking of Ramp 2, at Quang Tri Airstrip, "Viceroy." They are boarding a Huey slick, and he must climb in first so that they can position his weight for the takeoff. They are arrogant as all of these helicopter personnel are, and he could easily kill them but they will take him where the killing is unlimited and wonderful, delightful killing fields where he can take many, many human lives, and he ignores these childish men.

The starter makes an awful, pained noise and the turbine begins running up and the blade above them begins wh-yuuuuup, wha-yuuuuuppp, whaaa-huppp, yup, yup, ypppppppppppppppppping as it picks up speed and the noise is a deafening blast furnace as the machine groans and shudders and improbable as it always is lifts in a whomp-whomp-whomp of spinning blades and noise and heat and confusion and he can overhear the pilot say, "Yeah, Diamond 21, Viceroy Tower, we gotta' *load* and we're up and on our way to Hillside Killer." The pilot smirks.

"RRRRRRAAAAAAAAWWWWWRRR-RRR," the radio crackles, [Garble] Diamond 21." And he hears the static garbage of intercom noise.

Hillside Killer is a location where they are inserting this four man fireteam. Hillside Killer is actually a man light as Chaingang will move out on his own, a one-man fireteam in effect, and he smiles from ear to ear as he contemplates his lonely and thrilling jungle ambush that awaits him.

The other team members on board Diamond 21 will rendezvous with personnel from Central Park Killer, which is the location where the preceding bird has just overflown the landing zone. He has no interest in the overall mission of the ridiculous team, or whatever may happen to these other men. He works alone. He grins in anticipation.

But now his dream compresses and he does not have to ride in the noisy bird and feel the sickening descent down or hear the awful noise or the frightening time when he must drop off the skid and slam through the air his hundreds of pounds hurtling down to crush his already-sore ankle and he has no memories of dropping into the LZ or the bird hovering then lifting as the team disperses into the jungle.

He is moving deeper into his dream, and the dream takes him into another night and another ambush, and it is daytime and this is one of the favorite dreams—he has one of his best ambush dreams—and white humming lines hypnotically take him deep into his cozy and familiar jungle.

He is dreaming of a lovely moment, a killing of two humans in the jungles of Vietnam. It is a mission like all the other missions; he participates only for the night patrols. Ignoring all the rest of it. He walks drag so that no carelessness can harm him. He always remembers to close the back door, to look both ways before crossing the street, to walk softly and carry a big stick

They have just crossed a field and he has walked slowly, letting the others blunder ahead, hoping some of them will be killed. They seem foolish to him and he cannot admire their soldiering. It is pleasantly warm and he enjoys the feel of the hot sun as he slowly crosses the field and soon finds himself in jungle. Big trees just like he hoped for. He communicates with trees, actually holds intelligent conversations with them, and he will ask these trees for information.

The openings between some of the trees are very narrow and he realizes how he can use this later. Vines make movement more difficult, impeding it completely in some places. There are thickets, thorn bushes, all kinds of impenetrable jungle come out around the path he follows, the route where the others have gone now a wet, oozing slime of bootprints.

Water! Water and a trail have only one meaning. Ambush. He can smell little people everywhere. The main pathway goes off to the left but he can hear and smell the water to the right and he follows the scent. There is a creekbed under a protective arch of tree limbs that form a roof of sorts, having grown out from either side of the narrow stream of water, making a perfect green tunnel.

The word AMBUSH screams at him again. His skin prickles in pleasure and anticipation. He knows he can wait here and kill some of the little people. He sees nothing in terms of our side/enemy or North/South. He kills ARVN and Cong alike since in truth there is often no way to separate the two. Such distinctions don't concern him anyway. He hungers for an ambush of the little ones that the others call dinks and gooks and slopes. He hungers for their life source, lusting for bloodspill. This is the dream of the dreaming monster.

He does not exist, of course. They will promise you that and look you directly in the eye. His profession has been phased out, obsolete, they will assure you, long extinct like the cretaceous iguanodont, a profession made superfluous they'll tell you, rendered nonexistent like vaudeville, a bygone artifact like three-cent stamps and Davy Crockett caps. There is no much animal as a professional assassin. In Russia, maybe. But not here.

And so each time we learn of a professional assassin we are told he was that one exception to the rule. A rogue elephant. A once-in-a-lifetime deviation that was bungled or exposed and never tried again. The fact you have learned of his existence proves how inept we are at such things. No. Outside of show business and literary invention or perhaps some ancient leftover of whatever the goombahs are calling Cosa Nostra these days, he is an invention. A fictional device. And that is the official line. What else.

The real killers are seldom portrayed in popular fiction. They are seldom pretty enough for consumption. The word *assassin*, literally, means one who does murder under the influence of hashish, and today it evokes the pop-culture portrait of a black-suited ninja dropping down out of the trees to kick the bad guys into little pieces. Real killing is seldom so neat as one sees it on the screen. There is lots of blood and gore and horror. And "wet work," the profession of slaughtering, takes its toll on the killer as well as the victim.

The real irony is that our spymasters and those who control our intelligence monolith wish that they had a vast agency of highly efficient superkillers to draw from. How operationally marvelous it would be for all of them if they could only reach out and draw upon the wealth of diversity, the richness that our pop fiction would have you believe exists. We do have killers, of course, and have had for a long time. But their track record is far from great.

Unlike KGB or the Israelis we have not maintained a special section of security personnel whose sole function is to kill. We have had to build a small pool of talent outside the security umbrella, in the elite branches of the military, in certain areas of law enforcement, and even marginally in the private sector for "termination with extreme prejudice."

In 1960, with sensitivities raw, the national security heads decided to create a small and highly clandestine unit that could be used for assassinations. At the time our intelligence services taught the deadly arts but only as an adjunct to tradecraft. We had no counterpart to SMERSH's Active Measures Department that operated covertly as a unit trained to do sanctioned murder by governmental decree.

It proved as difficult for our controllers to find contact killers as it had for outraged wives wanting someone to cowboy their cheating spouses. So our security people turned to what is laughingly called organized crime, on one hand, and the military on the other. One of those military experiments was MACVSAU-COG, a hot mouthful of alphabet soup cooked up by an action arm of the National Security Council. Mack-Vee-Saw-Cog, as it was pronounced, was the first of the so-called secret sanction groups, and because of its special status of a "paramilitary" unit the most clandestine.

MACVSAUCOG was classified out there in the vortical swirl of smoke beyond the ULTRA TOP SECRET YOUR EYES ONLY classification. The main course was counterinsurgency warfare. The first thing it served up to its proud masters was a nasty little piece of business called the spike team. The spike team was designed for one purpose. To assassinate covertly. And it was built around one man, a four-hundred-plus pounder who was then waiting to hear on an appeal, doing Death Row time in a federal prison in Illinois. He was a "discovery" of unusual proportions in every sense.

Marion Federal Penitentiary has a number of nicknames, one of the more accurate being The House of Pain. It is the only correctional institution in the Federal lash-up with a level-six rating. A con inside Marion is serving an AVERAGE sentence of forty-and-a-quarter years. Slammed down tight under a twenty-two-and-a-half-hour-a-day lockdown, behind a fortress of eight guard towers and chainlink and sharp razor wire, are some of the toughest, most feared, wild-eyed killer cons in the federal system. In 1961, over there with the 340-some animals in Max, was a creature named Daniel Bunkowski.

At the time of his incarceration Daniel Edward Flowers Bunkowski tipped the scales at 422 pounds. At six feet seven inches he was a find. A unique combination—both seemingly retarded and a mind that was incredibly keen, a rational-and-"sane"-appearing sociopathic mass murderer. If his ramblings under drugged hypnosis were to be believed he had killed more than any other human being alive. So many killings in fact that even he wasn't sure how many lives he had taken.

A respected sociologist had seen something in his personality, some camouflage, some signal, and he had begun a series of carefully structured tests on Daniel and come away amazed. Bunkowski's IQ was not measurable. It "warped the curve." He was an autodidact, a self-taught killer whose alarming proclivity for violence was surpassed only by what appeared to be a genius intellect. A computer was spoon-fed the results of the testing and the consensus with respect to Mr. Bunkowski. And the computer served a select and highly covert series of on-line terminals.

There was even a bizarre, and far from scientific opinion advanced by one Dr. Norman there in the shop. He was of the opinion that this behemoth of a man had managed to escape detection and capture for so long a period, murdering wantonly and randomly as he had, because he was presentient. A physical precognate. None seriously believed this other than Dr. Norman, but it made the Bunkowski dossier even

more interesting to certain folk in the clandestine service, for whom every poisonous cloud has a silver
lining.

After more tests, interviews, drug-and-hypnosis ses-
sions, interrogations both rigorous and benign, exami-
nations, and debriefings, the aggregate data was poured
into the computers and the mavens gathered to pay
homage to the *deus ex machina* of tradecraft, and the
printout filled them with certitude. Theoretically, at
least, this Bunkowski person was ideal for the pur-
poses they had in mind. And they began creating a
spike team around this unlikely discovery.

Here is how you create a Daniel "Chaingang" Bunkowski. Take a little boy. Take his daddy away when
he is a baby and substitute a succession of drunks,
hypes, perverts, and assorted human filth. Make
Mommy a drunk too, and now give the baby a particularly vicious "stepfather" who doesn't like to hear
baby cry. He likes to put Danny in high places where
he will scream in terror, and leave him locked in
closets for days yes *days* at a time, and because he
is a bad little boy and survives chain him into a
special little metal place you've made for him. It is
his discipline box. And at night when "Uncle" comes
to visit Mommy later on, and Mommy is gone,
Uncle will chain him under the bed and bring him
out to use him and then jam him back under the
bed on his chain, feeding and watering him in doggy's
bowl. And when you beat him use your fists first,
and then a nice electrical cord, and later on a short
piece of rubber hose so Mommy won't see too many
bruises. Force the little boy to do every despicable,
unspeakable, depraved, degenerate thing in the pervert lexicon, and then invent a few just to keep
interested. And don't forget to torture him every so
often with clothespins, pieces of wire, matches, burning
cigarettes, a soldering iron—anything that will inflict
sudden and devastating pain. And then when he is a
big boy put him in a home where lots of bigger kids

can use him too, and that is how you make a Daniel Bunkowski.

Now tease and torment and assault and abuse and abandon and finally try to kill little Danny. And if Danny surprises all of you and SURVIVES . . . oh, my God in heaven . . . if he's four-hundred-and-some pounds of deeply, brutally disturbed manhood, six-feet-seven of spring-hard legs bigger than tree trunks and fingers that can rip a jawbone loose, tearing stabbing ripping like steel tools, and if he's spent about half of his horror of a life institutionalized in one way or another and if he's free to roam and kill, well by God on high you'd better get up and pray because he is A DEATH MACHINE and vengeance is HIS and you'd better believe he has a hundred ways to hunt you down and turn you into an unrecognizable bathtub full of red pulp and dripping, steaming dog shit.

And this is what is dreaming the dreams. He is dreaming it is night and he is camouflaged, traps set, waiting beside the neat green pipeline, a perfect roofing of leafy, verdant cover that hides the trickle of water. He is CHAINGANG again in his dream. A silent, still, unseeing, unmoving, lone killing unit. Waiting. Impervious to the tiny things crawling on him and buzzing around him. Waiting in the absolute blackness of the deep Vietnamese jungle, listening to the mosquitoes and the symphony of night noises, the dark overture that will tell him of the coming of the little ones. And the steel cigar fingers of his giant right paw ever so gently touch the special canvas and leather pocket that houses his three-foot, taped tractor chain, and he takes the last inch of slack out of the wire that triggers his grenade trap. And he waits with infinite patience, a beaming smile plastered across his big, dimpled countenance. And this is what he dreams. Of humans coming there in the darkness.

He dreams that he waits without moving. Scarcely breathing. His vital signs slowed to a crawl. A deadly, totally dedicated, ruthless killer. Efficient. An atavistic throwback to the precivilization when man killed to

live. He lives to kill. And he is waiting in the blackness with a loaded M-60 LMG, a violent hell of hand
grenades wired into his frag trap, a razor-sharp bowie,
and a yard of heavy chain. And in this dream he
smiles his grotesque, dimpled smile, remembering the
red mist and the taste of fresh, bloody human heart.

Jack Eichord
Meets the
Lynch Family

For three days and the better part of a fourth Jack Eichord sst on his butt at a borrowed desk in the squad room alternately reading the file on Sylvia Kasikoff and making fruitless phone calls of one kind or another. He was tromping over old ground. As police work it was probably worthless, as a time killer it was only slightly better. Boring stuff. People had moved, phone numbers had been disconnected, people had days off at work, work numbers had changed, out for illness, busy but he'll call you back, and so on. There's nothing worse than having to spend hours and hours on a telephone, especially when the results were zipadee-doodah.

A lot of calls were long distance, and everything involving a direct dial call seemed to backfire, and every time Eichord got a phone operator it was as if he'd played Operator Roulette and lost. That's like you have all these operators waiting, in theory, and you dial 0 and the most vile-tempered, arrogant, stupid, offensive, abrasive, sententious, officious and slow-witted bitch at AT&T gets you. After a couple of days of this he was getting phone paranoia, and subconsciously concocting little scenarios in which the phone company, pissed at divestiture, decides to seek revenge on the populace at large and instructs all its operators to be as obtuse, recalcitrant, irritatingly brusque, and shitty-tempered as possible.

On the third day something happened to the lines and all 1-plus calls were answered by operators who kept insisting that he "report your trouble to Repair." After a few of those he gave up on phone calls, both local and LD, and concentrated on pouring through old police reports, crime-scene photos, interviews, newspaper write-ups on the Lonely Hearts Killer, lab reports, transcripts, all manner of fun reading from official CYA tap dances to autopsy summaries. There was a ton of paperwork to digest, and he'd barely scratched the surface.

At approximately 1400 he packed it in and took his map into Vernon Arlen's office and got directions on how to get to the Lynch home, filled his battered attaché case with unread homework, and headed north for suburbia, despite having been unable to get an answer at the Lynch house for the fourth day in a row. It beat sitting in the squad room sucking up used smoke.

About this time he always thought about stopping in some nice little neighborhood tavern for a cold one, just to relax in familiar surroundings, mellow out for a few minutes, and enjoy watching the working folks come in for their boilermakers, a little shot n' beer or two on the way home, and a little double for a tightener on the way out the door what the hell. He loved the booze smell of bars and he'd nurse his Light and let the effluvia seep into his bloodstream by osmosis.

Or he'd stop into some little bistro for a little happy-hour pick-me-up. A nice dark saloon, atmospheric and dense with smoke and that rich, brain-battering booze aroma that he loved. Even as he drives through the gray Chicago streets the ambience swirls around his imagination engulfing him in the memories of that mixture that is uniquely happy-hour bistro. Lentheric, VO, Johnny Walker Red, Chanel, Gibsons, margaritas in icy glasses, a Harvey Wallbanger; assorted scents and flavors of urban decadence waft through his imagination.

His mind's eye pictures a nice, dark saloon with that heavy old wainscoting, an ornate backbar full of crystal, a shiny, gleaming brass rail. Leather stools. No chrome. No plastic. No disco bass thumping. The music drips out of the darkness and booze smell, the notes cool and fluid, golden colored and intoxicating like the stuff in the glasses—and it drips into a drinker's wet daydream. The music cuts through the swirl like a silver stiletto plunged into wet, black velvet, piercing the boozer's back with blue-note jazz. Unsmiling, tough, a little twisted maybe, convincingly alcoholic, sustaining the buzz and nurturing the feel of a serious drinker's saloon.

But now he is out of the mainstream, driving with frequent checks to find the next street marked on his map, on a route that looks like any midwestern small town, cleaners and package stores and video shops and Radio Shacks and fast-food places in an endless blur of neon, gray streets and the beginnings of a pretty sunset in the background, as he negotiates the unfamiliar territory, fixing it all in his mind so he can find his way back after dark. And now through the commercial section and out past the junkyards and salvage places and nurseries and on his way to the suburbs.

1619. Eichord has been parked across from the Lynch residence for an hour. He's read reports with half an eye on the street traffic, after having rung the bell and waited a couple of minutes. No barking dogs. The street is quiet save for a pack of kids on the way home after school. He watches a couple of jets go over and leave contrails in the stratocumulus, and he moves his head from side to side to get the cricks out, hearing the second vertebra pop like a finger snap.

Twenty minutes later and he's got his long legs stretched out diagonally across the front seat, and wishing he'd brought a thermos of coffee. So far this day is shaping up to be a king-size cipher. So much of police work is in the waiting. Surveillance, to some, can be one of the most hated jobs. A plant is one of the necessary evils in the job. He looks at his watch again. He decides to stick it out another twenty minutes, then go catch a cheeseburger and get some coffee and come back. She's got to come home sometime. There's only one newspaper on the lawn so that's an encouraging sign. No neighbors home yet either. This place would be a natural for some B&E guy who wanted to take down six or seven places in one afternoon, just for the silver and the shotguns, and minimum risk.

Nobody home. No cars in the driveway. Kids' toys all over the yards. Where is everybody? Other than a handful of cars and that pack of kids he hadn't seen a human face. One of the houses had a FOR SALE sign in the yard. Lawn a little shaggy, but every other yard looked like it had been trimmed with a scissors right before the last of the fall grass. Leaves all raked. Neat City. He waited with his mind on hold and watched one of the most beautiful, dazzling sunsets he could remember. The sky high up still lightly blue with a little peach color and then down where he could see the horizon a ribbon of the most beautiful red lighting up the dark bluish gray with a bright, breathtaking slash of color. And he was enjoying looking at it when Edie Lynch drove up into her driveway.

"Are you Mrs. Edward Lynch, ma'am?" he asked her, smiling pleasantly as she turned to face him by her front door.

"Yes."

"Sorry to bother you again, Mrs. Lynch," he said, showing his shield and ID as he spoke, "but we're investigating some related matters and I wonder if I might ask you just a few questions. It wouldn't take but a minute." She seemed to deflate visibly as he said the words.

"Oh. Yes."

"Can I help you with those?" he offered.

"Oh, no, that's all right, just let me get this one bag in with the milk and things and—Lee Anne, get that little sack on the backseat for Mommy please—and I can get this." He took the larger of the sacks from her as she spoke, and she shrugged a thank-you and smiled as he followed the woman into the house, the child running up the sidewalk after them with a sack of what looked like paper towels.

"That's fine," she said, "just sit it down there, thanks."

"Go ahead and put your groceries away, ma'am, no problem."

"That's okay. Just—uh, Lee, honey, go in and start cleaning up your room now, please, and I'll get the other things." She turned back to Eichord. "I don't want to talk about it in front of—"

"I understand. I won't take up much of your time here, but I'm just coming on board this investigation and if you can I'd just like to go over some old ground with you from the time of the tragedy that happened. Just to make sure I have all the information."

"They asked so many questions back then and I'm sure you'll have more than I'll be able to remember now down there in your reports, but I'll try to answer whatever I can of course." She was obviously very tired. He didn't ask but he wondered where they'd been for the last few days.

Glancing down at the report cover he was holding, he began without any hesitancy, getting right after it. "I have to take you back to some sad, painful old ground, and I want to ask you to help me reconstruct that evening," he began softly, soothingly, speaking in measured tones, building a layer of trust as he always did. Within a few minutes he'd be calling her by her first name, asking her calm, easy questions in preparation for the heavy stuff that was his sole reason for going back to this ancient, cold trail.

She repeated all the information that she'd given countless times before, embellishing one or two things, forgetting here and there, very straightforward in her willingness to retrace the ordinary events that had led up to that fateful night as well as she could remember them. And then he pitched her his change-up, and the long, slow curve that preceded his high hard one.

"What were his exact words if you can recall when he left that night?"

"He said he was going out for cigarettes and he'd be right back."

"No. Edie try to tell me the exact way he said it to you that night."

"Well . . . he said." She paused, trying to get it right. "I'm going to run down to the 7-Eleven and get some cigarettes. Do you need anything?"

"And you said what?"

"I said no thanks," she said, shaking her head.

"How much did Ed smoke—how many packs a day, do you remember?"

"Not too much, I guess. He never smoked over two packs a day."

"Do you remember the brand?"

"Parliaments," she said, somewhat exasperated at the question.

"Edie when Ed was found he had a half a pack of Parliaments in his pocket. We found cigarettes here in the house according to the reports. Now, that could just mean that he hadn't had a chance to get to the store yet when he was attacked. But it could have another meaning." She raised her eyebrows and made a little frown of irritation. He let the pitch go. "It could also mean that Ed wasn't going out for smokes that night."

"What do you mean?"

"What it could mean is that he'd gone to meet somebody."

"No. He said he was going to the store, I just told you that."

"But husbands don't always tell their wives the truth." He was watching her very carefully, boring into her with those hard eyes and keen reason.

"Well, Ed and I weren't like that. He was always truthful with me."

"What if—just to make a hypothetical situation, Edie—what if he'd wanted to meet someone that night. Another woman, for example, and he didn't want you to know. How certain are you that he wasn't going out to meet someone that night?"

"That's the most ridiculous question anyone ever asked me. We had a good marriage and Ed was a fine, upstanding man. I can't imagine why you would come around asking something like that."

"I apologize," he said to her softly, "but I have to ask that question for this reason. The man who attacked your husband may have begun committing crimes again. If there is a chance that there might have been some other witness that night, someone who might have seen—oh, let's say someone suspicious looking and they could help us in that regard, I know you'd want us to have that information."

"I can assure you that isn't a possibility. Ed was going to the store that night and that's all there was to it."

He ever so gently began turning the questions back around to the safer area, times, places, things she'd be more comfortable answering. Slowly some of the strain and irritation went out of her face and he was getting ready to wrap it up, hoping to leave a less bitter taste as he faded back out of her life, when an irrepressible bundle of cuteness came bounding down the stairs and came up saying, "Hi! Mom can we eat now?"

"Hi," he said, smiling, as her mom shook her head.

"No, dear, we'll be eating soon. This is my daughter Lee Anne, Mr.—"

"Eichord. Jack Eichord."

"Mr. Eichord is a detective working on Dad's case."

"Mr. Acorn?" she repeated quizzically.

"Eye-cord," her mother corrected.

"I'll bet you never heard that name before, did you?" he said. She shook her head in response shyly, smiling, standing very close, one of those people who will go through life never meeting a stranger.

"Lee Anne is a pretty name."

"Thank you."

"How old are you?"

"I'll be nine."

"That's a great age to be. Do you like school?"

"Uh-huh. I like Mrs. Spencer the best of all. Are you a real detective that's like on television?"

"I'm a real detective."

"Can you come talk to my bear. He's been very bad and needs to have a police detective investigate him."

"I happen to specialize in bears. What kind of bear is it?"

"He's a talking bear."

"Sweety," her mom interrupted, "Mr. Eichord doesn't have time to—"

"No. It's fine. Really," he said quickly. "In fact that's the main reason I came out here, to see what some of these bears have been up to." And Lee Anne was sort of helping him out of the chair and showing him toward the room where the bear was even as he soundlessly gave Edie the signal that it was okay with him, if she didn't mind, and she did a little shrug and head move kind of thing that said okay, but really said, well, whatever turns you on, because she was still angry inside. And before anyone could change their mind and let better judgment and wiser heads prevail, Jack Eichord, who a couple of minutes before had implicitly suggested Mrs. Lynch's late husband might have been having an extramarital affair was now in the bedroom with her daughter. Fate works in strange, mysterious ways.

"What is this talking bear's name?" she could hear him ask.

"My name is Ralph," her daughter answered in her bear voice, "and my brother's name is George."

"Just give me the bare facts, please," Eichord said, and the bear giggled.

"Now I've heard rumors that you have misbehaved. Could you tell us the bare essentials?"

"I bite sometimes."

"Oh, my, Ralph. Biting is absolutely un-bear-able," giggling, "of course this is barely admissible evidence."

"My brother George is a talking panda."

"That's very interesting. I'm afraid I'm going to

have to frisk you for weapons, Ralph old boy." Squeals of delight. "Uh-oh. Afraid this has become a ticklish situation. I don't think you'll be able to bear up under this sort of interrogation. If you promise to behave, I'll let you go with a warning, but no more biting. Okay?"

"Okay," she said.

"And no putting up bearicades, either. It's too embear-ussing, if you know what I mean." Lee Anne was laughing at the routine and he kept it up. So she had to show him George and Eichord had a long talk with the panda, and finally ended up back downstairs. Edie had been listening to every word of it and suddenly realized she'd been grinning from ear to ear for the last few minutes. They came back into the kitchen hand in hand, Lee leading him quite contentedly, both utterly charmed by the other.

"That was very nice of you to take so much ti—"

"Mom, I asked Mr. Eye-cord to stay for dinner is that okay?"

"I really can't," he said before she could have a chance to be totally flustered by it, "but that's very sweet of you, Lee Anne. Thanks." He seemed nice. He seemed different now too.

"I have to get back downtown," he said, and so very obviously didn't that before she could catch herself she said, "We'd like for you to stay and have a bite with us. We're only having hot dogs. How about it?"

She smiled at him and he felt so warm all of a sudden it kind of stunned him and the usually glib Jack Eichord just stood there like a schmuck and went, "Uh—" Brilliant, he thought. "No. I appreciate it. That is very nice." He was heading for the door. He felt like he was slogging through wet cement.

"Please," she said, with sufficient sincerity that he turned. She was finally snapping out of her anger enough to have sensed what it was he had been going for and she realized that he was probably a pretty decent cop, trying to do what amounted to an impossible task. And she saw herself as having been a little bitchy, whether justified or not, and she decided she'd make amends.

"If you don't have to be somewhere for supper right away, please stay. We'd enjoy having your company. Just hot dogs. Nothing fancy and no trouble." She told him with her eyes that she wasn't being polite and he stood there saying yes and felt a small hand pluck the hat out of his hand and the suffusion of warmth from a family start reaching out and touching him unexpectedly.

And something funny happened. Suddenly they were looking at each other and seeing a man and woman instead of the adversaries they'd been looking at before. And everything tilted a little, and Edie felt so funny as she was putting little slivers of cheese inside the split franks and putting them inside the microwave, and she was so dumbfounded at what she was suddenly thinking as she looked at this detective, this perfect stranger, thinking to herself the oddest damn thing, wondering what he'd be like, and she took a deep breath and couldn't make the thought go away.

And he looked at the back of her standing there in front of the oven with an apron over her dress and all tall and slim on those long, great-looking legs, and the look of her just came out of nowhere and destroyed him. He knew it was only because it had been so long since he had been in a situation like this, a real home, when it wasn't the home of one of his colleagues, and with an eligible young woman cooking him dinner, a lovely woman in fact, and not some one-night stand he'd picked up somewhere or the other way around. And the sight of her in heels, all that leg, and the little apron, with her back turned, just demolished him. And inside he went, Jesus, man, get a hold of yourself, are you nuts or what?

And inside Edie was thinking with her back turned, What am I letting myself in for here? And sensing that he was looking at her and not really minding it so much but just wondering what was going on and then thinking she'd been imagining the whole thing. It was ridiculous. Shape up. And with a tilt of her head and a feeling of relief she turned and their eyes locked, and hell the old cliches like "chemistry" have been so abused you can't even say them with a straight face but that's what it was, a chemical thing between them happening in spite of their best intentions, happening for no reason, coming out of nowhere, a thing that worked its way out of the secret heart of a person somehow and warms on its way up and then comes out of the eyes all hot and hungry.

This didn't even make a lick of sense she told herself and what are you doing and hold on and whoa and oh it's too late now, she thinks, sinking down into something that is pulling her like the current of a river of mighty whirlpools, and she tries not to let it show and feels the hot red flush of her cheeks and almost laughs at it out loud.

And he goes, Now wait you've got to be kidding here I'm not believing this, you go to somebody's house to ask some questions and you're looking at this woman like some love-starved teenage kid and this is some lady who lost her husband a couple of years ago and just what in hell do you think you're doing and they'll laugh you right out of the place if you and oh my God I'm falling and that wonderful awful feeling as he senses what is happening between them, wonderful if it's real, awful if it's one-sided and then the chemistry is just so strong that neither of them are trying to hide it.

And the dinner is cold and they're still there at the table just talking, talking about nothing, who remembers what, who knows what, just watching each other's mouths move, carrying on a conversation. Christ, he thinks, even the word *conversation* means *sexual union*, and he bites the insides of his lips raw to keep from laughing and telling her and yet knowing she'd understand. And now he knows that something is going to happen between them because it already is starting and she isn't saying yes or no but she is aware of something and he's going to make it happen.

It is very important to him now not to blow it. Not to do anything stupid or oafish or frighten her in any way. This is something special. Different. He feels something and he can't really analyze it because of the hot, flooding rush of desire that flows through his loins as he looks at her and he wants this woman and aware as they both are of the incongruities he can't stop himself.

Somehow they manage to part company that night, and of course he can't go out that door without leaving a connection, something, how the hell can he leave it so he can ask for a date, ask her out somehow, and he mumbles something about paying her back and he'd like to take her and her daughter to dinner next time mumble mumble, and now Christ almighty *he's* blushing like a little kid this is just unbelievable and she wants a man for the first time since she lost Ed and neither of them has said anything more provocative than the most mundane conversational things and yet—and oh and yet—they finally manage to part, leaving each other as happy if confused, very friendly strangers.

Winslow Charles Maitland ll

W. Charles Maitland of Symington, Maitland, Eaves, and Cox turned the page and scowled. Nobody called him Charlie anymore. He had outlived his only cronies, the one or two in the firm and at the club who had enjoyed that particular distinction. The article in a decidedly left-wing newspaper was a bit of blather on the Op Ed page and it was causing W. Charles Maitland to scowl and giving him just a touch of gas. Maitland scowling was a fearsome thing. Maitland scowling in court had been enough to send more than one young legal eagle nearly into a state of cardiac arrest.

The gist of the article was that the United States system of jurisprudence had become a sort of ultimate parasite, and the author of the piece was not the first to observe that the legal system seemed to view society as simply a food supply to keep the parasite alive. It was just this sort of irresponsible, crapulous—enough! He flung the paper as far from him as he could, which was about four and a half feet.

He tasted the claret and set the glass down, blotting his lips on his bedsheet. He had barely touched a swallow of the wine. Even that tasted bitter to him now. He removed his glasses and rubbed his sore, reddened eyes. He put his glasses back on and reached for the volume on the bedside table.

The old man held the rare book in his gnarled, arthritic fingers, caressing the raised gold binding and the beautifully embossed leather cover. He knew the volume the way you know your own children and he ran his hand across the smooth leather lovingly and quoted, "Where the bee sucks, there suck I. In a cowslip's bell I lie." And nothing. After something. On something. He felt a sharp pang of sorrow. An ineffable sadness of loss, mostly from losing his memory, which he had always prized, and from the impending loss of his life, which had become of surprisingly little consequence.

He trusted only one doctor, and the man was now near senile and at death's door himself. So he had gone to other, younger doctors whom he didn't like or respect and he learned nothing from the tiring tests that he couldn't have guessed in the first place. He was dying. It was a matter of time. A month. Two months. He was tired so much of the time now. The sickness did that to you.

These were only his reading books, the books he kept in his apartment in the penthouse the firm kept on Lake Shore Drive. His own main library was now a museum in another city. He had cased sets of every major rarity. He touched the book as you would stroke the hand of an old friend, thinking of the book in the manner of an antiquarian bookseller: Complete set. Bound in 22.24mo, full crimson, straight-grain morocco, gilt floral borders, back gilt with fleurons, leather label, inner dentelles gilt. A nothing little book, he thought, as he caressed its spine with his gnarled fingers. He opened the cover and read.

"Cum novo commentario ad mondu—" and his eyes ached with the effort. A nothing little book. With a great effort he managed to get out of bed and stand. He shrugged his expensive dressing gown off, letting it fall to the rich carpet, and hobbled over to the closet and got a black, cashmere coat. After some not inconsiderable struggles he got into the thing and padded across the room. out into the large penthouse apart-

ment and over to the glass wall. One entire wall of the living-room area was floor-to-ceiling glass and it was a breathtaking view of the lake and the vista of Chicago after dark.

Seeing it wasn't raining or snowing or doing anything wretched, he padded back across the big room and went out his front door to the elevator. He liked to go for short walks and breathe the nice, nasty smell of the taxi fumes and the downtown as they came wafting through the high-rises of the lakefront's most prestigious executive residential neighborhood. In the elevator he placed an illegal cigar in his mouth and sighed.

His memory had slipped badly in these last years. He could no longer remember anything from one moment to the next, quite literally. The elevator purred to a stop and the door slid open almost soundlessly. He stepped out and walked through the lobby, exchanging nods with the moron doorman, and realizing as he was nearly run over by a woman walking her preposterous poodle that he was still in his bedroom slippers.

What the fuck is the difference? he thought to himself and began walking down the street, hobbling along with his walking stick, a rich, dying old man headed nowhere. And he was still walking five minutes later when he had the little feeling. He was not one to ignore feelings. He had parlayed hunches into a fortune. And he had the feeling that someone or something was following him, stalking him. It was just a feeling he had. He hadn't seen or heard anything.

The street was no more or less deserted than it usually was at this hour and he walked like this almost every night. He could no longer take more than four hours or so in bed each night. But something was different tonight. He detected a presence of something nearby and he couldn't quite place it but the feeling was unsettling.

His own nature had been predatory, and he himself had been a very dangerous man. If you are dangerous and you make enemies, you will often make very dangerous enemies. There were others like himself, powerful predators, who might still wish to do him ill. It was mildly upsetting but he was too far gone to be alarmed at anything.

Still and all, wouldn't that be the last straw? To be mugged out here on the street during his constitutional. Dying of goddamn cancer and get mugged. More than a body could stand. He decided he'd head back to the apartment and about that time a bright silver thing sliced out at him slashing out of nowhere and the phrase "nuncupative will and testament" darted past his consciousness as he tried to curse this thing but the blood from his severed throat stopped this last obloquy of thought in a bright red, surprisingly hot spurt as his heart pumped valiantly pumping his life force out into the darkened street.

The First Time Together

She had forgotten what it was like to wait for the phone to ring. Just as he'd forgotten what it was like to have to build up your nerve to do something. Two more unlikely people never waited to make a date. Both of them long beyond the dating stage. Marriages. Children. Whole histories and lives that the other one couldn't possibly fit into. Just insanity, she thought. And she wondered, for the third or fourth time, when he was going to call her.

He was so damn excited getting ready to go see them that it started irritating him and for a few moments he almost considered calling the whole thing off. He was rushing around trying to get dressed here like it was for a night on the town with a movie star and he was taking some housewife and her kid to some burger joint or whatever. Get a hold of yourself. He took a final look at himself in the mirror, said to hell with it, and tried to keep from running to the car.

No matter how much he told himself that it was purely comical, he couldn't dampen the excitement he felt and the warmth that spread through him at the thought of seeing this woman again. *Unordinary* was the word that kept coming to mind. This was some unordinary woman he was having dinner with to-night. He caught himself humming with the radio and shook his head at the rearview mirror as he sped through all the lawbreakers hurrying home after a hard day at the office.

He seemed to get there a lot faster than he remembered, and his heart was pounding when he pulled up in front of the suburban Lynch home and got out of the car. She and Lee Anne both heard the car door and Lee yelled out,

"Somebody's coming," as her mother went to the door.

She opened the door and smiled as he came up the walkway and said, "Hi."

"Hello." His heart was in his throat. "Hungry?"

"Always." She was completely staggered by the look of him and he was poleaxed right out of his shoes at the sight of her. Neither of them had anything to say and they just stood there dumbly in the doorway as a little face peered around her mother's skirt and said, "Hi."

"Hi, Lee Anne. You hungry?"

"Sure."

"We're ready unless you'd like to come in for a drink first."

"No thanks. I'm set if you guys are." And they headed for the car.

"Where are we gonna go?"

"Anywhere you say, Lee Anne. What sounds good to you?"

"Show Biz."

"What's that?"

"You get pizza. You know. And there's these—uh, mechanical animals, uh—and—"

"Maybe Jack doesn't like pizza. Maybe he'd like to go somewhere else."

"Show Biz sounds good." Lee Anne was obviously pleased at the prospect.

In the car he and Lee Anne had a long conversation, Lee leaning over the seat with her head between them as she answered all of his questions up to a point. He was trying to be conversational but it had been a long time since he'd spent much time in the company of a little child. He was inadvertently doing his cop thing as he rapped with her and for a short while she was polite and tried to respond to the mini-interrogation.

"So. You sound like you've been busy since I saw you last. What do you do besides go to school?"

"Do?"

"You know, where do you go, like, at night after school. Do you have meetings? Do you go to church?"

"Yeah."

"Lee," Edie prodded, "tell Jack what you do on Monday night."

"Monday night I go to piano and Wednesday is GA, and—"

"GA?"

"Girls in Action. You know—church?"

"Um-hmm. Good. And what else?" he asked absentmindedly.

"Thursday is Brownies. *That's enough!*" Edie sank down into the seat. But Eichord only laughed.

"Yeah. You're right. That's plenty," he said smoothly, calmly, and guiding the conversation as he did so easily, and they were talking about something else.

By the time they'd scarfed up the pizza and some of the atmosphere and Lee Anne was already getting anxious to go visit her friend, the child of Edie's best friend at whose home she'd be baby-sat this evening, Lee and Eichord were really hitting it off. Jack thought she had to be one of the friendliest kids and the brightest youngsters he'd ever met and they were both pretty impressed with the other. Edie thought that's the way it is with eight-year-olds they either love ya' or they don't and this one was thataway about this cop. When they headed for the car, the little girl reached for Jack's hand and so it was only natural that he also took Edie's hand and they walked down the sidewalk that way all holding hands.

The first touch of the fingers and then holding each other's hand was like plugging their fingers into a light socket. They wanted each other but there was no sense of pressure, it was something each of them knew was coming and they knew it was going to be good, and it was just a question of the right moment. One of those times when it's not in question at all, really, even though neither one of them had made any kind of a thing about it.

The electricity between them was a living thing that flowed down through their arms and into each other's bodies and it was so beautiful that Eichord loved the moment and tried to will it to just go on and on with the three of them walking like that toward a rented car, him holding hands with this lady he barely knew and her little girl, all plugged into some inexplicable, surging electric current and inanely he thought about the old gal who told him she had electricity flowing through her and he felt like saying, "Doesn't everybody?" And inside his head he let out a silent whoop of pleasure, stopping it before it could get out around his grin, and he looked over at Edie and she was smiling too as they walked to the car touching.

This rush of energy was setting both of them on fire and it was probably a good thing the kid was in the backseat, Eichord thought, or I'd be all over this woman like some kid in a goddamn drive-in. That thought was enough to calm him down a little bit and she could see him visibly withdraw just a notch when they got in the car and she sat very still and tried to think about anything. What did she think about normally? For just that moment she felt like someone else had invaded her skin. She wasn't used to any of this and she wasn't sure that she liked it. And that's the way it went for the next fifteen minutes or so until they got Lee tucked away at Sandi and Mike's.

She said she didn't care what they did and she let him pick a movie and he didn't care either and he'd seen a pair of twin cinemas on the way to get the pizza and so he headed back in that general direction, driving automatically as work and The Job intruded on the evening. His thoughts turned to the latest murder, a wealthy and influential head of one of Chicago's oldest corporate law firms. What triggered it was he had picked up one of the papers and tried to find a movie he thought she'd like, and in tiny print some art house was advertising CLASSIC SERIAL MURDERS and he did a double take and went back and read in fine print CLASSIC SERIAL TRAILERS and this is what he remembered as they drove along in silence.

Two flake cops named McCluskey and Scheige had caught Charles Maitland while they were playing Hawaii Five-O over at the First. Every day they'd play something, these flakes. Like one day they'd be Kikes 'n Robbers, and all day long it would be Jew and Nazi gags. And today it was all TV cop crap, Columbo and Kojak bits all day long. And McCluskey was closest to the phone when it rang in Homicide and on the first ring Scheige had gone,

"That could be the phone."

And his partner went, "McGarrett, Five-Oh?" like he was answering a phone, and then smoothly picked up the receiver and said "Homicide," breaking Scheige up, and then listening and hanging up and telling his partner, "Jesus. Somebody just killed old Charlie Maitland the lawyer. Let's go."

"Well, book him, Dano," Scheige said, pulling on his coat. And within half an hour somebody had Eichord down at the crime scene looking at the old man's fresh corpse, and sniffing around the already-cold trail of another Lonely Hearts murder.

This one was a little different, and not just the MO. The target was W. Charles Maitland II, one of the richest heavy-hitters in Chicago or for that matter Cook County politics. Wealthy, but like so many rich men, power hungry in a profession where power is the abiding lust and common denominator.

As one of the founding senior partners in Symington, Maitland, Eaves, and Cox, he had carefully sculptured a stratum of political machinery that Eichord was told would now come crashing down around the cop shop like so many tumbling boulders in an avalanche of payback. Someone would feel the wrath of the gods, and his new colleagues informed Jack that the trick was to make damn sure the buck didn't stop with them.

Charles Maitland had been the living embodiment of Lord Acton's oft-quoted truism that absolute power corrupts absolutely. He had lobbied in the mecca of corruption, trading in weaknesses and follies, dealing in conflicts of interest and political vulnerabilities, in the foulness of old-time Cook County ward healers, fund-raisers, feather bedders, judges, a couple of congressmen, a senator here, a governor there. Maitland had bought and sold people like rental properties, paying so much down, buying them on paper lock, stock, and porkbarrel, paying them off in time payments, amortizing them, netting thirty, depreciating their corrupt asses, and now this merchant of corruption was dead. Someone had killed him and butchered him within two blocks of one of the most carefully guarded high-rises in Chicago, mutilated Charlie Maitland within TWO BLOCKS OF FUCKING LAKE SHORE DRIVE and people wanted fast answers. There'd be shit rolling downhill and you could count on that, Eichord was told.

The movie was Burt Reynolds in something or other and the other one was something something Part Two, and it all looked so totally irrelevant and predictable and bogus and boring and they just stood out in front of the giant marquee, looking up at the one-sheet for this piece of Hollywood dreck, and he turned to her and said, "Uh . . ." and she looked at him and he locked his little finger with hers and she smiled at him and he said, "Just how badly do you want to see this award-winning motion picture anyway?"

And they both broke up. And he made a couple of other suggestions and she kept holding on to his finger and then they were holding hands and walking back to the car.

The motel couldn't have been worse, first off. It might have been okay if he'd been some cocksman and had planned it all out, rented a nice Best Western or something up front, had the room key, a nice out-of-the-way room, and driven right up to the door. But he'd pulled into the first motel they'd found, some little dumpy Mom and Pop No-Tell Motel, and she'd had to sit there alone in the front seat cooling off while he watched some dour old character who looked like a hype he'd once busted spill ashes all over himself and fumfer around making sure Mr. and Mrs. J. Eichord, Eichord Company, Self-Employed, cash-in-advance, weren't going to get away with the broken twenty-one-inch Zenith in 312. And by the time they got in the room it was like oh good Christ what are we going to do now and the prospect of actually *undressing* in this fleabag was so depressing and remote that when he sat down on the lumpy bed she went over and sat in the sixteen-dollar sling chair by the window.

There's a little production of hanging coats up that he does, and then he sees her sitting there kind of forlorn and he just goes over and takes her hand, talking soothingly, very softly, talking about nothing, and they're sitting together on the bed and it just doesn't seem that natural to be in a motel room with him, she thinks, but she is a grown woman and nobody's forcing her to do this against her will, and she tries to relax, and he kisses her very softly on the cheek, and then again, and then it begins between them for the very first time.

Very *very* chaste, unsexy, brother and sisterly smooches. Just holding each other, tentatively, with him doing most of the movement, leaning in to her, exchanging a couple of little-kid-type kisses, and from out of nowhere he's shooting this *enormous* fucking boner into her leg as they are halfway lying in bed, one of her feet still touching the dirty carpet, and they both break up laughing and that helps some and then he's embarrassed and rolls over on his back wishing it would go away and knowing now what a mistake this whole thing was.

And she can sense that this is a very nice man here, a good man, and they can at least laugh together, and she leans over him now and kisses him softly on the lips, and he says it's all a mistake and she says don't be silly and he says I know you don't want to do this and she goes it's probably bad for a man to get a great, throbbing erection and not—you know—climax, and when a man is aroused like that she should reach an orgasm. You know, it's no big thing. We don't even have to do anything together or make love yet. Why don't you masturbate, and it sounds so silly they both break up again.

But she persists with it and she knows what she's talking about, she says, it's probably bad for you to be aroused and so on and so forth and he says yeah very hoarsely yeah it probably is and she kind of takes things in hand herself and begins rubbing him gently and oh my oh oh oh my godddd GODDDDDDD that feels so good so wild and now he know he's going to be going off like a rocket and he unbuckles his pants and slides his pants down and the embarrassment is gone and hell, he thinks, let her do it and she has matters in hand. A mercy cuddle, he thinks, that's what this is turning out to be.

"Edie, that's almost it, but don't let the top come up like that. You wanna' keep your hand real slick there, see—and just keep a nice steady movement up and down on it, not too loose and not too tight." I should know, he thinks, after years of devoted whacking off. "Yeah. That's *oh that's it!* That's more like it. *Do that. Oh yeah. Don't stop!*"

Thing about sex. Even when it ain't too good it's great, he thought. And so they began inauspiciously, to say the least, with a mercy jerk.

Chaingang

He has formed a kind of grudging respect of sorts for the little people. He readily admits they soldier better than we do but that's saying nothing. Our childish, arrogant bumblers are reckless and inefficient in the field. At least the little people have some soldiering ability. He loves to kill them—to ambush them and feel the life flowing from their wiry little bodies. He likes to chainsnap them, crack them open like rotten fruit, slice them, eat their strong life source. Eat their raw hearts.

Once in a killing field where he had gone alone he had discovered one of the major tunnel complexes. First he had found the entrance, a tiny spider hole that he couldn't get more than his leg through, and then some sixth sense led him to the blue feature that ran two hundred meters to the north and he had removed his ruck and shirt and pants and gone in the cold water, diving down with his blade and chain, a waterproof flashlight tied to him, diving down looking for the other hole.

He found the exit on his third dive. He was a powerful swimmer and could easily hold his breath over two minutes, and he feared nothing. He knew Charlie loved to dig down next to blue and make a slanting escape tunnel that would exit out below the water table. Depending upon the season of the year they could be impossible to detect. But inside the tunnel complexes there were traps, blind alleys, secret passageways that only the little people could squeeze through. He found the exit but he could see there was no way he'd be able to cram his bulk through the tiny exit hole. But it was here that he devised the beginnings of his plan.

Yet it was not until he had escaped their efforts to terminate the spike team and destroy him, escaped back to a warm, green place where he licked his wounds and by the sheer effort of his will brought himself back up out of the pit of raving lunacy that still reached up to claw at him, it was not until then that he began to transfer the dream to paper. The plan didn't totally crystallize until he'd finally reached the comparative safety of the mainland "back in the world" and was roaming, killing again as before.

He had been inside the car for a long time and it was cold and noisy in the foulness of the car, but his thoughts were elsewhere. For long hours he'd day-dreamed of the woman he had killed and the amazing and stunning luck of the draw in choosing her. She had proved an incredible, rich, spectacular choice, a truly beautiful woman whom he had been able to keep alive for many hours as he took her down into his hellish horror of unspeakable filth and terror and then killed her with delicious restraint.

Cody Chase was her name. He whispered it to himself inside the darkness of his pyschopathia. Cody . . . Chase. Imagine someone being named that. A bright, animated, physically breathtaking young palomino who thought for so long that she could outthink him, out-run him, outguess him, outfox him, outsmart him, outwait him, and then as it went on perhaps just outfuck him, outsuck him, outbeg him, outcry him, outbleed him, and then—she'd finally run out of outs. And that was when his pleasures began. When he could look into those dazzling blue soul reflections and see them turn tombstone gray with fear and know that she was now vulnerable to him the way he wanted. She at last realized that there was no exit. And in her vital, strong, willful abandoning of that last hope he let her rally then and began playing with her, teasing, showing her some of the first, simplest steps in the sometimes stately sometimes frenetic always awesome last dance of death.

He fantasized about another Cody Chase and the refinements of what he now practiced as an art form, nuances and embellishments, small improvements, little tricks to make the next bitch's hell all the more depraved, the more unendurable. Cody . . . Chase the outrageous untouchable bodacious temerity of the cunt to have a name of such lithe, sensual, elitist elegance and to flaunt herself in front of this great, fat, waddling blimp so far beneath her station in life, this disenfranchised, disgusting slob of a wretch who actually had the gall to breathe the same upper-class air as she. Cody fucking Chase in her Neiman's haute whatever, bathing him in fashionable scents and promises flirting with him simply by her bold and undisciplined movements taunting him with her long, shaggy, impeccably coiffed blondness, enraging him with her waspish, tight-pussied, high-assed, firm-breasted, long-necked, slim-legged, pampered, fastidious, *God God dammmmmmmmmake her crawl make that bitch eat the foulest shit hurt hurt hhhhhrrrrrrrrttttttt her and then kill her slow easy slow easy make it lasssssssttttttt ohhhhhhhhh* the white-hot waves were coming now and he must be very careful.

The words echo around inside that snake pit of a mind. Cody . . . Chaaaaaaaaaaaaaaaaaasssssssssssssssse . . . sibilant and snaky slithering syllables sliding around the twisted corners and crashing on the rocks. To find her like that and as always to move her to motivate her so easily the ultimate ego stroke to a monster man like him to gently cover her in a blanket of confidence masquerade and lies to play with the bitch that way proving himself that way simply turning her head around and then turning her again leading her so easily, she was so sure he was one thing and she was so maneuverable as he put her in exactly the position he wanted all the time making the cunt think it was *her* decision, selling her, closing the deal, getting the slut's name right there on the dotted line. And then taking her as he had planned from the first.

He could hardly breathe at the thought of it. The excitement of the kill had got him hot again as he relived it for the third, fourth time, remembering every tiny detail, running it back, playing it over again in his thoughts.

"Why would anybody get in a car with somebody like that?" he'd once heard some ignorant ass ask during an imbecilic television program that never even began to touch on the real guts of the mass-murder phenomenon. "Who would get in a stranger's car?" some nitwit had asked. Why, YOU would. ANYBODY would, you dumb, arrogant, insipid ignoramus. If the right strings are pulled, anybody will do anything. If a more powerful mind, a masterful and dominant intelligence, decides you will do something, you will accede to the wishes of the greater being. Because you are SHEEP.

No one had ever refused him. If he wanted to convince you that the sky was orange instead of blue, he would simply first put on his orange sky coat. He could pull on a characterization, a personality, a facade, the way you pull on your clothes. It is something any good actor can do. You can see the difference between genuine acting and reacting very simply: just turn down the volume on your TV set and watch the players. Most of them are unconvincing without the dialogue and a supportive story line to propel them. You have no sense of who or what they are. But the good ones—that's another thing. And they can even do more than react. They can act—alone—in a vacuum.

A true actor, a good one, pulls on a character and motivates that persona from an inner wellspring of some kind. And the reality of their own lives may be used in whatever the outlandish personality they are adopting for the moment. You can see the difference in the convincing sureness of the portrayal. He had the actor's skills, but learned the hard way, learned as survival tools as a baby, learned in dark, stifling, deadly places frightened out of his mind, learned so that he would please, and so that he would survive another tortured day. He is a chameleon when it suits him to change outwardly.

So you first see the same great, huge, waddling, terrifying bulk but not the same at all because this creature means you no harm; *au contraire,* he is a friendly, lovable, jolly fat man of great need and somehow has had the luck and taste to know that *you* of all God's critters out there in the swim this day, that *you* alone can help him in his dilemma or need. And all of this before a word is spoken. All of this in the posture, the diffident stance, the crinkled, dimpling smile, the radiant and puffy Pillsbury Doughboy cheeks all full of innocent, gigantic, Santa-caring and tenderness, or reflecting wonderment, confusion, loss, opportunity, the marketing need of that second's sales pitch.

And then the words come. A river of noise a flood of information a rushing inundation of data a damn ocean of input that you are suddenly awash in, all this raw verbiage lapping at the shores of your mind, saturating your thoughts, a tidal wave of talk assails you and the actor is never off the mark with the words. First the word. The word is always right, apt, mesmerizing, in character, convincing, captivating, so flattering to *you,* custom-designed to lull you, stimulate you, make you forget the simple reality of this frightening specter suddenly inserting itself into your life, always reasoned, impenetrable in its logic, unwavering, so certain that you will respond like so, and perhaps a gentle physical pat from this behemoth, guiding you, nudging you, HANDLING you as the stream of words hits you and you drown in the linguistic undertow of this powerful and evil intellect.

And the weirdness of the world helps. It's such a crazy place now who is to say that this huge, sloppy, grinning bear *isn't* a bizarro television producer, Cody, and hell everybody's always told you for years that you're beautiful enough for the movies and gee golly he seems to know what he's talking about and what—what's that?—you want me to go with you to the studio *now* so you can—oh, the photographer is only going to be there another half hour—oh, no, that's all right—I guess I could run by there. Where's the studio? No, I don't know where that is. Follow you? Well. Okay. Ten minutes? And he has them just that easy. Always some quick, surprising, even credible bullshit that sells them, convinces them instantly, that deep, basso-profundo smoke screen clouding minds as he lays down his con. And it just takes that one second—that moment when you drop your guard, Cody, and you get in the front seat with him for just that second just to—you know—go over one last thing before we go in there and start working with the photographer and you see the big, wicked, razor-sharp knife pointing at your belly and smile now, real nice, real friendly and you plaster a smile on and he's bent you over out of sight and a little careful tap just to keep you down on the floorboard for a couple of minutes until he can get over in the alley there and load you into the trunk—you know, Cody . . . for LATER.

And the scary thing is they all seem to have it now, baby. Even the dumbest baby raper has learned the verbal tap dance, the combative vocal retroflex, the conversational tennis match that will get in the pants of your mind, Cody doll. The satanic cat butchers, the psy-war voodoo priests, the benign seal murderers, the optical illusionists in the Pentagon, the young one-liner pickpockets from the coast, the rock stars from hell wearing pentagrams next to the skin, they all, *all,* have it down cold. You've got a whole gang of folks can get over on you just slicker 'n pee on a doorknob, Cody. But the big man—he's the great grandmaster of the bullshit ryu—the doctor of death with a Ph.D in psyche. The king daddy rabbit of the ultimate, big, fat mindfuck.

And in the cold, rattletrap car covered in printing and chalkmarked graffiti, he thinks about this magical moment that lit up a corner of his black life and the total conquest of this magical piece of serendipity with the memorable appellation Co-dee Chase, and it stirs in him again, and he wishes for something else. Dessert. A quickie. A bo would do. A bo like the young one he'd taken off just a couple weeks back. He could oh, oh yes, he could take a sweet young bo now, sixteen like the last one maybe, going back to Muncie or Middletown or someplace like that to face a parole violation and scared to death of doing some time that would leave him with "an asshole the size of a baseball."

He remembers how good it was, but so quick, and how easily he could snuff a young bo right now all filled with his desire and his scarlet fury that never seemed to quite get quenched and how it would heat up this cold and noisy car and how good it would be to have one to put under right here and right now and this is what the monster fantasizes about as he stands in the doorway of the moving boxcar as it pulls into the outskirts of Chicago.

This is a different view than the roadrunner sees from the cab of his eighteen-wheeler, and somewhat different than your perspective from the blacktop. The signposts are a bit different as seen from the rails. He just spotted the top of a barn not long ago that advertised M R L CAVE and as he thinks about the pleasures of a young fugitive hobo his subconscious is automatically analyzing the permutations, MARVEL, MARBLE, MIRACLE CAVE, CAVERN, MURIEL CAVE, MURIEL CAVEAT EMPTOR as his strange and amazing storehouse feeds his twisted terminals. But this is what he hates.

The two guys in UP Car Control are busy swapping gags about a shipper they can't stand when the big 110-car train comes chugging into the hump, and the one is saying to the other one, finishing up a railroad gag, "So you know how to cheer up a depressed flat?"

"Yeah. Ya' articulate it," the other one says and they're laughing when the car comes by so they don't see the thing in the doorway. The car is at the tail end of a half-dozen boxcars hooked into a string of gondolas and hoppers out of Stockton, originally, and Chaingang has popped the door of this Santa Fe box and now he's tossing out his massive duffel and gritting his teeth as he tumbles out the hatch, hoping just hoping some fucking yard bull will spot him jumping and come try to stick him.

He hits all five hundred pounds on his good leg which is now about as swollen as the bad ankle and he promises himself no more trains as he smacks into the hard, stinging earth. But you don't see this if you spot the big man jumping out of the Sante Fe boxcar, because what you'll see is the sight of a huge man ever so gently—and delicately you might say—dropping from the train and tumbling like an acrobat, rolling so gracefully, jumping and going with the momentum of the train's speed and his bulk and rolling like some great clown man laughing fatso dancing bear jokester. You'd probably think to yourself, isn't he light on his feet. And you not even realizing that's five hundred pounds on the hoof, pal, dropping from a moving boxcar onto the rocks and rolling, and that's a lot of rock-and-roll.

But then when he gets up and starts limping for his duffel, which neither you nor I could even lift off the ground (the sleeping bag alone weighs twenty-two pounds), then you see that it is all he can do to get back on his sore, throbbing ankle. But his mind is already concentrating on the job at hand as he heads unerringly out of the vast railroad confluence and along a side road then crossing a busy thoroughfare until, about nine blocks from the yard, he's reached a county road sign. He looks down the road and sees one of the small utility buildings he's been looking for about two blocks from where he stands now.

He decides to leave his duffel here and go back and get what he needs, but at least he knows now where he will spend the night. He is cold and his ankle keeps sending shock waves toward his brain and he ignores the pain, as always, and continues to concentrate on the matters of priority. First, he gingerly hops over the deep road ditch and hides his duffel in a bed of weeds at the beginning of the adjacent field. He breaks a huge limb off of a nearby tree and using it as a cane begins hobbling back toward a small grocery store.

A car of young women slow as they near him and he can see them looking at him and laughing and the driver honks the horn and they speed by him. He got a look at the one on the passenger side. A chipmunk-cheeked high school girl of fifteen. He thinks how he could tape her mouth shut so she couldn't scream and the different ways he could make her pass out before he took her under like the way he'd tie her hands and then hang her up nude so he could work on her, hang her up there with those nice tan legs all spread open and those little nipples are erect and how he'd start pinching them real easy and then fingers like vise grips like steel tempered steel *pliers pinching and twisting and ripping this little cunt nipples and clitoris off tearing that pink skin bleeding ripping that shit off her front there as she twisted and fainted and tearing at the skin on the inside of her upper thighs and peeling down peeling her skin like you would peel a ripe fruit* and he smiles and almost laughs out loud at the prospect of such a thing.

He has a case of fragmentation grenades in his duffel. He starts to fantasize about some of the things he could do to the girls in that automobile as he limps painfully toward the little store. He thinks how pleasant it would be to grade and brand that little USDA prime trim that just whizzed by him, stamp a brand on it then, a hot brand to mark the U.S. Government Inspected Prime and watch a hot iron burn its shape deep into the tortured, bleeding rawness of the jerking, squirming pink flesh, that pampered, untouchable young flesh and how he'd like to give it his special brand. Something to get their attention as they hung there like meat waiting for him to take his turn with each of them, letting his wild imagination invent new games to play with their bodies and souls and how easily and pleasing it would be then, later, to take their young, tender hearts.

He steps to the side of the building that advertises STRAWBERRY SODA and PROFFER'S BRAND MEATS, pushing on the dented metal door marked GENTS and letting it stand open behind him as he extricates his penis and for no reason begins urinating on the sink then guiding the stream of awful-smelling urine across the room and into the wastepaper can where it pounds like a hammer and only his inability to arc his stream that high prevents him from pissing on the empty towel dispenser. He walks back around to the front of the building, a combination grocery/package store/gas station, and pushes on the tin strip that says RAINBOW IS GOOD BREAD and lets the door slam behind him as he strides toward the food.

"Hah-dee," a wrinkled, middle-aged woman says from the shadows behind the counter where he can hear a vapid game-show host mouthing some vocal feces and he ignores her as he grabs the first packages he can reach out of the refrigerated tray, a large box of pasteurized American cheeze and a package of sliced ham and he rips the ham open with his teeth and tears the top off the cheese dropping the cardboard into the vegetable tray beside him and pinching the end off the foil, ripping a huge four-inch hunk of cheese off and wadding it up in the slices of ham and swallowing about half of it instantly, pulling a bag of something resembling potato chips off a nearby shelf absentmindedly and stabbing a finger into it then ripping it open and shoving a pawful of something into his mouth, just about ODing on sodium and preservative as he swallows a great mouthful of an awful chip of some kind, slamming one of the refrigerator doors open and grabbing a half gallon of milk and draining four-fifths of the half gallon in one long gurgling, ravenous chug-a-lug.

"Ah-gols-ah swear ah never have seen nobody drink

thet much milk all at a time like that! Ah swear!" she says nervously as he continues to ravage and plunder the shelves, ripping open some cookies and another pair of meat-and-cheese combinations, walking toward her as he crams an entire package of sliced swiss and bologna in his maw, scarcely taking time to chew before he swallows and says:

"Where's 'a beer?" coming toward her like a human King Kong, this human garbage disposal that nearly hits his head on the ceiling of the room now swilling the last of the milk as she says:

"Rat there inna frig, ova' to the rat." Wrinkled old cunt, he thinks as he lets out a loud belch and opens a Michelob on his teeth the way he always likes to do when somebody is watching him and spitting the cap off, letting it hit the floor as she looks at him and says halfway under her breath:

"Ah hope yew kin pay fer all that food," but thank God he doesn't hear or pay any attention to her as he chugs the cold beer and belches most offensively again, taking a quart of Wild Turkey off the shelf and sitting it on the counter. She no longer worries about the bill as this last item legitimizes his movements, and not only is he apparently going to pay, this is the first thing he has done that resembles the actions of an ordinary human, actually picking out something and not consuming it there in the store. She looks up at this mastadon and with the luck of the stupid says:

"Gols, yer a stout one. Whatcha' weigh there?" He looks down at her like she is a dog turd he has just stepped in. For just one second her life is in some serious danger but she says it again, "How much d'ya *weigh*? Ah betcha go ovah three hunnert 'n fifty?" He can't help it, a blast of noise explodes from him, the monstrous balls of this wrinkled old prune-faced hag, Chaingang can't restrain himself he actually laughs, saving her life as he goes off to get canned goods saying over his shoulder:

"Four thousand pounds, Lucky." He rumbles good-naturedly. He likes the old crone. Also he doesn't

want to have to relocate as he has a nice place to crash
tonight all picked out. Very safe. Still, as he steals
food from the shelves, he thinks how amusing it would
be to take one of the large cans of V-8 juice there and
pound it into her temple until she died and how easily
he could snuff out her dull existence. Perhaps he'll
come back tomorrow and do the old bitch a favor. Put
her out of her misery.

He takes a can of Chef Boy-Ar-Dee Spaghetti and
Meatballs off the shelf and puts it in his left hand with
the other cans he'll pay for, then slips a jar of deluxe
olives, a can of Bush's Best hot chile beans, and a
large can of Dinty Moore Beef Stew into the voluminous
chain pocket of his coat. He goes back to the cold
section and gets a quart of milk, as he puts fourteen-
dollars' worth of various meats and cheeses into his
other pocket. He goes up to her and pays for $6.95
worth of food, a quart of beer, and the quart of
Turkey, and walks out with another twenty in canned
and packaged foods. As a shoplifter he has no equal.

He has a large sum of money in his pocket but he
never or seldom ever pays for everything. It is, as he
sees it, a matter of principle. He loves to steal and is
an accomplished thief. Had he not opted to be a
murderer and let his warped life gravitate around crimes
of violence he would have been a spectacular major
thief. He knows everything about antiques and collect-
ibles, fine art, numismatic coinage and precious metals
and stones, stamps, weaponry, both arms and edged,
music, virtually any field in which memorabilia is of
value falls under the omnivorous umbrella of his computer retrieval system and general expertise. The thing
is he has no interest in material goods or money.

Waddling along, a little less uncomfortable now that
he's taken the edge off his enormous appetite, he
heads back to the fence row where his duffel is hidden. Carefully, very carefully, he reaches under the
duffel bag and his viselike fingers get a firm grip on
the spoon of the 'nade that is wedged under the corner
of the bag. Carefully he eases it back out and with the

fingers of a skilled surgeon slowly slides the pin back in the retaining apertures, bending the cotter pins back with a fingertip as you would bend a wet straw. That done he shoulders his burden and limps on down the road to his private cabaña.

His accommodations for the night will be cramped but secure. He is burglarizing a concrete block building owned by Ma Bell, sometimes referred to by the misnomer *utility building,* used as an equipment repeater station. It is carried on the Illinois Bell Systems books as RS-724-B, and locally referred to as Repeater Hut 724; 724 is a middle-aged hut and has a fairly sophisticated security system which is buried straight down under the ground with Ma's long lines, the building being used to boost signal for tolls.

If you take a crowbar and pry the heavy steel door open, a silent alarm is activated in Chicago Central and the dispatcher calls the boys in blue to investigate. Depending on the time of day and the fates, you have anywhere from two minutes to half an hour before you're in the backseat of a patrol car. Ma can't take a joke when it comes to screwing around with her repeater stations.

Of course you can get lucky. About once in every thousand times somebody does any work on the equipment they forget to hook the alarm back in after it has been disabled and that would be a free ticket to ride, roughly the equivalent of winning $100,000 playing Blackjack in northern Nevada.

Chaingang knows things like this and so he removes a small black case from his duffel. It contains a full set of Deluxe Taylor Picks, a set of homemade picks and levers, a small mini-key unit, a massive ring with 250 masters for everything from old time skeletons to the latest GMs, house keys, ornate keys, you name it. His case contains half a dozen jimmies and slim jims and pry bars. He also carries a cold chisel and a small sledge which he sometimes kills with when it suits him.

And he is inside standing there very still breathing in the electronic noises and just checking out the vibes, inside Ma's Repeater Hut 724 before you can say in-like-Sean-Flynn. And something is awry. Something doesn't quite, let's say, parse. His astounding mental computer is whirling away a mile a minute, tired as he is, and he is rethinking the last hour of his dark life even as he scans his close quarters for the thing that has disturbed him. Is a hidden surveillance camera now taking his picture? He blinks and begins to still his vital signs slightly, involuntarily and automatically, putting himself on hold as he scans and excogitates.

It is a presence, a feel that something is out of place. What went undone. What detail was overlooked. What carelessness will be paid for in heavy dues. He senses being watched somehow. It is very strong and he never ignores these things these hunches these vibrations—call them what you will. His strange and amazing instincts that have kept him alive a thousand times in as many ways are nudging him. It is something outside there.

He cracks the door slightly with his killing hand, his right hand, hanging at his side. He flexes the huge, steel cigarlike fingers making a massive claw and then relaxing the hand. He has a grip that cannot be believed. Once, enraged, he squeezed a flashlight battery as you might squeeze an empty beer can. For many years one of his small amusements was to try and squeeze his own hands so hard that it would take him to the edge of his pain threshold; a small eccentricity born in lonely, dark places.

He thinks of little babies before his brain registers the noise and then he realizes what it was—the faraway call of birds flying south and no, no, that's not it—he can hear babies crying now, and then even before he has found the box he knows what it is and he hopes with the part of his soul that is still human that he will not find something bad in there, something that will make his rage go all bright scarlet and bubble over into a sudden kill fury. But when he determines that there are no passersby about he goes over to the large tree next to the hut and peers down into the box. It is a pair of tiny, starved pups of indeterminate lineage, huddling together to try to stay alive as they take heat from each other's tiny, emaciated bodies, shaking and quivering as this huge shadow looms above them.

He allows himself to breathe for the first time in the last sixty seconds or so, and shrugs his great shoulders. He goes back to his duffel and returns to the box. In a couple of swift, sure hand movements he has opened the can of beef stew and he dumps it down into the corner of the box and watches as the starved dogs attack the cold stew with a ravenous hunger. They tear at the food insanely, as starved things always do, and within a few seconds the larger chunks of food are gone. He tries to decide whether or not to open another can, wondering if they will become sick gorging themselves, but he opens a small Vienna Sausage tin and tears the sausages into fragments, mincing them up with his big fingers and dropping them down on the dogs. Some of the sausages go into his mouth.

He goes back inside and spreads his huge sleeping bag out as much as he can in the open area of the hut, and then he goes back outside and picks up the little puppies with surprising tenderness, feeling them wiggle in his fingers as they whimper excitedly. He is glad he didn't see the one who dumped them as he could have gone berserk. Once before he saw a man dump an abused dog. First, he had put the dog to sleep, and then done a very bad thing. He had made the man ride with him in the man's old truck back to where he lived and they had gone inside his home. He had tied up the man's wife and two children and made them watch the things he did to the man as he slowly killed them, taking his life inch by inch in his maddened fury.

Inside the repeater hut he spreads a newspaper for the dogs, out of habit from his own tortured childhood, but when he lies down in the bag he pulls the puppies to him and they snuggle next to him still whimpering with joy. He opens a package of meat and cheese and the three of them devour it together, the enormous man whose bulk takes up the entire interior of the small hut, and the two tiny, starved mutts, wiggling all over him as he feeds them bits of his dinner. And that is how they finally go to sleep after they eat, the two little abandoned pups and the man called Chaingang, all huddled together, each of them as close to knowing love as they will ever know in their lives.

In his deep sleep the monster dreams of a beautiful woman with whom he has shared a wonderful and intimate experience, and he thinks of her several times during the night. But in the morning he will wonder if indeed the one named Cody Chase was real or if it was only a fantasy he has dreamed.

Jack
and
Edie

The second time was like the first time, a repeat performance of their first ersatz lovemaking. He caught himself thinking a lot of thoughts that he really wasn't that crazy about but what the hell. He was nuts about this woman. Eichord wasn't used to it all anyway. The fervor and the damn consuming passion of a love affair were so alien to him. He saw himself as an old middle-aged man and the pounding of the old valentine was something he couldn't get used to. Christ, he thought, am I falling for this old girl? Old girl is what he said as he looked at her smile lines and tiny wrinkles and the dishwater hands, kicking himself even as he thought the disparaging thoughts.

He made himself concentrate on the tiny lines of aging, and the creases and the imperfections. Think about the wrinkles and don't let yourself get swept up in the mass of long, silky hair or those gorgeous knock-out eyes or those legs that just seemed to keep going. Don't look at all that stuff. Don't, whatever you do, don't dare look at that mouth. No. That would be a serious mistake. Not if you want to shake this fever and get well. Shake this Saturday-night fever of yours, old man.

So he concentrated on her hands, and it was all he could do to keep his lips and tongue and teeth off those wrinkled hands of hers, those sweet fingers of a slim, good-looking, vibrant adult woman who had done her share of work. Pulled her part of the load and then some. Washed some dishes and diapers. Those hands that were now doing something that he couldn't get used to.

He was no cocksman. No way. But his women were of a kind. He was used to women wanting him and telling him that. Saying "I want you." And "I want you inside me." Variations on that theme. She didn't want that. Not yet, she said, it just wasn't right, and he tried valiantly to understand, and the electricity kept on surging between them, unmistakable and definitely high voltage, but still she kept a grip on the situation, kept it in hand.

It was certainly not that Edie found the act repulsive or even mildly repugnant. No. The thought of sex with this man was exciting and something she would eventually learn to anticipate the way a foodaholic looks forward to the next banana split. But it was just the inappropriateness of it, somehow, of what she still thought of quaintly as going all the way. To do it now, with this newfound lover, this new friend, so soon after their meeting, it was—well, it would be rushing that final stage of intimacy. Yet for all of her ambivalence she wanted it, needed the closeness, and knew he did too. She wanted and needed to solidify this thing that was zigzagging through the ether between them like tiny lightning bolts, this hot, new electric charge of desire and mutual attraction. And so for the time being this would do.

She knew about men. She knew she could make it do for him too, at least for whatever time she had to wait before she gave more of herself to this man. It made no sense, whatsoever, she fully realized. But somehow in the confusion and the befuddlement of her upside-down life that was slowly coming back up to sail on an even keel again, she saw this as something they could both live with. She knew this man wanted her very fully, and also she sensed that Jack

Eichord would do nothing to chance losing what they both had found and were finding with each other every day. There were no ultimatums that would come from Jack. And just the knowledge of that did much to relax her and help her begin to drop the barriers that so far had kept their sexual touching an adolescent thing.

And so it went. And when her arm started getting tired she did what all women do, she came up with a much better idea. Edie went out and got an old pair of panty hose and cut the foot out of it, don't laugh now dammit, and smeared Vaseline (the widow lady's K-Y Jelly) all over it and really went to town. Wow. Some widow, lady.

And the next night after that they were together again and she got him off with a Baggie, and by the end of the week she'd gone down to the neighborhood shopping center and bought a box of nylon socks, breaking up when the clerk asked her what size. Very small, she told Jack later. Well, even when it ain't too good it's great. And this was fine and sure as hell better than no sex life at all.

And it meant a lot to Jack on the friendship level, as well, since he felt like it was so important to her to obtain his physical well-being and comfort. Having lost a husband as she had, he sometimes wondered just how distasteful the act was to her. He knew she was not of the bisexual persuasion. She liked herself, as all of us do, and then, he felt, men would be a natural second.

Eichord was convinced she was neither daughter of Lesbos, celibate, nor neuter. He teased her that she was like Erma Bombeck—a trisexual—only able to resist his advances because she had attained some strange plateau of sexual weirdness as a result of watching too much "Donahue." She was multivalent, omnidirectional, and despite her obvious unwillingness to get it on with Jack in the normal way, she was sending out these potent and charged signals that ranged the continuum from onanistic to downright orgiastic.

"You know me," he had said to her, only half jokingly, "your friendly neighborhood pervert." He nudged himself at his willingness to pick up anything that looked like kiss-me vibes from this lady. Fires simmered within her, he assured himself continually. Then with a dollop of guilt adding to himself that such a response was typical to all of us macho-type clods. We're ready to think that of anybody with female plumbing, be she diesel dyke, nympho, fridge, or mud-wrestling kinkorama queen from the planet Uranus.

Eichord pondered the meaning of it all, his lonesome semen continued to solidify into cementitious mucilage in the toes of discarded socks, grossing him out not a little, and doing zip for the old demon ego as he felt himself falling deeper and deeper into some kind of a pit with high, slippery walls. It bothered him. Not enough to stop, you understand, but guilt can be a weird thing.

He was on his way north from Chicago, nine hours of very boring and fruitless paperwork behind him, and he'd been down at work since dawn. It was late afternoon and the day, and the job, and the strange new love affair, and the serial killings—the whole schmear just collapsed in on him as he drove, and when he found an open, overgrown field he pulled his car off onto the somewhat muddy shoulder and got out, mindful of a new pair of shoes, and started aimlessly down the pathway that bordered the field, taking in the air in big, deep lungfuls.

It took him almost ten minutes to amble across to the end of the field, but he was in no hurry. He wanted to think, to air out the cobwebs a little. He had never felt so many things going down at the same time, important things, that is, and he knew that even as he walked, somewhere out there a mad serial killer was about to take another life. That was on one level. On another level he couldn't stop thinking about this Edie. What a woman. He was falling in love with her. And he didn't care about the other stuff right now.

He felt better and was walking back to the vehicle

when something nudged at him the way things often did to Jack. Something he'd seen. A loose, out-of-place detail, some fact that sat up and waved a red flag at his subconscious and said, hey . . . look over this way. It was a small thing. The cardinal shrub that he'd seen there by the overgrown field. A small piece of paper, burned to black ash, caught up in the branches of the shrub. It was black, roughly the size of a softball but a strange irregular shape that nagged at him. One of those things you see and it suggests something like a psychiatrist's inkblot test. What did it remind him of?

He was in the front seat and putting his key into the ignition when it hit him and the realization washed over his soul like an icy wave. The shape of the ash, just a fragment of paper from someone's burnt trash floating across a field to catch and hang suspended in some branches, the fragment was the shape of that Buddhist's heart in Saigon, the one who had set himself on fire. They had saved the heart, a charred cinder about the size of a baseball, a hard, black reminder of cruelty and injustice. And the words banged around in his mind just as he pulled back out into traffic—self-immolation.

But that night was the night it finally came together for them and that was their first night from then on. It began as it usually began, with Jack holding Edie and feeling that soft, lovely and pliant body mold into him, and laying her gently back against the bed and kissing and feeling that same kind of surprising rush whenever their bodies pressed together, and running his fingers into her long hair, and feeling her touch him first on his rib cage, and then up and around, but then instead of him rolling over beside her she was helping him pull her closer, pulling him into her and before he knew what they were doing he was inside Edie and they were lovers for the first time and it was like being burnt by a flicker that suddenly caught fire and threatened to engulf them.

She went wild and surprising both of them equally it was genuine fire. He tried to kiss her and she tried to kiss him, really kiss him, and it was like for the first time. Everything was the first time and as they came closer together with the hard, rocking movement their lips barely brushed and the fire was so hot, *real* fire that it scorched each of them with its astonishing, delicious heat and they cried out and whimpered from the flame of it, and he was shooting, spent so quickly it was an embarrassment or it would have been but even as he was shrinking inside her she whimpered—ungh—un—no—oh—no—please, with such urgency and held on so tightly starting again in a kind of gently insane frenzy, beginning, moving and quivering with those little, mewing, whimpering, soft animal sounds and her breathing all over him and her hands moving against him, fluttering over him, clutching him, and the close, sweet hotness of that soft bush, and her wetness and that sexy voice whispering and whimpering and my God the fire it was so hot.

Jack knew he was dead. No way could he move. He was drained. Never anything like it in the history of the fucking world. Never. Not with anybody, anywhere, at any moment in time. He was empty. And in sweetest agony he rolled over slightly and looked at her for the first time and she was brand-new and in their intimacy he saw her for the first time then and she was new for him and he looked at that body of hers. Oh, he thought, I'll never doubt you again, oh Heavenly Father. No, Lord. Because you made trees, and flowers, and streams, and rainbows, and snowflakes, and oh, my. You did a job on her too, let me tell you, he thought. What a woman.

It was a prayer of a kind that he thought as he rolled over and looked at this miracle beside him. Lord, anybody who can turn out one of these can't be all bad. What a lady. He saw those legs for the first time, the dazzling curve that became a flatness of stomach and rolling upward into a magnificently formed chest that met a perfect throat and then she rolled over and moaned and Eichord saw the most beautiful ass he'd ever seen and he thought of himself as a connoisseur of

female butts, a heinie epicurean, a derriere gourmet.
He told her as much, his voice cracking with the effort
of verbalizing speech.

"You know something?"

"Hmm?"

"You've got—the loveliest—oh, yes, the loveliest
rear end—in the world. Did you know that?"

"I'm glad *you* think so," she whispered back to him.
"I guess I never thought about it much."

"You mean, seriously, guys haven't always told you
that you had a fabulous ass," he said, without thinking.

"Well. No. I mean, I guess I knew I had an okay
rear end, but—" she trailed off.

"Uh-huh. An okay rear end, is that what you think
you have?"

"Yeah. Okay. Nothing special. Nothing to get that
excited about. It's just adequate. An okay rear end."
She smiled.

"If that's an okay rear end," he said hoarsely, "the
1959 Eldorado had an okay rear end. I mean we are
talkin' Hall of Fame classics here, lady."

"Oh, sir, you make me blush," she murmured, still
on her stomach.

"Yes. I can definitely see that." He lay there transfixed. "I know where I want to have dinner tonight,
beautiful," he said.

"Where?"

"Ummmmmmmm," he replied, rolling her over
on her back again. And soon she was making those
sounds. Doing it again. Making those hot little whimpering noises that turned him on like crazy, and it all
caught fire again and the embers that he thought had
finally gone out were fanned into a burning flame once
more, and he was rock hard and inside and they were
both slick with sweat and love juice and bodily fluids
in a wild, white-hot heat of the moment.

Neither of them could quite believe it. He was totally immobilized again. Not just drained. His crank-
case was empty, folks. Bone dry. He was exsanguinated.
Dead and buried. Motionless as she traced outlines up

and down with those hot fingertips and Jack knew Edie
was smiling as she ran those fiery fingers across him,
playing with him, and it made him laugh and they were
in each other's arms and enjoying their discovery so
much.

The humor of it was just ineffable and illogical and
they both felt giddy, hysterical, a little confused,
mindfucked, spent. They came apart and just looked
at each other, sweat drying on their bodies, and just
glued themselves to the sheets, too blown to even
smoke. And he felt some *very* weak stirrings again as
he ran his hands over those hard nipples and before
they knew it they were together once more in a drunken
kind of slow, languorous, loving, easy thing. Moving
to some unheard reggae beat, some bedsprings ca-
chunk, ca-chunk, in a very gentle, soft, concupiscent
pushing, his hands on her moving over her in the
darkness, exploring hidden treasures in the ruins of
the fires, and later he felt her erupt like a volcano,
washing him in molten lava, burning him again with
the wetness from her loins and he moaned with delight
into the sweet candy of his lover's mouth.

Edie
and
Daniel

At some point, or as the Watergate-era co-conspirators would say, at some point in time the lines of lives destined to come together will come so close the interstices narrow to nothingness and the vectors almost cross. It was that way with Edie and a monster, whose lives would nearly touch. And yet, amazingly, neither would realize it. Nor would the cop Jack Eichord, whose own vector had already crossed one of the lives and was reaching toward the other to complete this overlapping triangle as diagrammed by destiny.

At 151130 Central, Mrs. Edith Lynch was registering a complaint with a rather unresponsive and tired employee of a major department store and was saying:

"—that it wouldn't be any problem to return it."

"It isn't any problem," the woman was saying, "but I have to get the number to put in the computer, and if you put the invoice in with it when you sent it back to the catalog center, then how can I help you?"

"But I have the number right here, as I just told you, the thing is that the two numbers don't—"

And at 151130 Central, Daniel Bunkowski was squeezed behind the wheel of a stolen Mercury Cougar, window down on the passenger side, tape deck blasting. He was on the outskirts of Chicago, trying to negotiate the heavy Chicago traffic in the uncomfortable Merc, black vinyl over silver, license X-Ray Tango Romeo-1969 belonging to one Olin Neidorf of Mount Vernon, Illinois, now deceased. Mel Torme was emoting from the car speakers:

He heard something about writing the words again, as Bunkowski ejected the tape savagely and twisted the radio dial to a teenybopper hard-rock station, blinking his reddened pig eyes and concentrating on his driving. Just an hour or so now and he'd dump this piece of crap.

And at precisely 151130 Jack Eichord was sitting in the squad room at his borrowed desk doodling on a yellow legal pad. He had just finished a doodle, what looked like a doodle in any event, based on the commonalities of medical records of certain individuals and he was beginning what someone might have termed his E doodle. He sometimes just sat and drew the letter *E*, never bothering to reason why. He thought and schemed by what might have been called the doodle method, but he had never put a name to it. It was simply part of his process of analyzing data.

He would sit, sometimes for hours on end, a felt-tipped pen making neat, precise marks on a legal pad or whatever paper was available as he allowed his ability to free-associate time and space to analyze. He would throw his brain into neutral, just sit there doodling, let it all come naturally, thinking quietly and as organically as he could let himself, eliciting all manner of arcane lore, evoking any number of trivial facts, educing commonality and pattern where there often would be none.

The E doodle had many variations, and was worth zilch as police work goes but for some reason it often preoccupied him during these reflective times and so he invariably gave rein to it. Here was the way his latest E doodle looked on paper:

E   SylvEEya (phon.)   AvEry Johnson
    Kasikoff   CharlEs Maitland

Edna Porter GiavinEllo   VErnon ArlEn
Edward William Lynch   Richard SchEigE
Edie Lynch middle name EmalinE
Eichord   Bill JoycE
LEE AnnE Lynch

At 175500 Edie was drinking a cup of coffee with her friend Sandi who was saying, "—so glad you are."

"Me too, you know? I mean even if this doesn't last—"

"It will; don't say that. Think positive."

"I can't think at all, that's the problem."

"Oh, I'd love to feel that way again. It's been so long since I went love crazy." They both giggled.

"That's what I thought too, but now I'm so head over heels that I—"

At 175500 Daniel Bunkowski was pulling into the area known as Oldtown, looking at the odd human landscapes of hippies, winos, coke snorters, and antique dealers, and listening to a completely insincere resonance extol the highly dubious virtues of a chain of waterbed stores. He smashed at the radio dial with a vicious backfist. He was ravenously hungry. What do I want? he thought. Chinese, he told himself. A big sack of egg rolls with lots of sweet and sour to go with it. And a quart of Wild Turkey to wash it down. And later maybe play with one of these bums.

At 175500 Eichord was drinking his ninth cup of cardboard-tasting coffee of the day and block-printing a huge letter *U*. It was printed or drawn to look like a letter carved out of stone, and it was the last letter of a twelve-letter two-word phrase that it had taken him nearly ten minutes to draw on a sheet of paper. Each large stone letter had its own shadow and he had carefully inked in the black shadows of the words that filled the page.

ETAOIN SHRDLU

He completed the artwork. Crumpled the paper up into a ball and arced it overhead to a large metal wastebasket to his left. A homicide cop behind him said, "Two points."

"Foul," someone else said and the first unseen voice added:

"Two free shots from the foul line. Keep your hands to yourself," in a mock W. C. Fields voice.

181730. Edie and Sandi are coming out of a store and Edie tells her, "I sure appreciate you picking up Lee Anne."

"No trouble. But I sure don't like you staying down here so late at night even if it is only one night a month."

"I'll be fine, worrywart. I'll get Mr. Whatsisface from the center to walk me to my car if it's too late, or maybe Jack will pick me up. I'll be careful."

"Okay. But call me later just to say hi, okay?"

"Okay." She knew how Sandi worried. Sandi should worry about herself, she thought, in an uncharitable moment, considering the way she dresses and comes on to guys sometimes. She put the irritating thought out of her mind and click-clacked on her high-heeled long legs to the center. One night a month she did a stint of telephone answering on the Runaway Hotline. It was from six to ten P.M., and she would make sure to have someone walk with her to her car as the center was in a pretty bad neighborhood. Of course, the whole world was a bad neighborhood now at ten o'clock at night, she thought.

At 181730 Bunkowski was parked in the parking lot of a convenience store having just used the pay telephone outside the store to place an "order to go" of forty dollars' worth of egg rolls. When the girl who took the order hung up the phone, she had relayed the message to the cook saying:

"Somebody's having a big party tonight."

The big party is still crammed behind the wheel of his uncomfortable stolen Cougar, and he is drawing in a large book that appears to be a bookkeeper's ledger of some kind. He is working on a diagram with the printed caption "#610," and he draws freehand but with perfect, sure strokes. At the moment he is designing a wooden ladder device. He is working on his book of Chicago escapes. He is about to use the book, the results of many hours of methodical preparation, for the first time.

The ledger is a piece of genius. Evil genius to be sure, but true genius nonetheless. Bunkowski has no problem murdering. It is in him, his second nature. His only problem as a killer is how to escape the modern, sophisticated police technology. How does a man who weighs almost five hundred pounds and stands six feet seven inches, a man who looks like an insane cross between an enraged gorilla and the Pillsbury Dough Boy, how does someone like that achieve a low profile? Where can he go to hide?

Bunkowski has prepared carefully. He emulates his former enemy, the VC, and so he prepares now to build and enter that other world, the world he will make for himself below the city. The Cong who hid by day, going down into the tunnels beneath Vietnam to sleep and nurse wounds, would come out at night. They would come out to resupply, to intimidate, to gather intel, to harass, and of course to hit and run. To kill. And so this is precisely what Chaingang will do.

We exist in today's high-tech society by the infinitely complex interwoven web of utility services that run beneath the urban megaplex. We maintain our level of civilized societal convenience and comfort through our sophisticated telephone cables, our electrical hookups, our water supply lines, our sewage disposal pipes, our arterial service tubes, our transit modes, our pipelines to and from the urban masses of working humanity, the huge and generally unknown subworld that exists below the surface of the city streets.

191800. Daniel Edward Flowers Bunkowski is diagramming rung supports and listening to traffic. Edith Emaline Lynch is walking through a room that smells of cologne and stale popcorn, and listening to ringing telephones and subdued conversations, and Jack Eichord is walking down stairs and singing jumbled bits of half-recognizable songs.

"Sinatra, you ain't." A voice from an open doorway above and footsteps behind him on the stairs. Jack turns with a smile in place as he sees Arlen.

"S'matter, Lou, you don't like music?"

"Come on. We got another one," the lieutenant says as he rushes past him.

"Christ." Eichord hurries to keep up with him as they run to a unit. It is a call that was first handled by a single patrolman in a roller who answered the call on what he thought would be another domestic dispute. It was a young boy. Teenager. Cauc. Sandy hair. Husky build. The heart gone. The MO appeared to be identical. Body mutilated. Burn marks. Looked like a torture-homicide. Only one thing different. This time there was an eyeball witness.

"She's pretty shook up," the cop was telling them, "but she saw this dude clear when he got out of the van to dump the kid. Big mother. Sounds like our man."

"Description?"

"Better. A description and a fucking license number."

213430. Edie is talking with a thirteen-year-old girl named Pam who is pregnant, alone in the Big City, and afraid to go home for what her father will do to her. Edie is begging the girl to stay on the line as she signals for a legit counselor to pick up the telephone. Eichord is on his way to a Chicago suburb with a convoy of vehicles closing in on a Ford Econoline which has been spotted by a state rod who is at this second in pursuit. The two-way sounds like World War IV. Bunkowski is in a field next to a construction site building a sturdy wooden ladder. He saws through a two-by like it was made of balsa wood.

Garrett Aldrich, the director of the center, is busy on the Crisis Hotline and Edie decides to walk to the car by herself. No big deal. The street is still busy with traffic and brightly lit. She click-clacks out of the center and along the sidewalk. She has her key ready and unlocks the car door instantly, immediately locking the door after her. She sits behind the wheel thinking. For the first time today she really thinks about how fast everything is going. How deeply she and Jack are getting involved with each other's lives, and the implications on both herself and Lee Anne. This is what she is thinking when she looks across the street and chances to see him.

It is a man. A huge man. He is running out into the street with a big ladder over his shoulder. He takes a kind of hook and lifts the manhole in the street, drops the ladder down into the hole, and begins squeezing himself down into the opening as Edie stares, transfixed. He happens to glance up by chance and sees a woman in a parked car sitting there looking at him as he squeezes his huge girth down through the manhole opening in the street. The time is 222030.

Edie sees the big man look up at her and freeze. She feels intense fear and intuitively grinds the ignition key, jumping to discover she'd already started the car's engine. Without glancing back at the strange menace, she trods on the accelerator, dropping the transmission lever into drive, and shoots away from the curb. When she glances into the rearview mirror, it is too dark and her perspective has shifted enough that she fails to see that the man has come out of the manhole opening and has moved with deceptively quick strides toward where Edie had been parked.

She sees none of this as she turns the corner, breathing more normally as the weighty presence of dread lifts from her like an invisible stone, and she puts the menacing weirdness of The Manhole Man out of her mind. She has much more interesting and rewarding things to concentrate on as she wonders if Jack will call her late tonight as they discussed, and when they will see each other again. But at 222030 Eichord's thoughts are far from romantic. He is all cop, standing with other men at the scene of an arrest. They have taken a suspect into custody and the air is electric with the possibility of these men having caught the Lonely Hearts killer.

"So what's the problem, Jack?" one of them is asking Eichord.

"It just isn't that tight."

"Wrong-oh."

"Say?"

"Shit, man, it's absolutely dead bang. What more do you want here? We've got that sonofabitch."

"I don't think so."

"It's dead bang, Jack," another cop says.

"No. I don't believe it's dead-bang sure at all."

"We've got an eyeball witness. We've got a perp with a psycho package. We've got a blade man. A resisting arrest. We got a body. We got blades. He fits the whole MO. We got opportunity. We got motive. Dead-bang solid."

"No." Eichord shakes his head.

"Come on."

"Huh-uh. He's not our man."

"Eye-fuckin'-witness, Pops."

"That's the dead boy. Okay. That's what we've got. He did the boy all right. But as far as Sylvia Kasikoff I gotta' tell you guys, I just don't like him for it at all."

"Talk," Arlen says.

"You're gonna find out that it isn't the same blade. He took the heart out with a scalpel. A little—what the hell was it?—a Benson and Hedges—uh, some name like that—the little blade?"

"Brookstone and Jensen surgeon's scalpel."

"Right. He did the boy with it, bet money."

"So he used a scalpel this time. We've got the big hunting knife that he used on all the others. Maybe it was getting dull. Whatever. So he used a scalpel. Same difference."

"When the lab tells us the hunting knife was the blade, *then* it's dead bang. No. I don't think we got the main heart man here at all. I think we got a copycat."

"Jack."

"Lou?"

"What throws you off on this guy . . . I mean, how come you don't like a guy who takes a heart for Sylvia Kasikoff all of a sudden?"

"The burns. I dunno. Something about the fact that he tortured the boy. It's like he was playing with him and then did the heart number to throw us off the other. Make it into a Lonely Hearts. And he just cut the heart out of the chest cavity and pitched it. The other times somebody took the heart and did something with it, disposed of it elsewhere or *used* it someway, like in a ritual thing—whatever. I just don't think we've got him at all." But it wasn't the burns. It wasn't that at all.

"Jack. I think you're going to be very, very surprised with the lab work on this. That hunting knife has got a big blade. I think we'll make it for the others. You want to put a big steak dinner on it?"

"You got it." Eichord laughed. "And let's pray you're right."

The cops are in a good mood in spite of Jack's dissenting opinions, and everybody is heading for the cop bar and a big celebration. Eichord is going too, never a wave maker, letting the comaraderie and self-congratulatory fever take him against his better judgment.

It is 222600 and against his better judgment Daniel Edward Flowers Bunkowski decides to ignore the woman who saw him and, tired and ravenous, has gone down into his nightworld. At 222600 he is nineteen feet south of Chicago Submain K-138C-10, in a tiny submerged room that hangs beneath the manhole next to K-138C-10's valve-box cover, where he sits quietly, staring into the shadows of a lantern, oblivious to the overpowering stench as he consumes forty-dollars' worth of cold egg rolls, and thinks about his dark future.

As his conscious mind thinks his horrifying and disgusting Chaingang thoughts of rape and murder and mutilation, on another level his subconscious registers the recent events in his computer and a tiny voice whispers to him, "Well, you've done it again. You've made another mistake." And subliminally he feels himself sinking deeper into the quicksand of retribution that continues to tug at his massive body so relentlessly.

He mashes another cold egg roll into the sweet-and-sour sauce and inhales it in a gulp, staring into the black shadows with tiny eyes like hard, dark marbles set in a face of dough. The coal-black pig eyes of sudden death. Evil . . . safe now, down in the sewers.

And Edie Emaline Lynch is rolling northbound. Her vector has crossed that of the monster. She is humming along with a love song on the radio, thinking about an almost-stranger she is nuts about, this Jack Eichord, who is at this moment laughing on the outside, gritting his teeth on the inside, and about to succumb to his personal demons.

Eichord
in the
Spotlight

"What?"

W H A T ?

The word explodes into the stillness of the room, shocking him awake like a pitcher of ice water thrown on the naked body of a sleeping human. He is jarred awake physically but remains deep inside the clinging and impenetrable covers of one of those unbearably realistic-to-the-last-detail nightmares that some people seem to visit in lieu of confessionals.

Jack Eichord was an ardent and longtime fan of the movie genre known as *film noir;* dated, dark, nighttime guided tours of forties and fifties urban underworlds. He loved the old black-and-white late-show procedurals, full of seedy PIs in search of elusive Maltese falcons. One of the early ones was a thing with Victor Mature and Betty Grable called *I Wake Up Screaming* and he thought the title to himself as he woke up screaming the word what.

W H A T ?

He is screaming the world *WHAT?* at the top of his brain's lungs, just as the room explodes in noise and he penetrates the curtain of the bad dream enough to snatch the ringing telephone off the cradle and whisper through a sleep-parched mouth the hoarse, cracked greeting:

"Wha'?"

"Jack? Are you awake?" she asked.

"Huh?"

"Is this Jack?"

"Huh? Yeah. Yeah. Edie?"

"Were you still asleep? It's after ten. I'm sorry. You got in late, I shouldn't have called. I'm sorry."

"'S okay."

"Jack! Congratulations!"

"Huh?" What, he thinks, I wonder what time it is? He is totally befuddled.

"It's all over the television and newspapers this morning. You're a celebrity. Except the one paper got your name as John Eichord instead of Jack, but on TV they didn't have your name on the one channel; they referred to you as 'the famous expert on serial murders' or something like that and—"

"What?"

"Huh? Pardon?"

"Edie, can you hear me all right?"

"Yes, honey. You sound like you've got a cold or something. Have you got a bad connection? Can you hear me?"

"Yes, I think so. Listen, what are you talking about? What's in the papers and on TV? What are you saying?"

"You, my darling. You're a big cop star now." She laughed happily. "Oh, Jack, was he the one,"—her voice took on a cold edge—"you know, responsible for Ed? Or is it too soon to know that yet?"

"Edie, I just don't have the faintest notion of what you're talking about. Start from the beginning."

"Are you serious?"

"Yeah. What is it?"

"You solved the Lonely Hearts killings."

"I'm not believing this. What in the *hell* are you talking about?"

"Well . . . didn't you?" She is confused now. "They said the man you arrested last night was the one who did all those . . . crimes. The Lonely Hearts murders. What are you telling me? Are you saying you don't know what any of this is about?"

"Edie, listen, this is very important. *Who,* exactly now, who says I solved the murders?"

"Channel Four, the American, ABC-TV had it on their—uh—"

"No. I mean who—what official—name the names. What . . . Where did the TV and newspaper reporters get the story? Was it from Lieutenant Arlen or who?"

"The police commissioner, I don't know. It's all in the papers, Jack. Didn't you arrest someone last night in the killings?"

"Yes. A suspect. But he didn't do the other murders. This was an isolated homicide. Who said it was the Lonely Hearts? Did the commissioner actually say it? Can you find it there in a paper and read it to me?"

"Hold oh." He could hear the phone make a noise. " 'The announcement of the arrest was made by Chicago Deputy Chief Samuel F. X. O'Herin, who attributued the quick capture of the killer to the fine police work of the Chicago police force and to the outstanding direction of Special Investigator John Eichord, a consultant from the national Major Crimes Task Force. Deputy Chief O'Herin announced the arrest at a special news conference during which—' "

"Oh, those dumb bastards."

"What is it, Jack?"

"Those stupid sonsofbitches. What in God's name do they think they're doing? They're not going to be able to put this over on the public. The next time he kills they'll know it was all so much bullshit." But even as he said it he knew that wasn't necessarily true. No one had clout like law enforcement. And in certain localities—like Cook County, Illinois, Tarrant County, Texas, isolated pockets of California, Florida, Mississippi, Missouri—the clout was unreal. There was one notorious area of New Jersey where a badge was an absolute license to kill, and the truth was . . . Hell, the truth was he was beginning to wonder if he knew *what* the truth was. He finally got the squad room on his second attempt to dial, so sleep-befuddled he was.

He'd almost gone all the way down into it last night, standing there in that smoky cop bar with those fucking flake homicide dicks and those worn-out groupie retreads, laughing loud, plastic laughs at cruel cop wit, almost falling off the edge of his glass down into that sweet, bitter, stinging, intoxicating piss-colored liquid world he loved so much. Almost let it take him. No special reason. Just the power of the moment. A juicer never needs an excuse; you just go with the flow. It had been close. He'd pushed his tolerance right to the wall. Very stupid.

His hand was shaking a little as he waited for Arlen.

"We tried to phone you; you were either asleep or out," they said to him.

"I was right here, Lou," he told the lieutenant.

"You sleep sound. A clear conscience."

"What's the story?"

"Yeah. Well, it's out of my hands, as you can imagine. This is right from the chief's office. It's a whole big number and you're it. They've talked themselves into going that route with it, going public with you, and they're going to make our boy downstairs for Kasikoff, right or wrong."

"That's the craziest fuckin'—"

"No," he went on bitterly, "don't even bother. I've already told everybody who'd listen including that asshole I work for that this is a wrongo play. My opinion or your opinion is of zero consequence here. You are going to have it laid in your lap and that's it. You're to take a meeting with the brass at eleven this morning. Which means you have some forty minutes to get the cobwebs out of your brain, the sleep out of your eyes, and have your heroic ass down here for the pleasure of the big boys. I'll see you after your briefing—'kay?"

"Yeah. I'll see you. And I don't fucking like any bit of this."

He was there in half an hour, scraped face and

yesterday's suit, clean shirt, prepared to wait in the outer office for the requisite four-and-a-half-to-six minutes, but getting the red-carpet treatment and being ushered right in to The Presence.

"Jack Eichord, is it,"·the older man effused, bathing the room in peppermint-flavored mouthwash, good cologne, and the memory of old cop sweat that lingered in the carpeting and draperies from a thousand such meetings. "Congratulations on solving our big whodunit!"

"Thank you, sir, but I don't believe it's solved yet."

"Sit down here, Jack. How about some coffee?" He buzzed and a male secretary came in with a tray even as Eichord said no thanks.

"Two sugars, is it." It wasn't a question. "Jack, of course it isn't solved yet. Of course not. But that's what *we* know. And that's for our official ears and eyes only. The public. They're going to get a slightly different view of the Kasikoff case." A younger man came in without knocking or being announced. Jack had seen him before. The division PR man.

"Rolly, you know our famous Jack Eichord, don't you." Again, it wasn't a question. "Rolly Margulies is our liaison man with media. Our public information officer and all-around fixer," he said the last with a cold chuckle.

"Absolutely."

"Gladaseeya."

"Rolly, Jack is naturally concerned about the problem of our misrepresenting him as having solved the Kasikoff killings."

"Jack, if I may, I know what you must be saying to yourself this morning, but believe me, we've all thought this one out and it's the best route to go. We need you to go along with us on this one hundred percent. It's the only way. We have to put up a solid front to the media people. We're in bad trouble with this one. The fact that Charles Maitland was slaughtered right outside his own penthouse and we didn't, quote, do anything about it has got us up to our balls in the hot wax.

There's people can use the Lonely Hearts thing to make the PC and the whole force"—he gestured to take in Deputy Chief O'Herin who glowered across the desk at them—"look bad. Tar us all with the same brush. Inept, all the usual criticism, totally unwarranted, but the public is scared to death right now and they're buying it. This is a way to take the heat off the whole department."

"I can understand that much. The problem is, when this guy murders again, when he takes another heart, you're back in the soup. In the hot wax, rather. And now you're going to look like not just inept cops, you—we're going to come off as lying, inept cops. I don't see this buys us anything but lots of trouble. There's no way—"

"Let me cut through," O'Herin said. "We've got a handle on it, Jack. When the perp hits again, who's to say that it isn't a string of copycat killings?" The deputy chief's rosy cheeks shone with scrubbed, talcumed innocence. Smooth as a baby's ass, Eichord thought.

"It's a trifle thin, to me."

"Well, we're asking you to live with it." Eichord shrugged a response. "This is right from the PC himself. So let's play it this way and take it as it goes from there."

"What we need you to do, Jack," Rolly said, "is to be our mouthpiece on the thing. You're technically not one of us and it will be much more credible coming from you. You need to tell the press how we narrowed down this lead, and that lead, good solid police work, blah-blah-blah, and finally homed in on our suspect. You can sell it easily. You were in on the arrest of Mr. Triarnicht last night, and enough reporters know that so it will be plausible that you were directing the apprehension of the perpetrator. You know he did the boy, so that part will play easily too."

"Have you forgotten that when the lab reports come back they're not going to match that hunting knife to the other Kasikoff killings?"

"Well. That's a shame about those lab findings. It seems something happened over there. They're so busy, you know. Buried in work alla time. I hear the lab work got—misplaced for the time being. So I wouldn't worry too much about any confusing findings interfering with the position you'll be taking."

"I don't think it'll fly. That's my opinion." He gestured minimally with his hands tightly in front of him.

"Fine, Jack," O'Herin said, "and we respect that opinion very highly. But with respect to the public facade you'll go along with us on this, right?"

"Sure." He seethed.

"We're going to want you to do an interview. There's a talk show that is watched by all the media people called 'Chicago Sunrise,' you may have seen it. Little gal named Christa Summers does it over on Channel Thirty-one. They have a local celeb of some kind, a political figure, athlete, whatever—and usually at least one guest journalist to ask questions. Nicely moderated show—no hatchet jobs or any of that—very uptown, upscale kinda' thing. We want you to go on the show and let her interview you about the killings."

"You've got to be kidding me."

"That or you sit and give interview after interview to every big paper and radio and TV reporter in the Chicagoland area. Or hold a big ball buster of a press conference where you'll have to field all kinds of cheap shots from the hardballers. Nail yourself to a cross. You don't want to do that. This is the best way, by far. Nice safe interview. You do it one time and cover all the bases. Then it's all old news and nobody's on our case anymore."

"Until the next time he kills somebody and rips the heart out."

"We face that problem at that time. Okay?"

"You're calling the shots."

"Good man. Now let's go over a few points about how you solved the Sylvia Kasikoff case. . . ."

The interview, which would be played back on videotape the following morning around eight A.M., was recorded in a large studio over at the television station that night at seven. Eichord rode to the interview with Rolly Margulies. He resisted being made up by the makeup lady and went to the greenroom to be briefed a final time on some of the questions that Christa Summers would be asking him. He was the focus of twelve eyes as he sat listening to the woman read off a clipboard taking him through some of the Q&A's. There was a floor-director type, a station executive of some sort to whom he was never introduced, Christa herself, Rolly, a "gofer" who waited in attendance, and the woman who took him through the basic questions until he had somehow satisfied the twelve eyes that there were going to be no unpleasant surprises.

The greenroom was actually beige. The main studio where he was taken for the taping was blue. It resembled a huge, bright blue warehouse, the floor a litter of cables, cameras, cigarette butts, and the other garbage that a tide of humanity had washed up to the riser on which the show "Chicago Sunrise" took place. As soon as he stepped up on to the riser, a large wooden platform containing the set for the show, a bank of piercingly hot spotlights blinded him, instantly drenching Eichord in fear sweat.

But the big surprise would not hit him for several minutes. The big and most definitely unpleasant surprise for Jack was in the person of one "Uncle George," the character who would act as his Grand Inquisitor before the grueling interview session was over. Uncle George was one of the strange, aberrant, bizarro improbabilities that somehow managed to surface on isolated major-market television stations across America. He was the backlash, perhaps, to all the cutesy, wimpy anchorpersons with their blow-dried hair and capped teeth and soulless on-cam personalities. Uncle George Kcscztska was a tough, ugly, sadistic, kick-ass old curmudgeon who had become one of Chicago's favorite television stars quite by semi-accident.

It all began when Channel 31 ran one of its Editorial

Echo features about how far too much abuse was heaped on the IRS. It was written and voiced by the station manager, one Harlow Boggs, who actually hated the internal-revenue folk like most everyone else did, but who had designed the editorial to evoke a strong viewer response. He hadn't envisioned one George Kcscztska, pronounced Kicks-zitsca, who would come slinking out of the woodwork just quivering at the chance to get some free TV time under the FCC fairness doctrine.

Kcscztska did a pretape interview that met the standards-and-practices requirements, but then when it was time to tape his Editorial Echo something happened. A question, as always, of chemistry. Something lit up inside the old misanthrope. And when that red light blinked over the camera and he took his hand cue from the floor man, this television novice just knocked everybody out with his total poise, burning intensity, and searing intelligence.

He called his guest editorial rebuttal "An Open Letter from Uncle George to Uncle Sam," and by the end of sixty seconds airtime he had made both the United States government and Channel 31 look like the imbecilic institutions they truly were. And a certain segment of the viewers just went ape over it. The switchboard was flooded with calls, many of them wanting more of Uncle George. And so a TV star was born in the Windy City.

Back in the greenroom nobody had bothered to warn Eichord that this old, ugly geezer who called himself Uncle George Kick-Ass-ka or whatever was about to do a "Bed-Sty Ninety Percenter" on Jack. A Bed-Sty Ninety-Percent stomping being the old-time gang vernacular for a little boot party where the stompee is left alive, but just barely. Uncle George was going to do such a J.O.B. on Jack he'd be a drenched, trembling sack of protoplasm by the end of the taping session. All they told him was that he was the guest reporter or interviewer who would come in with a few "follow-up questions and remarks" when Christa had finished with the main interview segment.

Eichord was a bit wet-palmed and dry-mouthed, but not too shaky. Then a tall, thin woman wearing jeans and high heels, with one of the truly sensational rears in all of Christendom, came and smiled at Jack and made a move with a long, Dragon Lady fingernail, indicating that he should follow her and she said:

"It's time," with that little tilt of the head and funny smile and odd tone of voice that people always use when they lead the little kid in to have the impacted molar cut out. That same tone when the secretary at the IRS tells you the auditor is ready for you. The little look you recall from childhood when the principal finishes talking to your folks and it's *your* turn. The little quasi-friendly lilting tone that never fails to engender a rapid palpitation or at least a stab of apprehension.

He expected to be a little warm under the lights but it was actually rather cool in the studio. As he shivered reflexively he felt himself suddenly bathed in fear sweat, stage fright, and an unexpected, massive, drenching paranoia from left field. And as he tried to pull his socks up, adjust his tie, and blot his forehead a monitor beside him came to life with a shot of him wiping perspiration and he could hear the loud bark of audio on the cameraman's earphone as a recorded announcement introduced:

" 'Chicago Sunrise'! Starring Christa Summers—with her special guest, noted serial-murder expert Jack A-cord, who will talk about solving the Lonely Hearts Murders! And our guest interviewer for Hotseat Spotlight, the inimitable Uncle George! And now . . . for Lakefront Furniture City, he-e-e-e-e-r-r-r-r-r-r's Christa!"

Real original, thought Eichord as the red light on Christa's camera winked on and she was already asking him something and his mind kicked in just in time to catch, "Ay-cord or I-cord, so which is correct?" She was smiling with teeth that looked like they'd been carved from a single piece of white plastic.

"It's Eichord but—"

"The German diphthong, I should have known." She had a sort of semibreathless style, and she was quite attractive and show bizzy. And the combination gave her most mundane pronouncements an aura of discovery, and Eichord wished he could come back with some brilliant rejoinder but unfortunately he hadn't the vaguest notion of what a German diphthong was. And the only thing that came to mind was a dildo with a French tickler on it and he was sure that wasn't what she wanted to hear so he only smiled idiotically and perspired profusely as she continued talking.

Fortunately she didn't ask him any other questions, rounding up her introduction by saying, "More on the end of a horror story, the solving of the Lonely Hearts Murders with the modern-day Sherlock Holmes who brought the killer to justice, as 'Chicago Sunrise' continues—right after this!"

And suddenly the floor director made a cutting motion across his throat, which even Eichord could understand, and also relate to at this point. And people were running everywhere. The cameras were moving around in the sea of cables, twisted like a menacing nest of huge, black snakes that surrounded the riser where they sat, and several people attacked them, doing last-minute things to Christa Summers, two of them talking with her at the same time, which she seemed to find quite normal, and a woman blotted Eichord's perspiring head and someone did something to him, touched him with something he felt but couldn't identify, and he heard someone ask him if he would like a wet cloth and he almost laughed out loud at the insanity of the question. What in the hell would I want with a *wet cloth*? he thought, but he managed to shake his head and smile and he was just working up the nerve to ask if he could have a glass of water when the furniture commercial stopped and Christa calmly turned to him and said:

"I'm not going to bite, you know." And she gave a sexy, soft little mew of a laugh.

"Oh," he replied wittily, not having any idea what she meant. It was like the wet cloth. Why would he think she was going to bite him? Did these people around here speak only gibberish?

"You seem nervous," she was explaining to him, as you'd explain calculus to a third-grader. "So just relax or you'll make *me* nervous, and if *I* get nervous, and we're *both* nervous, I'll have to get the director down here out of the booth and *he'll* have to finish the show. And we don't want that do we, Don?"

And she giggled as Don said, "Speak for yourself," on the intercom, and everybody broke up.

And she was pretty good. Within a couple of minutes she'd calmed him down and the worst of the stage fright had begun to recede into the wings or wherever TV jitters go. Eichord was beginning to respond to her questions in actual sentences, and before long he was feeling somewhat at ease in front of the lights and the cameras.

He tried at first to really tell her about the phenomenon of serial murders but she already knew all the answers to the questions she was asking or at least she knew what she wanted to hear. That was the impression she gave Eichord asking things like:

"There's really no profile of a serial murderer, is there?" very confidently, and when he answered:

"Actually there are profiles. In fact one of the courses the agents teach at Quantico is called Logical Profiles of Serial Murderers and—"

"But what I'm saying, is that—" and leading him down another path altogether, in a way that an uncharitable person might think was designed to make herself look as infallible as possible.

She was very good. Slick. Facile. Quick with the teeth and sparkling cokey eyes and little hair toss. And she was no dummy. But she didn't seem to want to learn anything in the interview, which was fine with Jack. As soon as he figured out what she wanted he started giving nice, long-winded, winding answers to keep her on the safe stuff. And when she got on to dangerous ground he'd try to get her off of it entirely, leading the questioning away from the Sylvia Kasikoff thing as much as he could without appearing evasive.

She was experienced enough to catch what he was doing immediately but as long as it played she went with the flow of it. He was making her look as if she'd done her homework, even though she didn't like the way he kept steering her off the specific case-solving stuff and going into lengthy explanations when they were talking generalities. She knew how to get numbers and she kept him firmly on the killings. He had done a good job, he thought, of fielding the questions, bringing the conversational ball back to safer turf where he could talk about the serial specter in general. And then Uncle George took his turn at bat and the whole thing fell apart at the seams.

George sat down and didn't speak or even look at him. He looked at the floor until the standby cue came and then those eyes opened wide and he looked directly into the upper center of the camera lens as it blinked red and began speaking very fast looking into the camera eye but speaking *to* Jack Eichord, and in the first long, prolix, recondite question he used the phrase *meromorphic function* and Jack's eyes clouded over and he replied:

"I'm sorry but I don't know what you mean."

"What?" Uncle George demanded.

"I'm not familiar with the phrase *mar-uh-morphic function,* so how can I answer a question if I don't understand it?"

"Well, let me explain it to you then," George said sternly, becoming quite agitated. "The dictionary defines *meromorphic function* as a function of a complex variable that is regular in a region except for a finite number of points at which it has a limitless infinity as its terminus, from the Greek prefix *meros,* and am I going too fast for you and do you understand all the words like function and complex and variable and regular and region and finite and number and points and limitless and infinity and terminus and prefix, or should I go back and define *them*, which would take up most of my time and we wouldn't have to see you squirm trying to explain how the modus operandi of last night's murder was significantly different than that of the previous mutilation murders in the Chicagoland area, would we?"

And his face was bright red and Eichord thought he looked like a Type-A heart attack/hypertensive/apoplectic candidate for early hardening of the arteries who was about to have a stroke right here, folks, live and in color, and he said, "I'm sorry but I've forgotten the question," definitely getting off on the wrong foot.

So this was the brass's idea of a nice, upscale interview, upbeat, no hatchet jobs or anything—eh? And how did this old fart know the MO was different? From that moment on it was all downhill for Jack, who was no great shakes as a liar anyway.

After four or five minutes of this relentless diatribe they gave Uncle George the wrap-up sign and he looked at Eichord for the first time and said, "You've got nobody fooled, and frankly I find the police's playacting, public posture, premise, position, and presentation mendacious, specious, meretricious, and highly odious. And if you find that an impenetrable logograph, Special Agent Eichord, I'm saying it's a lying, stinking *mess*." Eichord thought of several witty comebacks but luckily managed to refrain from trying any of them and in a second or two the light blinked out and it was mercifully over.

Five minutes of this in private would be bad enough. But for Jack Eichord, hoisted as it were on his Smith and Wesson and left to twist slowly, slowly in the Windy, there in the white-hot glare of television, there in the hog butcher of the world, city of big shoulders, it was five hours of hell.

And when Uncle George had finished with him the whole deal was fairly precarious *in re* who would believe what. Clearly George Kick-ass-ka's fans, if no one else, would think this had been a ruse on the part of the authorities to placate a nervous (and naive) public. And one would have to conclude Jack had done little or nothing to convince a skeptical viewer. But one such viewer sat watching Eichord's performance in a quiet and deadly rage.

He was watching a twenty-three-inch RCA inside a small home out in Oak Park in which three members of the Volker family sat beside him. Ted Volker, and his wife Betty, and their nine-year-old son Sean, all sat on a sofa beside Daniel Bunkowski, who had pulled his chair next to them.

They all sat there quietly watching the bright screen there in the darkened room, the noises from the television set's speaker being the only audible sounds. Ted and Betty and Sean watched the show with unseeing eyes. And as Daniel listened to the pontificating about the serial murders and all the lies, he stared at the cop's image with his hard, little pig eyes and decided he would send some proof that the Lonely Hearts killer was still at large. He liked that phrase—*at large*.

He turned to the dead Volkers and beamed radiantly, and with a groan of effort lifted his great bulk from the armchair and went to work.

Eichord
the Hero

He told her the whole thing of course, screamed it at her, cursing, pacing up and down, she whispering and softly mellowing him out, cooling him off as he raged about the "fucking morons" downtown. But somehow she didn't really let it register. He could tell that by the way she kept talking about how the paper said this or the television said that. She liked it that he was a cop star, for right or wrong, it was hard for her to let go of it, so he finally shut up about it.

There were too many reporters around and she talked him into taking a somewhat extravagant suite in an outrageous but quite private "XXX-rated motor hotel" in a nearby suburb. And this is where she took him to lick, among other things, his wounds—both real and imagined.

And what wild fantasies of eroticism held him spellbound as he lay there on the satiny sheet, eyes closed on the sexy lighting and oblivious to the quietly insinuating background music? Two cops named Pat McTeague and Penny Butts. Pat and Penny. Sounded like two broads, he thought. I'm layin' here next to this fox thinking about two cops. I'm in trouble.

Penny Butts weighed 250 pounds and ate onions like they were ice cream cones, and Pat McTeague was equally attractive. He was a borderline alky with a face like a Rand McNally, topped off by this big Rudolph-colored honker of a hose-nose with veins so big they had their own little veins. His whole face looked like a huge, ugly busted capillary.

Eichord was thinking about them because it was them he sat with when the contingent from the squad room moved en masse to the cop bar the night before. Their conversation was mostly jokes, one of the less obscene was a particularly ornate thing with the following punch line:

"So the judge says, say what? And the lawyer says, your honor that's when the plaintiff took an alpha cyanoacrylate monomer and created anionic polymerization bonding my client's erectile member to the subjacent faying surface of the sleeping unit. And the guy yells, *Yeah, Judge, an' the bitch glued my cock to d' mattress too!*" Laughter.

They started ragging Jack about his heroism.

"Man that fuckin' McTuff can solve the tough ones, can't they, bro?"

"Damn straight, ace. I gotta' get on that team, man. Can you see my name when they do the TV series about me. 'McTeague of McTuff; has a fuckin' ring to it.'"

"I like 'McTuff Butts, Private Eye.' " Eichord laughed dutifully.

"Shit, man, I mean you fuckin' get *down* on them whodunits." And on and on. After a few minutes his smile muscles were starting to get that pinched-up feeling and he finally was able to con his way out the door and managed to ease out without looking like an asshole who couldn't take a joke. They were flakes. But the teasing was just their way of saying they knew it was out of his hands. They damn well realized it could easily happen to either of them, to anybody else in Homicide. Still, it rankled. He didn't like any of it.

The hero thing was serious business to him. He had come from a time that now seemed so remote as to be part of a lost world. He had come from the never-wuz yesteryear of a kid's dreams, back in the forgotten past of an America that believed in the mythologized hero. Larger than life. Pure of spirit. The good guy in the white hat.

Eichord had been a kid when the golden age of the heroic image tarnished in the onrushing high-tech era, disintegrating, the pieces of rust scattered by the fickle winds of time and evolution. But he still remembered the hero world that had formed his early years into something resembling a normal childhood. Jack re-called those giant-size images that his dad had taught him about. Stillwell! Damn. Salk, DiMaggio, Harry *Truman,* for Chrissakes—these were great, looming, awesome personalities like the six-sheets out in front of the Orpheum. And Eichord's generation had grown up with seriously revered heroes in sports, the mili-tary, science, and even—believe it or not—politics.

When Jack wasn't swimming or shooting baskets or climbing trees, he was reading about heroes. First the Hardy Boys and then the great autobiographies and then the military histories. He devoured *The Washing of the Spears* again and again. He read *Seven Pillars of Wisdom* twenty-eight times in two years, reading it night after night, reading paragraphs at a time, sight-reading great chunks of it over and over, letting it mold him, shape his self-image.

He was raised in the shadow of the Invincible Nord-Americano, the legend of the White, Anglo-Saxon, Protestant Male Hero. The elitist spear-carrier; the warrior responsibilities of middle-class noblesse oblige shaping him into the only acceptable professions of career military man, policeman or fireman, paramedic, whatever. He had to be at least symbolically in uni-form, and out there on the cutting edge.

And then something went wrong. And the weight of all the input and the information mixed with the liquid realities, and it all combined to take him under like an anchor, and he dropped into the impenetrable depths of Jack Daniels' Lake, sinking down to the cold, muddy bottom, another victim of the Black Water Fever. Another muddy thinker trapped in a hero's rusting, one-man sub down in the Land of Lost Souls. A booze-battered casualty of the heroic era.

So now, Eichord thought, here I am next to the soft and warm lady of my choosing, on exquisite sheets in a room of erotic mirrors and sexy lighting, basking in adoration and tenderness, drenched in musky aromas, hearing the soft, whispered phrases of love, and all I can think about are two ugly cops and their bad jokes, and all I can feel is the chill of the land of the lost.

And underneath all that, hiding down there in the dark substrata, I sense the foul presence of a human thing who kills for pleasure, taking hearts for God only knows what reasons. Ripping bloody hearts out of freshly killed corpses. And this thing is still out there, no matter what the newspapers would have you believe. And the cloud of menace hangs over the bed like a frightening shadow and I detumesce without dying the little demise, Jack thinks.

But Edie is here and the nearness now is what matters. So he opens his eyes and ignores the mirrors, and blocks out the thoughts of blond silicone twins and French maids and all the other silly, childish fantasy stuff that goes with a bed like this, and he relaxes and breathes her in. And in his new state of grace he feels his humanity slowly ebbing, then shifting current and flowing back into him, and the softly fluttering eyelashes, and the hot fingertips begin to work their electric magic on him again.

And his hands catch in that dark pillow of long hair and he pulls her near so that he can see nothing but the closeness of her, a mesh of flesh and bone and warmth and delightful mewings, and mouths and limbs and organs and souls rock and explode together and they go down into that hot pit of flame again, and let go in an achingly sweet and perfect, bubbling, delicious honey pot. And not caring then.

Now he only wants this moment to freeze. This second. This timeless, unimprovable, textbook-perfect, classic, heartthrobbing, madly exhilarating love explosion between them. Suddenly this is the only thing, the only important thing, the only thing that matters to him, and he prays that he can make the world stop and hold on to this, this joyous, shouting, lovely, love-drenched instant of full-tilt, kissy-face, huggy-bear, jailhouse tango blues.

Another Mistake

Ted Volker was one of those fortunate people who had a great mother-in-law, a pleasant woman who was close to her daughter and son-in-law, whom she treated like her own son, and especially her grandson, and who visited them almost every day. It was she who found the family the next day. And it completely destroyed her mind.

A mail carrier was first to hear the screams but thought it was coming from the television set. A delivery man was probably the second to hear her and phoned the Chicago police emergency number. After several minutes the call-in was routed to the dispatcher, and a few minutes later a two-man car responded. What they found was a scene straight out of hell.

They heard the awful, tortured, animal screams before they reached the door of the Volker household and the men looked at each other and one whispered:

"Holy Jesus," and they entered carefully, with their pieces drawn. The blinds were all shut and the small amount of available sunlight barely penetrated the gloom. A woman could be heard literally screaming her lungs out back in the family room and when they came around the corner the overpowering stench caused them both to gag.

Sudden, unexpected, surprising, overpowering, and terrorizing shock affects each individual differently. It all depends on the circumstances, the state of preparedness, the individual's predisposition to trauma, personal physiological thresholds; the thousand and one factors that either soften or amplify those shocks that human flesh is heir to.

There were three bodies on the couch, taped nude to the sofa and each other with silver duct tape like plumbers use, and each with the eyelids taped open— the silver tape pulled grotesquely over the hair and the faces, the eyes of the dead rolled up in unseeing sockets which gaped like holes in a silver death mask.

The standing woman continued to scream until just before the doctor started to sedate her when she passed out from exhaustion. She had lost her mind, and would never make another sound beyond those final anguished screams. Parenthetically, the police had no way of knowing, but her hair, gray before, had bleached absolutely white during the dehumanizing hours of unrelieved horror.

The living room, the dying room that is, was covered in what had been a lake of human blood. The blood had coagulated and congealed into a hideous crust of insect-covered filth and drying slime and the smell was the smell of the busiest killing room of a nineteenth-century stockyards slaughterhouse. The cops had never smelled anything like the smell of that room in the Volker house.

The beast that had done this thing had tromped through the grisly bloodpond leaving brazen, red 15EEEEE pawprints of massive, naked feet as he walked to the bathroom at the end of his work. Tromp, tromp, clomping along down the hall that still echoed with the awful silence after a family's muffled screams. The creature hearing nothing, feeling nothing beyond simple pleasure at the destruction process, a postcoital kind of feeling as he clomped along leaving big, nasty, sticky stains on the lime-colored shag. Huge, scarlet paw marks where his weight smashed down on those size fifteen flat, splayed feet.

He had clomped into the master bedroom, turning the shower on, urinating for some reason into the sink at some point, then taking a hot shower. He had masturbated again after the shower, while standing there with the water drying on his enormous body, this having been determined by semen residue found in the tub trap, then he dried off on a missing towel which he presumably used to wipe off all the hand-touched knobs and other printable surfaces. They picked up a fairly good left thumb off a mirror that it seemed he might have touched before he put his gloves on. They had run it out to the feds along with the other forensics. It didn't happen much but you never knew when you'd get lucky.

A mail carrier leaving a priority first-class package in the lobby of the division out of which Jack Eichord was working added his set of prints to the case. The other prints were also postal employees. The label on the package was hand addressed by someone who had used a felt-tipped pen, writing with hard, firm, angry lines that mushed the tip down, making broad and precisely squared-off letters as he carefully printed out JACK ICORD [sic] which he had heard over the television set while in the Volker house.

He had then wrapped the items in three individual plastic bags, then put those bags inside another container which he sealed using a heat-seal cooking device he'd found in the Volker kitchen. Seal-A-Meal had been the brand name.

When he had sealed up his items he'd wiped the outside of the plastic again, wiped off the heat-sealer, and put everything in the sack with the towel he'd used to clean up with, along with other miscellaneous things he wanted to dispose of. But there was a marked difference in his attitude and comportment. He was changing. He was no longer as concerned with perfection or professionalism. He was well aware that as he cleaned up after himself he was going through the motions. That extreme teeth-gritting focus of concentration had lightened up. It was beyond his ability to analyze. Perhaps he was going into some sort of an I-Want-to-Be-Punished phase, he thought to himself. No. But what? What indeed.

The swaggering, cranked little man was five feet, three inches tall and he was extremely tough. He had fought all of his life. His name was Tree. It was his street name. Little Tree, or Tree, they called him. Mr. Tree. He truly did not remember his own name. It was a name like Tree. His first name, his real name, was Buddy but nobody called him that. He had not been Buddy since he lived at home.

He had run away from home when he was fourteen. After being confronted by his father about his frequent sexual attacks on his new stepmother he had beaten his father unconscious and left home. He was a sometimes-member of an outlaw biker gang called the Flames that was currently trying to muscle in on the Chicago Warlords for a piece of the lucrative market in crank, or crystal meth.

"Fuckin' Deuce is lame, man." Deuce was the current president of the Flames and Tree was telling this to his only friend, another very short man who was known on the street as Leaping Lester. Lester was a cringing sort of a wimp who was always seen scurrying around the fringes of the outlaw gang members and groupies and hangers-on, turning up in the leather bars and redneck roadhouses and dope joints, trying to suck up to the Flames or anybody flying colors (wearing a biker-club jacket) and smelling rank. He was a biker buff. He was also frightened to death of Tree, and because Tree liked this attitude he allowed him to hang around. "Fuckin' Deuce had any balls he'd . . . we'd be dealing, goddammit."

"Yeah," Lester agreed enthusiastically, "that's right, man. That som'bitch's lame."

"He's a lame, jive-ass mother*fucker*."

"Damn right he's lame. I don't know why—"

"Got to kick his bogus Deuce ass out o' there and get somebody can deal real. We be dealing some fucking *weight* here, motherfucker."

"Fuckin' lame Flames. Shit, man, fuckin' Warlord faggots dealin' big numbers goddammit and that's—"

"Fuckin' Whore Lards."

"Yeah," Lester agreed, laughing, "the fuckin' *Whore* Lords."

"The Whore *Lards*, you dumb, midget punk," Tree said viciously.

"Yeah"—Lester giggled—"lard-ass Whore *Lards*."

"I'm gon' to get that shit from Apache and Saturday we'll get the meth and the hydrochloric acid 'n shit and go out to the point and have us a fuckin' *cookout*, motherfucker."

"Yeah!"

"Man, soon's I can get me another two grand we're goin' to fuckin' Big A, man."

"Huh?"

"Thas' right, motherfuck. Fuckin' *Australia*, man. That's where it is, pud. That's where the freedom's at now. Fuckin' Peter whatshisname, Peter-eater, remember that limey cocksuck?"

"Eh?"

"The limey, English fucker you pud. Well, anyway, that motherfucker says like it's wide open over there in motherfuckin' Australia, man. An' I'll take Debbie and you take that ugly bitch of yours and we'll go over there and live like fuckin' kings." Debbie was his slave; a pathetic, morose, robotlike teenager who worked with them as part-time janitorial help. Physically unattractive and unwanted, she played out the parts of his twisted psychosexual fantasies because, at least so far, perverted attention was better than none.

"Fuckin' Australia? Gawddamn, I dunno where it is even onna' fuckin' map."

"You dumb li'l runtcunt, you don't know where your shitty ass is either but you can still manage to wipe it oncet in a while, cancha'?"

"Yeah, I rectum so," he said, achieving for him what was a veritable Everest peak of wit.

Bunkowski had been watching them for about half a block, coming silently behind them, stalking them in the darkness. He could make out most of the absurd, moronic conversation as he drew closer now, and the light glinted off the chain that the one called Tree wore over his shoulder, the thing that had caught Daniel's eye in the first place.

Tree wore a huge chain, something off a motorcycle perhaps, an enormous thing that he ran through one of the shoulder loops on his leather jacket, and down into his pocket, to a heavy weight of keys, the other end of the long chain fastened to his belt. He liked to whip the keys out in a fight, and it was the silver chain catching the light that Daniel had seen.

He loved the idea of taking off this pair of drooling punks with his own chain, a yard of taped tractor chain that had killed and killed again, and he planned to smack these loud-talking, ignorant insects just as you might swat a pair of buzzing mosquitoes. He liked to kill any living human, but little people were his first love, little strutting cocky bantam-rooster braggart smart-aleck punk loud-talking, ignorant little people wearing chains were right up his alley.

"That shit we cooked up before was fucking decent, man. I mean it drummed on the inside of y'r head all fuckin' *day*. We can cook that shit and man, I'll be the fucking king of Australia." Tree had begun his fantasy-obsession about Australia several weeks ago, how they could go over and sell crank free from any laws, and so deep was the structure of his psychosis that each day he built another imaginary layer onto the foundation of his Australian dreamworld. He really believed at that moment, that any day now he'd be buying his tickets for the big boat ride to a ripe, wide-open paradise without authority or law.

"They ain't hardly no big gangs ovah there, man. We can fucking con*trol* the crank market overnight. Brew up our own good shit. Be dealin three, four pounds a day. Be the fuckin' *kings* of—"

They smelled Chaingang before they heard him or saw him, which isn't hard to understand when you consider that he was now spending most of his time down in a specially built trap hidden in a submain of the Chicago sewage system. Tree and Lester were no fragrant flowers themselves, but this—this thing could be smelled, sensed, half a block away, and as he drew near to them coming up behind them on the street even the most desensitized dolt would instinctively turn and look at the looming apparition coming up out of the night. In-stink-tively.

Tree had the first syllable of his precious Australia in his mouth when he went down, appropriately, right in the middle of becoming the king of Aus— he caught the first chainsnap from the heavy, taped links that came snaking, snapping out silently and catching him along the hypothalamus and the medula oblongata and taking his dream down for good in a wet, scarlet sheet of blinding pain and smashed cells, tissue, vertebrae, cartilage, nerves, spine, brain. Lights out. And Bunkowski's tree-limb wrist snaps it back and out again in a lightning bolo throw; a vicious, unstoppable, furiously whizzing, deadly spinning chainsaw of certain death flung with incredible strength, and yet, amazingly, missing.

Missing! Daniel Edward Flowers Bunkowski didn't know the word. *Missing* was not a part of his comprehension. The vocabulary was new. It took a giant heartbeat to sink in, that his killer chain had spun by MISSING *M I S S I N G* this insignificant wimp crashing through the side window of a parked Ford Escort in an explosion of spider-tracked safety glass. And in that heartbeat Leaping Lester did the only thing the little nerd was any good at. He fled. He got up on those filthy tenny-runs of his and he flat out boogied. He booked like the wind. And he was goneski.

And Chaingang, killer of five hundred, killer of families, killer of professional mercs, killer of head-hunters, killer of hardcore soldiers, the assassin's assassin—stood motionless in his tracks. Chaingang stood there over the inert form of the Flames' fallen warrior Little Tree, and watched as a lucky wimp named Lester did the thing he did best. And for the first time he felt a nudge deep inside the bulky body somewhere, this man, this beast that knew no such emotions as fear or apprehension felt something and he could identify it, alien as it was. Because he had M I S S E D. Because he had been seen. Because he had made another mistake.

And Jack Eichord the cop would not know of this for a time. He was busy in the middle of a meeting where he was hearing was what shit-assed, bad, ama-teurish police work he'd been doing. Not him person-ally, you understand, just any warm body involved in Kasikoff, anybody who'd managed to let this ballbusting mother come turn around and kick the PC's ass, which in turn caused the chief to get *his* ass reamed, which is how come the deputy chief had the end of *his* dick stepped on, which is why all these cops were working a sixteen-hour day and still stuck in the cop shop at this late hour in an emergency meeting of the coppers in the Sylvia Kasikoff investigation.

Because this morning the package came. The pack-age with the neat, block-lettered JACK ICORD, the one with the bad weight and the loose, harum-scarum feel; the one Jack was afraid of long before he examined the writing, long before he had them open it up in the bomb vault downstairs, long before he saw what was in the package the thing had sent him.

This was the morning the papers would go back to when the Lonely Hearts killings became a new head-line in the tabloids. This would be the day Eichord would remember for a long time to come, and a day that would keep him awake at night goading him, stabbing at him with the little ice picks of fear each time he thought about the package and what it meant. This would be the day that put him to bed more naked than he could ever remember being; more vulnerable to evil, his outer covering of hard cop removed, decorticated by the awfulness of it, stripped bare like a tree with the bark peeled away.

This would be the day the papers began calling the sensational case the Jack-of-Hearts Murders.

Need
to
Know

What they could have done, what they normally do, is throw the shredded paper mass into the incinerators and erase the computer memories and a thing simply ceases to exist. They are the people who first used *stonewall* as a transitive verb. When they chose to forget something or somebody, that thing or that person never existed. But because of the time and the pressures and the sensitivities and the climate, something still lived on to tell of the beast's existence. And it couldn't have been more telltale if it had in fact been a bloody smear right there on the printout.

"Extension 2228," Eichord said, waiting as the line hissed all the way to Washington.

Had they simply shit-canned it, what the administrators would normally do, that would have been the end of it. But some dim-witted, superbureaucratic type at a desk decided to classify the prints, blood group, and the related ident of those individuals involved in what had once been our military/clandestine intelligence shop's most secret experiment—once called Special Action Unit/Covert Operations Group, pronounced "saw-cog," a euphemistic acronym meaning assassination squad.

And so instead of "No Response" or "Insufficient Data" or whatever, instead of the normal absence of data the feds kicked it right back with an "Officially Deleted," which lit up the printout like a neon sign.

Eichord had been on the telephone for over two hours and his arm was so numb he thought for a second he might be having a small heart attack. And then the phrase *heart attack* slapped his brain around a bit, as a crisp, female voice snapped him out of it:

"Twenty-two, twenty-eight?"

"Sonny Shoenburgen, please," he told her.

"One moment please," she said, pleasantly putting him on hold.

"Thank you," he told a hissing Ma Bell, AT and fucking T, Western Electric, and God only knows what other congloms all seething in their postdivestiture irritation, all hissing at him from within the sanitized, swept, shielded, sound-secure landlines of one of the largest spook complexes west of the Atlantic.

Finally, after what seemed like a month or so, a different voice comes back on the lines, this one male, not quite so pleasant or friendly saying:

"May I help you?"

"Sonny?"

"I'm sorry but we have no one here by that name."

"Listen, I'm with Justice and this is an emergency so cut the crap and put Sonny Shoenburgen on, please."

"Sorry, but he's tied up in a meeting," the voice said after a very brief hesitation. "May I tell Colonel Shoenburgen who's calling, sir?"

"Tell Sonny it's Jack Eichord, E-I-C-H-O-R-D, and I need to talk to him very briefly but I need it to be *now*."

"Right." Another hesitation. "And you're with whom, did you say?"

"Justice department," he lied smoothly.

"Yes, sir, one moment please." The lines hissed and booed again. One moment could be anything. He had once waited one moment for Federal Express on a weekend call that had run twenty-five minutes of the most tortured Muzak to which he'd ever been subjected. Twenty-five ear splitting minutes of some of the most wonderful ass-kissing ricky-tick numbers imaginable. A moment in D.C. time could be fucking anything. He was reaching his telephone tolerance for the day. It was a thing that had crept up his left arm, then his right arm, into both ears, and was now drilling inward, inward toward the soft core of the brain.

"Yeah?" the voice said, quietly.

"Hello?" He had been on the line for some time, picking up his phone without a discernible click. Some cordless, shapeless thing that you never touched, Jack supposed. A telephone that was formed like a microorganism and surgically implanted, perhaps. These bastards had everything.

"Sonny, it's Jack Eichord."

"Agh, you worthless heap of dog shit whatcha' up to?"

"Up to no good. I—"

"You here?"

"Huh?"

"You here in D.C.?"

"No. Chicago. Chicago PD at the moment on a homicide case."

"Jesus H. S. Christ, Junior. Whenja' move to Chi-town?"

"Well, I didn't move here exactly. I'm on loan to 'm for a serial-murder thing. Through Major Crimes. I'm in some deep damn puppy poop too. I wanna' tell ya'."

"I don't doubt that for a damn second." The colonel laughed.

"I need some—"

"Hey! Since when are you with Justice, asshole."

"What time is it now?"

"Uh-huh." Shoenburgen and Eichord went back a long way.

"Sonny, goddammit, I need some help."

"What's up," he said more seriously, "ya' fall off the wagon again?"

"Haven't touched a drop in nearly ten years," he lied, knowing that if Shoenburgen heard he still tipped the odd beer, there'd be a fifteen-minute AA lecture. Nobody was as devoutly born again as a rededicated reprobate and nobody was as fiercely anti-alcohol as a reformed drunk. The two of them had that common bond.

"The problem is, old buddy, I need somebody with heavy intelligence clout to get information on a subject whose fingerprints have been yanked out of the federal computers and classified 'officially deleted.' "

"Deceased, you mean."

"Deleted. That's the way it came back to us. Officially deleted. I'm looking at it now."

"Never heard of such a thing. Wouldn't be any reason for it. Declassified. Or classified such and such. But we don't use that particular nomenclature. We have something not for your eyes, we restrict the knowledge, classify it, or in the case of something being removed we sure don't leave a big, fat red flag in the file saying SOMETHING WAS REMOVED. Only calls attention to that entry. What you've got is some sort of a clerical error. It isn't a file or computer classification any of the agencies use, that's for certain."

"How about your old gang before they disbanded?"

"I don't know what the connection of the subject might be to a murder case but—"

"Potentially we think it might be this guy's right for the Lonely Hearts Murders, which I imagine you've heard about."

"Shit, Pops, I haven't read a newspaper or seen a TV newscast in a month. With the current situation over in—"

"No matter. Listen, this guy's butchered God knows

how many victims. He's a real maniac. Cuts their hearts out. Leaves whole families mutilated. It's one of the worst serial-murder cases ever. We gotta' run this down."

"Okay. But nobody puts 'Officially deleted' on filed fingerprints. Certainly nobody here. Nobody at the Company. The Bureau. I never heard of an agency doin' it. If you see deleted in a sanitized or declassified document that's being downgraded after so many years,' just as an example, like something the agency has to make available under the Freedom of Information Act, you know damn well it's nothing very sensitive to begin with or it'd never got a new rubber stamp. That's the nature of restricted material. This is an error. Some tired clerk who—"

"No, hold it. We assumed that too. But I had our chief out here run that aspect down himself through the Bureau and it isn't a clerical mistake. That is some kind of maximum security deletion. Somebody with heavy-duty clout pulled a curtain down on that person; the error was that they shouldn't have identified the deletion. But what was apparently somebody's in-house response to an inquiry went public in the bureaucratic computer shuffle. I gotta cut through this, Sonny. Please, man, you need to help me on this one."

"Official channels, pal, that's the way to move. I couldn't do it any faster than the Major Crimes Task Force, fer' Chrissakes. Just put an urgent/special-priority request trace in motion through your chief of police or whatever and—"

"Will you listen, man? I've already gone that route. I've already banged up against all those walls. Hey. We gotta PC out here with ties to plans at CIA. Big personal pal of the former deputy director, okay? He called himself. They say it's out of their hands. Deleted at the highest levels of government. That's gotta be one of your people or a cabinet secretary, or somebody swimmin' around at the presidential level. I gotta have serious help on this one, Sonny. And I don't wanna say you owe me but *You Owe Me.*"

"All I can do is check it out, Jack. What's your number?" Twenty-five minutes later Colonel Sonny Shoenburgen was on the line telling him the same crap he already knew.

"Jack, your partial print check was run through McTuff, and NCIC, all the usual, and it got kicked out. Printout flags an official deletion and nobody can go behind that. Someone very senior has put the identity of the subject under a tight national security lid. Best I could do was run it back to the input point which appears to have been Fort Meade, but there's nothing more I can do on it, pard."

"Bullshit Sonny. I *gotta have it.* This guy is ripping the hearts outta people, goddammit, I need you on this, man. *You have to fucking help me!*" Eichord was yelling into the telephone.

"Well. Shit. What can I say, Jack?" A pause and he says, "I know a guy. I can't promise anything."

"That's not what I said to you, man, once upon a time. I don't like saying this, but dammit when you needed me, I was there for you and now I could have found out this much on my own, and I need to know who this fucker *is*, Sonny—and I need to know *bad . . . please.*"

"I'll call you back," he replied, with an audible sigh.

"When?"

"As soon as I fucking *can*, all right?" Sonny promised, somewhat pissed, and hung up the phone—not too gently.

A minute became an hour. Eichord, way, way beyond having any reluctance to push this one regardless of how badly it maxed out the colonel, called Sonny. Colonel Schoenburgen was on another line and would Mr. Eichord like to wait? Why the hell not? Five minutes and he's getting really steamed and he hangs up. Nervously, he's trying to figure what to do next. Two minutes later his line rings.

"Eichord."

"Okay," Sonny told him, "I had to call a big fucking favor for this, so don't do anything like this to me again, *Ever*, I mean this is *Payback*—in spades. You roger that?"

"Affirm. Whatcha got?" Eichord asked eagerly.

"I got a deletion for maximum national security reasons, which we knew. Military intelligence at the highest levels. It was part of a sanitization program that swept a lot of the dirty files clean at the time of the big shake-up over at the Company.

"From what I can gather this was a joint thing between Clandestine Services and the military people. Something that was in place right before the Phoenix Program. Not domestic, best I can make out. I'm going to give you a telephone number to call. Now listen to me, Jack old buddy ole' palsy-walsy, man—no follow-ups. None. I had to pay some fucking long coin of my own to get this son of a buck to hold still for it. I explained the subject is some nut who committed every murder back to the Kennedy assassination, so it's up to you now.

"He'll give you about two minutes on the phone so don't expect more and don't call me back because I won't be here anymore for you. Understand? That's it for me—even steven, agreed?"

"Gotcha. What's the guy's name and who is he?"

"Negative. You just call the number and ask him what you want to know. Don't fuck around with him. He'll hang up and that'll be it. I've given it my best shot." He told Eichord the number, which happened to be a Virginia pay phone, wished him a cool good luck, and clicked off.

"Yep," a gruff voice barked on the first ring.

"My name is Ja—"

"I know who you are, Mr. Eichord, I ran my own check," he said talking very fast, slurring his words slightly. "And as it happens I also know about the Kasikoff case. The man you're looking for is—and get something to write with now, although I assume you have a tape rolling too, is—I'll spell this name, B-U-N-K-O-W-S-K-I. Bunkowski, Daniel Edward Flowers and he's killed a lot of people. I assume he's still at it, right?"

"Right. What's the story on him and why was his identity deleted?"

"Can't tell you that. He was part of a program that was run back when we were experimenting with the use of mercenaries and such over in Southeast Asia, and this the early sixties, back before we got completely involved in the war. Around sixty-four, something like that, he came into the program, which was disabled after a very brief period.

"Deleting his identity was the right thing to do, the mistake was to have those blood groups and prints in the computers, but those things sometimes happen. I'm telexing you his dossier as it applies in your case, and sending the official photograph of Bunkowski down the line to you as well. Don't bother trying to reach me again here or through Sonny Schoenburgen because he will not be able to contact me again. This bridge is burned—no matter what."

"Hold it, mister. This Bunkowski may have killed *dozens* of innocent people and the entire city is about to be thrown into a grab-ass panic the likes of which you've never seen. So let's cut out all the national security bullshit for a goddamn second and give me some real cooperation here. I need anything at all that might give us some perspective on the man. I mean . . . what makes him kill? How does he know to pick certain victims? Who taught him to kill so well? What are his weak points? How is he vulnerable? How can we catch him? I need to know how—"

"What makes him kill? He likes it. Who taught him to kill? We sure as hell didn't. He was self-taught. What are his weak points? Well, he weighs about 450 pounds, Mr. Eichord, so if you wait long enough he'll probably EAT himself to death. Dossier's on the way. Good-bye, Mr. Eichord."

The machine rumbled inside, printing hundreds of thousands of impulse dots, and he waited for it to give him an electronic facsimile of a face. And he took it from the machine when it was through and saw, for the first time, the face of the beast.

Below

The smell in the trap was the smell of excrement multiplied by what? A million? Ten thousand? Was there an olfactory scale for shit stink? Was this 147.2 on the shit scale, 139,000 stink power? It was almost more than he could take and he could take anything. And so he uncapped the quart of bourbon and took a mouthful and swallowed it, loathing the taste and gagging nausea as he swallowed but welcoming the deadening of the sensory organs and the blocking of the afferent nerve impulses.

A particular sound, look, or odor triggered the most intense memories from childhood, or from his institutionalized years of concentrated horror. What for you or me might be only unpleasant, a smell of cigar smoke, the feel of a chalky eraser, the aroma of sachet, the hospital smell of antiseptic, could goad him into a killing frenzy. And the waves of hate and madness would sweep over him in a blinding raging red tide, kill lust taking him, pouring down on him in a scorching effusion of liquid fire and it was then he would require all of his concentration and skill and control because it was then that he would do the bad things.

The smallest most inconsequential thing. Like a finger pointing on a direction sign. The sound of wind rustling through leaves or metal-cleated footfalls and distant voices on the landing and he was back in the closet huddled in icy fear waiting, praying to gods that only he could summon, promising begging them to hear him and spare him as the loud footsteps and the quarreling voices drew closer and he saw the snake man again and the little boy Danny peed himself knowing fearing that it would be him again and then and then oh oh aaaahhhhhhhh nnooooooooooooo not oh oh don't hurt me oh don't let him Mommy Mommmmmmmmy urinating in little uncontrollable spasms wetting himself there in the foulness of the closet, daring only a brief peek through the crack, holding on to his little dog in the blackened space, hoping the snake man would not find him again.

And the memory does not come from that back center of the brain within the hippocampus, it comes down a toilet flushing in a high-rise, yes flushing out in an effulgence of liquid gold flushing and circumfusing, surrounding, enveloping his memories in the shit stink smell as it gushes, flushes, rushes down through tubes down to the sea in shits, down to timeless bowels down to Danny Boy oh Danny Boy the pipes the pipes are flushing down down down it comes flowing and circumfluent down through the caverns measureless to man down to a sunless sewer and clay and concrete and chemicals and the pipes and tubes and tunnels and submains and declinations of defecations into the main flowing under him and he is back in the closet and the hate the putrid mean bitterness of it drowns his mind in the memories of the dreaded snake man.

And Danny is waiting in the closet as the snake man rages and he catches words and threats as the arms with the snakes the serpents coiled around hairy muscled awful arms smash out knocking his mommy from the chair and the booze stink from a broken bottle and he sees the frightening blue writhing snakes and guns and scorpions and dragons and skulls and scarabs and eagles that coil, fly, crawl, levitate, creep, slither, stampede and explode around the smelly, rubbery, matted pelt of hairy flesh and scaly skin of the snake man whom he detests with a child's loathing, abominating and fearing him with all the contempt a little, tortured boy can feel in his bursting heart. And the snake man vows he will kill the little dog tomorrow and he will throw it out the window and maybe the punk too he laughs as he stomps toward the closet for something but in that instant as he starts to open the closet where the boy and the dog are cowering together the boy has stopped him somehow, and he tells the dog you will be safe speaking in his mind and all of this is happening on some inexplicable mental plateau that you and I will never travel in our comfortable chairs and clean, neat, orderly lives free from the mind-exploding childhood terrors that were the daily regimen of the little boy Daniel.

In the basement his memory lingers on the two bottles there in the row of dusty chemicals on the shelf down in the basement, the two bottles he always remembers as the smoking bottles because when they are unstoppered a dangerous, acidulous wisp emanates from the small, thick glass bottles and he takes them both and when the snake man is asleep, his eyeballs rolled back in his head, dead drunk, his small hands wrapped in rags take the bottles and his mind, HIS MIND oh, God, Jesus his mind warping the curves destroying the graphs lightning bolts of kinetic mystery, powerful energies on an uncharted level of will NOOOOOO THE ACID pouring the smoking liquid into the eyes and face of the sleeping blue snake man and knowing even at age nine what payback is and savoring it as the sleeping, drunken filth screams awake blindly plunged into an anguished world of mindless, unutterable horror.

"NOOOOOOOOOOOOOOOO! AAAAAAAAAA-AAAHHHHHH! ACID!" The snake man's screams have a lovely, nourishing echo even now. And he is in The Max again back in Marion hearing the two blacks go over the side hearing the screams as they plunge off D Tier. He is back with the most incorrigible bad-

asses in all of the entire federal system, back in the bull tank in D Block where a white effigy pincushion man hangs with BAAD sprayed on him, voodoo hoodoo admonition of the Black Afro-American Defenders who control D, and the two black bosses who run it brace him and light flashes on the knife and pipe and on some level of energy beyond understanding he destroys them.

Their arrogance to think they might threaten this force this presence who draws on a power source beyond any witless muscle or martial skill an all-conquering, indomitable energy flowing out as an implacable physical law of mass and motion and will twists rips splits breaks rends cleaves destroys snaps maims mutilates ruptures tears through spines like twigs, crushing bones like dry limbs, chainsnapping them breaking their weight-lifter necks which to him are the nothing pencil necks of geeks fools hulking bull morons

"DIE!" he screams.

"NOOOOOOOOOOOOOO! AAAAAAAAAAAA-HHHHHHH!" The scream again the scream of the snake man as this human garbage goes off the high tier in a stinking blackness of deathscream smashing down into the dumb mass of guards, inmates, snitches, killers, sissies, wardens, hacks, cons, jailhouse lawyers, fish, rapos, short-eyes, jerks, parole boards, and then the other one, still remembering the sewer stink of him as he died, and then he is down in the hole waiting execution, bread and water and rotting food and his own filth and roaches and the occasional rat for pets.

And his mind takes him back to The Nam where he is waiting in a quiet, one-man ambush on the grassy hill above a crossroads, a huge X of bandoliers over his mammoth, obvoluted gut, waiting under a tarp the size of a bedspread with a beer-belly spare tire of deuce-and-a-half proportions, black stony eyes hard and obdurate in a doughy face of baby jowls. And he feels no insect bite, suffers no heat stroke, has no thirst, experiences only pleasurable anticipation as he sees movement coming from down below but not from where he was expecting it, coming along the roadway. Instead, this is a movement he *senses* oh so that is why he has not seen it—he feels in the first pinprick of intuition and animal awareness it is not *below* him he only assumed that because he "saw" it as a physical precognate, sensing not seeing it and naturally concluding it was there in his field of vision but it was BE-HIND HIM and he turns and sees the soldiers there next to him raising their AK-47 and whatever else and his weapon is blasting them without a quarter second's hesitation tearing through the tall grass in a strange noise as it spits its song of death out at the men.

"(THWOCK-KLLLAAAAAKKKK-THWOCK-KL-LLLLAAAAAAKKK-THWOCK-KLLLLAA-AAKKK!)"

He fires carefully, firing on semi-automatic, and he feels the burning as he takes an inconsequential wound, his adrenaline pumping, concentration focus laserlike and relentless, taking them all down in the hundred ballpeen hammer strikes as the weapon shoots its deathstream puncturing and penetrating their bodies with nice red, wet holes as the NVA regulars fire and scream and it is the

"AAAAAAAAAAAAAAAHHHHHHHHHHHHHHH" of the snake man, eyes blinded by the acid, and he loves it he fucking loves it, only wishing he didn't have a suppressor on so he could hear the full, explosive power of the weapon as it fires its searing nails of pain into these arrogant, little men, the expulsion of gas blasting out in fast, anvil hammers, the hundred indistinguishable KLLLAAAAKKKKs of the bolt slamming another one into the spout in the metallic clatter, escaping gas, two-hundred-decible thwocks in one hundred strikes fired in four, five, six-round bursts so fast they sound like one long hammer blow echoing over a lake.

"(THWOCK-KLLLAAAAAKKKKKKK!)" Like a single, indivisible sound, and the metal smashes and explosions and the gas cracks and the screaming and the gunfire all mingling together in the scream of the snake man:

"AAAAAAAAAAAAAAAAAAHHHHHHHHH!" And he knows he must get out of here tomorrow, to the storm-drain catch basin he has prepared, and then he will go to the trap in the submain again. But he must leave the sewers before this smell drives him mad, he decides, not without irony.

Now the bourbon and the effort of the mind has tired him to the point where he can sleep, and he curls up under a filthy army blanket and a huge tarp, a humongous, deeply breathing mound snuggled down in the wooden trap, and he allows himself to dream of an LZ where the smirking pilot digs the skids into a paddy dike flipping him out and how he relished the moment of fear as the three men on board saw him almost pull the pin and toss one in, *almost*-catching himself just as he let them hold one for good luck, tossing in a short-fused grenade and telling them:

"Here, autorotate on this." And smiling to himself from ear to ear as he fantasizes what it would be like to hear the bird explode in a bright red ball of flame and silver metalstorm and he dreams he can hear the delicious screams of the dying as it blows.

"AAAAAAAAAAAAAAHHHHHHHHHHHHHH-HHHHHHHHHH!" And the screaming is a symphony that is music to his ears and he falls into a deep and lovely sleep, a great, snoring, beached whale, sleeping clown man, hybernating bear under the rising, falling mound of tarpaulin and blanket, asleep in the foul stench of the sewer, one massive paw curled around the thing in his special pocket just in case one of the giant rats might come near him while he sleeps.

The Jack
and Queen
of Hearts

He sat in Edie's kitchen drinking strong, black Yuban and running it all through the tangle of his head again, over and over, sorting the pieces. Rearranging. Trying to get some kind of a fix on this Bunkowski. He had the dossier memorized. He'd look at the photographs till his eyes burned from them. Now he was chewing it over. Sifting. Looking for the hidden common denominators. Mistakes. Feeling for the weird rhythms of the killer.

True to his word, Sonny had slammed all the doors down tight. The commissioner was about to tack somebody's chestnuts to a door over this thing. The brass couldn't believe that neither the top cops in Chicago nor the heavies on the Major Crimes hook-up could blast loose more background on a plague of heinous murders that had picked up this much national ink.

But that was because they didn't know from MAC-VSAUCOG and the tight, little band of hardcore head-hunters who'd discovered Daniel Bunkowski in the beginning. It was a burned bridge. Tantalizing. Maddening. But staring down into the chasm couldn't accomplish much beyond giving one a migraine.

He had made sex with his lover. He couldn't think of it as making love because it didn't deserve that appellation. Once he'd heard two hillbilly types back home who had a memorable predilection for crudity of speech talking about getting laid. One of them turned to the other and mouthed the ultimate redneck phrase for fornication, a turn of phrase so gross that it had seared itself into Eichord's brain.

"Ah shore 'nuff dumped a fuck inner," he'd said.

Jack shuddered as he thought to himself that was precisely what he'd done and nothing more. A kind of physical catharsis unrelated to love beyond the sense of desire. It was only a momentary cleansing and restorative to the nervous system. The kind of sex one had after death in the family. A defense mechanism. A release. A life-affirming knee-jerk response to pressure.

My God in Heaven, this woman could do it to him. Edie could take him and turn him around no matter where his mind was. He could be immersed in the bloodiest carnage of the Kasikoff homicides, his brain working overtime as he fought to tie into the wavelengths of this strange and horrible killer, strained to feel the nuances of the city's pulsebeats, concentrated on the subtle rhythms of the dark world that was his professional environment.

And inside the shadows of this world, deep inside where nothing human lived, the thought of her could light up his innards like a shaft of the purest, golden light. She was goodness to him. And her sweet and unexpected sexy ways could set him afire in the most unusual settings, and at unpredictable moments.

She stood with her back to him, stirring herbs into something, her hair as she turned swirling just as it had that day *Chicago Lifestyles* had taken the picture and he flashed on the experience of seeing the real and the photographed Edie simultaneously, the picture having been thumbtacked to a paper on their cork bulletin board, the photo trimmed and pasted with about a pound of mucilage to a neatly crayoned frame with the caption MOMMY AND JACK. Lee Anne's work, meticulously and lovingly rendered.

But it was a picture that had caused him to nearly

go insane with rage when he saw it and the story that had gone with it. He'd said nothing to Edie about it, but he wondered if she suspected how he'd reacted when he saw the story. He wanted to guard Edie and Lee Anne. Shelter them, and keep this thing they had private. A clever woman reporter for *Lifestyles* had put two and two together and run the photo into a semileering piece about the supersleuth and the widow of the victim. There'd been a brief exchange with a woman named Vicki Duff whose name appeared as the byline. She had said he was overheated, he recalled.

"You're going to think I'm getting overheated when you find out what is legal to print and what is not. You're going to find yourself in a caldron of some extremely hot water, and you're not going to like it." He was getting even more torqued as he heard her wise tone of voice.

"So you're implying that I broke the law by running that piece?"

"I'll let you know what I want to say to you in clear, understandable English. I think this is the height of irresponsibility for a journalist to run that sort of an unthinking, carelessly researched, insensitive piece of tabloid gossip in the middle of an investigation of this seriousness."

"It wasn't carelessly researched and you know it. You're a public figure, Jack, and you might as well get used to it. The First Amendment gives me the right."

"The First Amendment doesn't give you the right to put someone in a life-threatening situation by exposing them to unnecessary media attention just to sell papers. And not only is it irresponsible as hell, it may even be actionable. You have a right to put a fist in the air, but if it hits my nose, Vicki, that's battery. You also can't use the First Amendment as a shield for malicious gossip-mongering, defamatory misrepresentations of relationships done to hypo circulation, or—"

"If you've been slandered, you have the same recourse as any other citizen under the law, you can—"

"I know what I can do, and you know what you can do. I can see how very interested you are in being a conscientious reporter. But I want you to know you're skating on some thin and extremely hazardous ice. The bottom line is that—"

"I'm sorry, I don't have the time to listen to this, Jack. If you think I've misspoken in print, I'm sorry, but I didn't do anything other than report what I saw. Thanks for calling, and have a good day."

And the line was buzzing in his ear. What was done was done. He shut it all out as he looked at her silky, lustrous hair. Downtown that day the wind had caught her lovely hair and swirled the tendrils around her face and he'd felt such an unabashed and deep pride that it had filled him like wine, making him drunk with her availability and sweetness and caring. He had never quite become accustomed to the fact that she was his. And as Edie stood there on those long, slim legs of hers, still in high heels, cooking, her back to him, those sleek legs—the backs of those beautiful knees so tantalizing below the short skirt (thank the Lord those were coming back in fashion again) and the little apron tied so demurely around her tiny waist—it was overpowering and wonderfully exciting. He wanted her again now as he sat there drinking her in, and he thought of this lady as so very beautiful indeed.

She turned and looked at him, saw him watching her in that way he had, with what she had called his smoldering eyes, so darkly attractive and serious and sexy, and she read his mind.

"Not before supper," she teased, "you'll have to wait and get your dessert at the end of the meal just like the rest of us."

"Scandinavian peoples sometimes eat their dessert before the meal."

"Well, we're not in Scandanavia at the moment."

"Always quibbling about something."

"Ummmm." Some of the tendrils had worked loose again and it was getting to him. He stood up and walked over, moving up close behind her, snuggling up against this woman he cared so much for now, and encircled her small waist from behind, holding her against him.

She smelled so great, like—what was the fragrance? A combination of musk, fresh bread, and the sexiest perfume imaginable. He nuzzled against her neck and pressed himself into her.

"Oh, Jack."

"Dessert, you say."

"Ummmmm."

"You're something else; you know that?"

"Jack." She wasn't having any more of it right now. Something on her mind. And he watched her eyes harden with a question as she turned.

"Yeah. What?"

"The man."

"Huh?"

"The man."

"What man?"

"You know—who—who he is and everything."

"Umm. More or less."

"Do you, uh, have a picture of him?"

"Ung." He nodded halfheartedly.

"Do you think—" She let the question hang there in the air. The kitchen and the dining room, just a small open space with table and chairs, were empty of Lee. He was suddenly aware that she was over at her friend's house, and he thought it was odd that when Edie had asked about the picture of the killer he'd thought instinctively of Lee Anne, wanting her isolated from this.

"What?" he said.

"Could I see it?" she asked in a tiny, very soft voice.

"Oh. Well . . . yeah. I—uh . . . I guess you—uh, are you sure that's a good idea, babe?"

"I want to see what he looks like," she whispered in her quietest voice. If he hadn't been watching her lips move, even as close as they were standing he wouldn't have been sure what she said.

"Okay," he replied. He just kept standing there beside her, not moving, reluctant to let the mood disintegrate. Reluctant to show her the man. The thing had taken her husband and Lee's father away from them. This monster of a man. It seemed somehow a dirty, immoral act to show her his image.

"If—you think it's okay. I'd like to see it."

"Sure," he said. But he didn't at all. There was nothing okay about it. But he went over to his attaché case and popped the latches and took out a slim manila folder and opened it to the thing she wanted to see.

"Oh" was the sound he thought she made. A pair of coal-black, diamond-hard pig eyes stared out from the cruel, yet somehow childish, jowly face that confronted her. Even the two photographs, harsh and grainy and devoid of all attempt at reproducing the look of a naturally posed human being, even these identity mug shots from Marion Federal Prison failed to convey any instant sense of menace.

It was the childishness of the man's face, the dimpled baby-fat face that made him look so unthreatening. She felt a cold tremor as she realized this was the thing that had . . . killed and mutilated Ed. And then it had killed again and kept killing, taking more lives without rhyme or reason.

"Jack?" She started to say something and he was taking the photograph out of her shaking hands as the torrent of stinging tears began to flow from her eyes and she collapsed in her lover's arms and he held her for what seemed to be a long time as she shook with violent, bitter sobs of loss and anger. And as he held her whatever thought she had been thinking left her like a wispy, blackened, and charred fragment of a half-remembered dream.

"Come here."

"Nnnnnn." It was a keening, a pitiful, wordless cry. But she'd cried enough now, and he led her over to a chair.

"Come on, hon. Sit down."

"Huuunnnnggg, hunnnnngggghhhh," a sound like she was still trying to make tears come but the well was dry. He sat her down at the kitchen table and stared at the dossier, not so much reading as remembering word groups, and then busied himself finding the bottle that he knew she had in the kitchen someplace. He found it up in one of the cabinets with the crackers and breakfast cereal, a nearly full fifth of Seagram's, and he sloshed a little into a coffee cup, pleased that it wasn't for him but sorry for this sweet lady of his. He ran some tap water in over the booze.

"Take a little sip." He put it in front of her. It was all she could do to get the cup up with both hands and she tried a bird swallow and went "Wwwwaaaaauuuu-gh," shuddering and pushing it away from her as she shook her head and he took it from her shaking hands and emptied the contents into the sink. And he took the dossier again and with eyes unfocused let the phrases and word blocks commingle in his mind, staring at the face that perhaps not even a mother could completely love, a smile like the grillwork of a 1949 Roadmaster, teeth meant to tear meat, huge, misshapen teeth—never a cavity in the strange head—perfect, perfectly awful teeth rendered obsolete by civilized society, teeth meant to wrest the crimped top from bottles now made to unscrew. A human shark's teeth. All business.

A face like piles of dough, massive and oddly featureless. A soft face dimpled like a fat baby's butt, repulsive and kissable at the same time, free from facial hair or scars of combat. But there were scars and then there were scars. And Eichord knew that some people wore their scars the way Yakuza wear their dragons, discreetly. His scars, aside from broken belly veins that encircled his girth like pregnancy stretch marks, his scars would be borne like ostracized triad tattoos, old and fading pachuco gang cruciforms, worn secretly and surreptitiously. Socially unacceptable stains on civilized skin, his worst marks deeply subcutaneous— living reminders of unforgettable nightmares, burned down into the core of his twisted soul with the tortur-

er's cruel branding iron. Twenty-year-old scars that
would rankle and hurt like half-forgotten shrapnel working its way to the surface of this uniquely malevolent
human being.

There was something here, though, and he stared at
the word groups and data patterns, letting the mass of
fact and surmise free-associate and interconnect. Letting the life and times of Daniel Edward Flowers
Bunkowski lap against his brain, sometimes not touching, sometimes in actual contact, contiguous and se-
quential and chronological, and sometimes without
propinquity or connective. And he knew it was no
good trying to force it and he closed the dossier not
long afterward, going to her again and taking her in
his arms.

He told her for the first time that he loved her
without speaking the words, making his first commit-
ment to her and to the little child that now ran across
the next-door neighbor's backyard, pulling a kite against
the light breeze as a young, female hunting dog of
dubious lineage bayed excitedly at her heels, committing himself to them wholeheartedly now. Wanting "to
dump his love inner," he thought, smiling, to himself.

So close. Forty-seven minutes away, driving the speed
limit and hitting all the lights just right, only forty-
seven minutes away by vehicle, sitting in a cramped
framework of two-bys some nine feet below the city
streets, the killer sat watching them. Looking at Jack
and Edie. Then dropping remnants of a beef-and-
cheese burrito onto their likeness in the grainy photograph as he continued to scan the somewhat lurid,
breathless, and largely inaccurate account of the special homicide investigator and the widow of one of the
first victims of the Lonely Hearts killings.

The name Edith E. Lynch and her suburban Chicago address typed themselves on his mental word
processor and filed themselves neatly away for retrieval. And each word of the report and every word
spoken by the arrogant cop on the television program
struck at Daniel like the sharp stings of a rattler,

taunting him, biting at him until he stomped down on the filthy paper with a vicious, 15EEEEE heel obliterating the images that enraged him. And he imagined he could hear the cry of the snake man again. It was taking him around the bend. The kind of purple, swollen rage that made him do the awful thing to the Volkers that day. It was going to make him take the cop and the cop's bitch and create a special and mouth-watering feast.

And just at that moment, when the killer's grotesquely brilliant mind began to get the first glimmer of his next move, Jack heard the hound baying out in back and an almost-ignored fact popped a red signal up amid the flood of trivia awash in his brain, and he knew then—as he always knew—without a moment's indecision, he knew exactly how he would take this man down.

It was not until the phone call late the following night, Edie calling him at eleven-thirty, after a day that included another long interrogation of the biker punk and a series of fruitless and frustrating attempts to pry more information loose from the people at Marion Fed, Edie calling him just as he was hitting the sack, not until then that the whole thing began to come together and his own plan started to assert itself.

"Hey, babe!"

"Umm, yeah?" A voice like a mouth full of cotton.

"I'm sorry, honey. Had you just fallen asleep?"

"No. Just got back. What's up, love?"

"Ohhhh," she sighed audibly, breathing into the phone. "The man. The man's face you showed me last night. I've seen him, I think."

"Say again?" He was wide awake.

"Jack, I know how this is going to sound but I have to tell you. I don't know—I almost didn't say anything, but—I mean, something was so familiar about that face when I looked at it, but—I just . . ."

"Huh?"

"I just couldn't put it into the right pigeonhole, but then I remembered when I was talking to Sandi about going to the center it came to me where I'd seen him before."

"You talking about the killer?"

"Yes. The man's photographs you showed me from prison. What's his name?"

"Bunkowski."

"I think I've seen him. I know that face. I saw him down by the center the other night."

"What center. What are you talking about?"

"The Crisis Center where I do volunteer work." She gave him an address in downtown Chicago. "I saw that face; I know I did."

"You—uh, you're really sure about this? I mean, look—"

"No, Jack. I know what this must sound like to you, but yes, I think—I *am* sure. I'd remember that face. I know it looked different, he'd look older now, wouldn't he?" She wasn't asking him. "But even so, the face is the same. Heavier maybe. I saw him in lots of light. It was a dark night but there was plenty of light to see his face and it scared me. He was huge. I was just getting in my car and I saw this—I saw him going down to work in a manhole. He was dressed like a whadyacallit? A sanitation worker. Those guys who work in manholes?"

"You saw *Bunkowski*, you think, across from the Crisis Center going down into a *manhole*?" He was beginning to think he had hallucinated the phone call.

"I swear I'm not kidding, honey. He had on like—this pair of coveralls or something and this big—uh, ladder thing, and a sack. And naturally I just thought it was a workman. And it struck me as kind of odd he'd be going to work down in a manhole that late at night. It was like maybe ten, ten-thirty, something like that. And you know, I was tired and all. But I think that was him. I mean his size. He was *huge*. There can't be that many guys that big that look like that. Can there? I—"

"Edie. You're sure about all this now?"

"Jack, I'm not playing games. I almost didn't say

anything but I had to tell you. I think that was him. Really. I bet it *was* him. Honey?" No response. "Is it possible?" A long pause. She could hear him breathing. Thinking.

"Hell, I don't know."

But he was pulling his pants back on as he told her he'd talk to her first thing in the morning. And at 011500 Eichord and three other armed detectives, plus two backup units of uniformed cops, plus a chief inspector, plus Lieutenant Arlen himself, were standing with their weapons drawn and staring down into the eery shadows of a submain, looking at the remnants of the killer's last feast, feeling icy fingers of dread reach up toward them in the flickering lantern light and flashlight beams and spotlights as they looked down into the den where the beast lived.

Eichord felt two things. A thrill, not exactly elation, but that sort of an energy spritz—and fear. He was afraid. A nervous tic was pulling at his right eye like a Bell's palsy attack, and he could feel the side of his face twitch as he stood in the middle of the street staring down into this vista of another world. And he wanted a real drink.

Leroy
and
Albert

You know how it is when the table sort of turns to rubber on you, and the windowpanes liquify. Well, that is how it was behind the green door of Dr. Geronimo's HERBS, ROOTS, DREAMS, CANDLES AND . . . POTIONS on the south side. The fat, black buck with feet unstable did not pound on the table for that very reason. When a table gets all rubbery, you can just about do good to hold on to the sucker and that was the case here. Everything was liquifying, rubberizing, moving.

It was either blood pressure, the dropsy, the whim-whams, an evil spell or curse, migraines, incipient tuberculosis, a severe hitch in the gitalong, or one of those cases of spofus sporium you read about. It could be the half tab he'd just done, some old hippy sun-shine he'd moked up somewhere, fuckin' hippies sell you any kind of shit, on top of all the gangster he'd smoked and that good sweet Boone's Farm he'd done put a hurtin' on.

Whatever it was it had Dr. Geronimo all queeeeasy Jesus I'm gonna lose it any minute, he thought as he saw the green door open and a man with spiky Martian-green-and-pink hair come slithering in.

"Oh, no. Lord have mercy omigoodness oh Sweet Jesus in Heaven I'm trippin' out baaaaaaaaaaad."

"Hullo," the Martian said.

"Ommma gowaamba, mumbo-jumbo, bopovauni—"
It was the first incantation Dr. Geronimo could think
of. Pure nonsense, but hell, maybe the Martian wouldn't
know the difference and the fake curse would cause
him to flee. "Fepoapalula zawfram paradiddle oomgawa
b'wana melloroony," he intoned, waving his hands
toward the Martian in the hopes of warding off the
Evil Eye, voodoo hoodoo, and whatever bad jazz the
Martian might try to lay on him.

"How do?" the man from Mars with the pink-and-
green hair said pleasantly, liquifying slightly and waving as he dripped in the rubbery acid manner.

"I warn you extraterrestrial heathen slime, I am a
fully ordained witch doctor of the Comanche Indians,
licensed to kill by voodoo, and if you come any closer,
I will put a curse on the entire planet from whence you
come, not to mention any heirs and assigns you may
have left on your Martian spaceship. So stay where
you are oomala maxamillian shellaroony dizzy gilavauni
oomashabadoo," still with the hands waving, fingers
fluttering through the stale storefront air, warding off
Martian badjazz.

"Hell, Dr. Gee, I ain't from Mars. It's only me,
Woody." The man with the spiky green-and-pink hair
came a couple of steps closer.

"Damn you to creation, you dripping, poisonous,
pukeface, I'll put such an incantation on you that your
entire family will . . . Woody? Woody who?"

"Whatsa matter, Dr. Gee? J'a break your glasses or
sum'thin'?" the man asked him.

"Ummm. Er, ah, hold on now just for a minute."
The room was beginning to solidify slightly, and a
wave of nausea receded. The man named Dr. Geronimo steadied himself on the hardening rubber table
and squinted at the apparition confronting him. A
blurry focus sharpened and he could see that it was
indeed a man with spiky pink-and-green hair but it
was only Woody Woodpecker and not an evil futher-
mucking Martian hit man.

"Woody, my main man. Er—uh, I was jes' jivin'

witcha'—how's to it, brother?" he asked amiably, feeling his thumper palpitate with relief.

"Doin' fine, Dr. Geronimo, nothin' to it," he told the man behind the counter, who was approximately the shape and hue of a cannonball. "I need to ask your professional advice."

"Axe away, my man," Geronimo said expansively, as the rubber hardened.

"Well, I got me a girlfriend now. Well. Not a *girl*friend exactly. It's May Seebaugh. You know May? From over on Wells?" May was a bag lady.

"I don't think I've had the pleasure."

"A delightful flower. But to the point. Dr. Gee, I know you're a man of the world so that I don't have to feel shame at this admission, but sometimes, at a certain age, a man has problems with—" He trailed off as Dr. Geronimo surreptitiously attempted to glance at his watch, which was no longer dripping from his wrist in a Daliesque meltdown, but was hardening nicely into readable numerals.

"Urinary infections," the good doctor helped him, "prostrate problems, assorted plagues and social disorders, malfunctions, dysfunctions, nonfunctions—"

"I'm having trouble getting it up."

"And an Afro-dizzy-act is in order. Well, Woody, you have, as they say, come to de right place. I have something so fantastic, so incredible, so foolproof, it would stiffen the member of a dead eunuch. It is the most secret, hush-hush Afro-dizz ever invented. It is called Alura."

"How much is it?" Woody Woodpecker was fifty-seven and did in fact have pink-and-green hair. His real name was Albert Sharma.

"It ain't cheap," said Dr. Geronimo, a.k.a. LeRoy Towels.

"Say what?" Woody Woodpecker was reasonably intelligent or had been prior to the pickling of his thinking apparatus in a variety of stimulants and depressants that included but was not limited to vodka, gin, tequila, paregoric, Ripple, pruno, White Tiger,

Black Panther, Green Dragon, absinthe, Brut, Sterno, Chaps, Old Spice—the list is long. He had ended up with a partiality toward Mission Sweet Lucy and all he needed was a drink of men's room water and he stayed on a kind of semipermanent buzzer.

"Two hundred a cap," the cannonball-shaped entrepreneur told him.

"Wheeeee," Woody lamented, "shit."

"I know, my friend. But you have to understand, it's not like there was an unlimited supply. When these caps are gone, that is the end of the tune. This was the top-secret discovery of the Sexual Research and Development Unit of the CIA. It is called Alura, the letters standing for Autoerotic Lutenizing Reagent. Only a small amount of this was cooked up, for use by impotent spies so they could seduce women to get information. It'll make your tool so hard you can use it for a cat-scratch post. So two hundred for a cap of this magic is a bargain."

"Wow," said Albert Sharma, trying to figure out how the hell he could boost enough cassettes and shit to come up with two bills. Woody Woodpecker was the name he'd gone by for six, seven years since he'd been known as the Wood Man. But Woody Woodpecker seemed more appropriate, and it had a street rhythm so it stuck. Now he worked to the image, talked funny, told people his pecker was wood, stuff like that. Punks sometimes spiked his hair and the pink-and-green bit was a leftover from a recent Woodpecker do.

He was called the Woodpecker, and Woody, and before that the Wood Man, because he saw men in wood. This is what started Albert Sharma drinking in the first place—years ago. He could not look at a piece of wood without seeing faces. If you're a carpenter by trade, this can become a very unsettling experience, and one thing had led to another, and before long the Wood Man was down and out, among the street people. So it sometimes goes.

"What say, brother," said Dr. Geronimo, who

claimed to have lived with the Comanche tribe for many years learning potions, spells, and miscellaneous divinations and witch doctoring. But who had in fact lived with some stockyard workers in Omaha, from whom he'd picked up a variation on the fortune-teller pitch which he used in his current dreambook emporium. It made a nice little lucrative sideline to the roots-and-herbs thing

"I ain't got the two hundred. But you know Deuce, doncha'?"

"Yeah," he commiserated, "a deuce ain't easy to come up with, but that's the price."

"No, doctor. I say you know the dude calls hisself *Deuce*? Deuce Younger?"

"Say what?"

"You know, man. The biker dude. Guy runs the Flames?"

"Oh, yeah. I know the man. So?"

"I got something."

"Yeah?"

"I heard he put three hundred on the street for anybody could give him the one that hit Mr. Tree."

"Now, Woody, you're a good old gentleman, and you best be not messin' with them boys."

"Yeah, but I need that stuff. And if he gave me three hundred, I could buy a cap of Alura, and me and May could take a real honeymoon together."

"Uh-huh."

"See." He leaned close to Dr. Geronimo, bathing him in terminal halitosis, Old Spice, and body rot, as he whispered conspiratorially, "I know something."

"Huh?"

"I know where he lives."

"Who, Deuce?"

"No. I know where the one who kills lives."

"Yeah?" he said, feeling suddenly very sober inside. "Where?"

"Under the street," Woody Woodpecker said, proudly, in a cracked voice.

Instinctively Dr. Geronimo knew that Woody was

not lying and he was getting a scent of some money here, and he wished he had not purchased that nasty old hippy sunshine and picked today to do that half tab, because he was going to need his wits about him if he was going to get into this particular can of worms.

"Under the street," he said, his eyebrows raised in question.

"Under the street. I know where he goes. And I seen him kill Mr. Tree with a big chain thing. An' I seen him try to get that one called Lester, and then I watched where he went. And me and May watched the hole where he went down and we never seen him come up there but May seen him come up about a block away, just by luck. And then we figured how he hides down there in the water mains and sewers and that. Can you get hold of Deuce Younger and tell him I can show him where the one who kills is?"

"Now, Woody, you're sure about all this, are you? Hey, bro', this is very important. I mean you 'n May didn't get hold of no bad Lucy and trip out on some Phantom of the Opera thing?"

"Huh? Fat man of the opera? No, this guy's down in the manholes, ya' know. I can take Deuce right to him. But I gotta' have my money like I heard they put on him. The three hundred. Okay?"

"Hey. Fine with *me*, my man. But I'll have to call around for ya. I mean, I don't know where Deuce is just like dat." He tried to snap his fingers and missed. "But yeah, I'll try to run him down. Thing is, I'd have to have a small finder's fee for that. Say thirty-three percent of recovery?"

"What's that mean?"

"If you get three hundred I get one hundred. It's only fair, Woody. That way you get your cap of precious dick-stiffener, and I get a hundred-dollar bill for helpin' get you together with the Flames. What do you say?"

"Uh, yeah, I guess that's okay."

"All right. Now Mistah Woody, we need to be abso-posi-lutely 101 percent on this, dig?"

"Yeah?"

"You can go find the guy that kills people. He's still there. Under the street, I mean."

"Yeah."

"You *sure* because I don't want Deuce Younger and a half-dozen biker maniacs upside my head cause you made a *mistake*, ya' know?"

"No mistake, Dr. Gee. I seen 'm go down 'n come up. Not always the same rabbit hole but I know he's down here. I know where he stays," Woody Woodpecker whispered, "but I want the money first." The doctor nodded, and another strange alliance came to pass.

And the cannonball-shaped black man scratched his head and thought for a minute, looked closely into the wacky countenance of the Wood Man, and asked again, "No mistakes about this?"

"Huh-uh, Dr. Geronimo. I know where the big man who kills people stays underground. How fast does that stuff act anyway?"

"Yeah, um-hmm," the man told him, reaching for the big directory.

"Dr. Gee."

"Huh," he said, leafing through the pages looking for the Wathena Salvage Yard. "Yeah."

"Thàt Alura. I mean, how fast does it act?"

"Instantly," LeRoy Towels told the wino, not without a degree of impatience as he picked up the telephone and paused one last time while he considered whether or not to dial.

"*In*stantly?" Woody asked incredulously.

"You do a little of this baby"—he nodded vaguely as he stuck his finger in the dial—"you be ready to fuck a junkyard dog."

The
Flames

There were four Flames lounging around the filthy shack that served as an office for the Wathena Salvage Yard, of which Pop Meiswinkle was the proprietor on paper. He'd purchased the yard, as he liked to say, "lock, schlock, and bagel" from the Wathena Brothers when the elder sibling had come up with a bad case of lead-poisoning complications as a result of acute seenus (as in "I was out with my girlfriend and my wife seenus").

But in the ensuing months he'd been taken over by a corporate raider named Deuce Younger, who made him an offer he thought was worth consideration. Something along the lines of "we run the place and give you a cut or one night we come in here and slit your fucking throat from ear to ear and bury you in an LTD."

So the Wathena Brothers Salvage Yard and chop shop had become a pit-stop flip-flop in the hot-car ring that headquartered in Cook County, Illinois. In the true spirit of free enterprise the biker club The Flames had diversified to the extent that they not only controlled a respectable slice of the methamphetamine market, but they actually made a fairly impressive dollar in the salvage business. When the enterprising team of Dr. Geronimo and his trusty aide Woody Woodpecker arrived at the yard, Deuce Younger was in the midst of a weighty corporate conference with his top counsel.

"That dirty cocksucking bastard motherfucker," he was saying, refering to a colleague in the salvage profession. "He comes in here what—maybe every six months with that portable car crusher, and you know, you can't say shit to the motherfucking asshole sonofabitch, and he backs that tractor trailer in here like he owns the dump, and you know, man, I can't stand here and count every fucking car that comes along. We started with what was it 172. Something like that. End up with a 164 count—that greedy cocksuck stole eight fuckin' cars from us. *Eight goddamn fuckin' vehicles, man.* I don't fucking believe it."

"Fuckin' unreal," a Flames bodyguard agreed.

"And you can't say shit to the bastard. You know how it is. What the fuck are you gonna say? Call the cunt a liar. You gotta have him. Shit."

"Still, I'd like to kick his ass," one of the Flames called Retard said.

"Cocksucker. He'll crook you into the fucking ground if you turn your back on the lying sonofabitch dickeye."

"That motherfucker come over to Billy's and he loads up twenty-three of Billy's cars. He puts them little ones in between the big ones. And when the cocksuck pulls out, he tells the ignorant motherfucker he only has eighteen cars. I never seen *anything* like the sonofabitchin' crooked piece of dog shit, why I'd like to—"

"An' you know if you got a little compact crushed in there between two big boats, shit, you can't tell what the hell you got on the stack. And Christ, even the dumb bitch pussy works for Billy said that's the tallest fuckin' stack of eighteen cars I've ever seen." Raucous laughter drowned out the knocking on the door.

But two Flames working on their bikes saw the two strange figures over by the shack and walked up to them saying, "You guys need somethin'?"

"Yes, sir." Woody spoke before Dr. G. could talk. "I'm Woody Woodpecker."

"No shit," said one called Mingus, "an' I'm Donald fuckin' Duck. You got business here?"

"Right," said the cannonball-shaped doctor of herbology and occult sciences, "we're here to see Mr. Younger on an important matter."

"Uh-huh," Mingus told him, "you wanna' haul fucking ass, darkie, and take this old bum with ya, we got *enough* junk around here." Both the men really broke up at that one, guffawing and slapping each other as if it had been the *bon mot* of the century.

"Sir," Woody Woodpecker said, looking at the wooden door of the shack, "I hope you're aware of the problems posed by a door such as this one. You have what appear to be smiling faces but"—he moved closer to the door—"there are two evil ones right there. And look at this"—he pointed at a swirl of grain in the beat-up wood—"a pair of real ogres, a skull profile with huge fangs, and a frowning and eyeless head that I think you'll find is—"

"Get the fuck outta here you crazy old freak and take this fat little spade with your raggedy ass before we kick your goofy ole' booty!" the wild-eyed biker screamed, his fellow club member trying unsuccessfully to stifle his laughter.

"Let me handle this, please," Dr. Geronimo told Woody. "Now, sir, we do have an appointment with Mr. Younger, and if you gentlemen want to find out the location of the man who did that awful thing to Mr. Tree, I suggest you tell him Dr. Geronimo is here to see him." The giggles stopped.

"What'd you say about Tree?"

"I was trying to tell you we're the ones that are here to help Mr. Deuce in his efforts to obtain justice in the recent tragedy."

Inside the shack the business of the salvage company had taken a discursive turn as they discussed the problems of enforced incarceration. Retard was addressing the conference room:

"D'jew all hear bout Greasy?" It was rhetorical, as he continued to address his rapt audience. "Fucker sent his brother back a letter telling him he's getting married."

"Where is that crazy motherfucker anyway—down in Jeff City or some damn where?"

"Leavenworth, ain't he?" someone else said.

"Naw. He's just a kid. He was doing juvey time when he busted outta' Booneville or some kiddy jail and they put him in Algoa. He was on the run from fuckin' Algoa when he was up here." They laughed.

"You shittin' us, man?"

"Fucker was in the middle of a six-year bit. Had three years left and this asshole talks him into makin' a move. Three years. He boogies. That's why we never saw the cocksuck. They nailed him up here runnin' around." The board members thought this was quite humorous.

"Anyway, his brother gets a letter from Algoa. He says he's getting married. Brother writes back that's cool, let's see a picture of the bitch." A knock at the door interrupted the story.

"We're in the middle of a meeting," Deuce hollered out at them through the door. "Yeah?"

"So he says, send a picture of the bitch." Laughter. "And his brother sends him one. It's Greasy's bitch awright. He's got him an eighteen-year-old faggot named Ronnie." Hysterics in the room. A moment of gay abandon in the workaday drudgery of a busy corporate staff.

"Believe this shit? Said he looked like a wife awright. Looked like a pussy'd bend over 'for you could get its pants off." Screaming in the room. "Any fucker'd boogie in the middle of a fucking six-pack in fuckin' Algoa! Shit!"

"What a fuckin' dummy." Roars of laughter finally recede to the point they can hear the loud, insistent pounding.

"What the fuck is it, goddammit," Deuce asked.

"Yo, Deuce." Door opens and they can see a lot of faces. Mingus goes, "Think you'd better check this shit out." He comes in and shuts the door on the others. "Jigaboo calls hisself Geronimo or some fucking shit. Got some old wino with him. Claim they heard you put three bills on the street for anybody give us something that would get the one did Tree. They swear they can give the fucker to us." Very quiet in the shack and all eyes on the door as Deuce nods to let them in.

"You two get y'r butts in here," Mingus commanded as Dr. Geronimo and Woody strode through the door with as much dignity and poise as the occasion allowed.

"Mr. Younger," the cannonball-like man said, "this gentleman knows where the man you want lives. He can show him to you, take you right there."

"Yes, sir," Woody Woodpecker said. "I know where the man who kills people stays."

"You do, eh," Deuce said softly.

"Yes, sir. If I show you, do I get the three hundred dollars like they say?"

"Where is he?"

"In the sewers. He stays in the sewers."

"Get these fuckin' bums outta here f'r chrissakes," one of the corporate vice-presidents suggested gently.

"No. Hold it." Deuce smiled. "I go with my vibes. My vibes never lie. I feel good about these two." He looked at the Wood Man with a pair of eyes like the business end of a double-barrel shotgun and smiled after a few moments. "I say hold the calls. I think we got us a winner."

Chaingang

Daniel Bunkowski is asleep. RY-7/INLET 20 is a rectangular storage tank approximately twelve and a half feet below the city streets, and situated at the intersection of pipes that lead to a system of storm drains that connect to a main catch basin. If you could see the pipes from the air, they would look like a large letter Y with the bottom stem connecting to the O of the storage facility. The larger facility is very deep, and it is into this area that the overflow ultimately goes from those rainstorms that would otherwise fill the low-lying areas with the spillage from rains, melts, or flood backwater. Bunkowski is asleep in the smaller storage tank that feeds the water into a channel that opens at the center of the letter Y.

He is asleep in the trap he has constructed in the neck of the storage tank, but that is only his physical bulk. Danny boy is far away, dreaming of another time and place. A place known as Echo Sector, in the lowlands of Quang Tri province, Republic of South Vietnam, where a kamikaze truck full of men roars along a very dangerous stretch of road. The truck, by coincidence called a deuce-and-a-half, is driven by a sullen, acned, sneering youth with bad teeth who drives at one speed, accelerator to the floorboard, and stops by running into things.

"Stop," Chaingang yells around the side. Nothing. A fist the size and solidity of a solid steel pineapple begins pounding huge dents in the truck. "Pull over!" Chaingang has seen something. The truck slows marginally, the sullen kid looking for something to drive into to get the wreck to quit moving, but Chain is already limping back toward his ruck.

"Get some," they yell, and there are other taunts and names shouted at him as the truck roars off. He smiles as he thinks how easily he could have tossed a frag in their direction, just for luck, counting it very close for a nice and deadly air burst—just so—and in the dreamsleep he grins at the imagining of the exploding charge and the screams of surprise.

He waddles off in the direction of the nearby treeline with an M-60, and a ruck that weighs more than any of the men on the truck.

He is carrying an M-60 LMG, and wearing six crossed bandoliers. Each holds over a hundred rounds of ammo. He is literally covered in fragmentation grenades. His taped chain bulges from a special pocket. He wears a bowie the size of a small machete. His ruck is a mobile home.

It is packed in this manner: ponchos (2), liners (2), tarps (2), his special extra-large mosquito netting cover which is folded as carefully and methodically as a chute, then packed inside a four-millimeter Mylar sleeve, cammie cover, detonation equipment, wire-cutter pliers, det cord, fuses, an M-18 smoke grenade, igniter, John Wayne (opener), utensils, extra socks, extra bug juice, pills, matches, C-4, and on and on—many small items.

Then there are his "pies." He calls them the little pies and they are vaguely pie wedge in appearance. He loves them. He knows how the little people like to come in at night slithering through the ridiculously easy-to-penetrate wire protection of the sissy soldiers, how they like to turn them around so that when they are detonated the enemy gets an unexpected present of flying, killer steel. They are called claymores, each weighing three and a half pounds, and Chaingang carries six of them.

His mobile home carries everything from a coil of rope to a special plastic box holding the swivel rings he will use to rig his grenade trap.

Across the layer his ruck is crammed with thirty meals of instant rice and shrimp, beef, pork, spaghetti, which are the top-grade freeze-dried lurp (LRRP-Long-Range Recon Patrol) rations called Long Rats. They are prepared simply by adding ordinary cold water. He then carries small Tupperware containers full of salt, sugar, coffee, and other staples that can be used to expand his rations by the usual diet of rice and fish and native groceries. The back of the ruck is covered in plastic bottles containing twenty-two liters of water and two liters of Wild Turkey. He also carries several items of gear in miscellaneus belts, pouches, and the like such as bug juice, battle dressings, and the other impedimenta that will allow him to rove as a self-contained hunter-killer unit.

He is a six-hundred-and-some pound one-man mobile fighting unit, loaded for grizzly, and carrying everything from Tobasco to toothbrush to toilet tissue in a ruck you couldn't get off the ground. Then there's what he carries by hand. In his left hand, or on his shoulder over a special pad, the M-60, and in his right hand, a huge plastic spool of wire. This is his one-man ambush wire.

He knew when he saw the dense treeline's edge even from the distance that he would kill humans again tonight and many, many of them. He can feel it and sense it in a moist, white-hot swirl and blur that washes over him before he can control it. Not yet. He holds himself in check as he thinks how it would have been so easy to waste the occupants of the deuce-and-a-half as it sped off.

It is getting dark fast and he walks faster, not limping now, a huge smile plastered across his countenance. Dimples and grins. This is his thing. He was born to do it. He will go for a big kill tonight, if his

luck holds. His goal is to take off a whole platoon of
the little people single-handed. He knows ways it might
be done.

He hopes someone will come tonight. If it is only
one or two, he might kill one slow, play with him a bit
before he puts him under. Make his lights go out real
slow. He remembers the one he lit up the other night
and almost laughs out loud. He shifts his 60 to his
shoulder and takes the wire spool for a second as he
pats his pocket for chain, then rings, what did I do
with the swivel rings? Ah yes, in the ruck.

Moisture drops from the foliage. It hits the ground,
soaking into the Vietnamese earth, making the trees
grow taller, coming back up into the trees to water
them, so they'll have bigger leaves to drip, to catch
more moisture and on and on it goes in the never-
ending, self-regenerating cycle that always stirs his
interest. He thinks of trees as people. When he spends
a lot of time in the jungle in one location, he becomes
so familiar with the major aspects of the trees and
grass and vegetation and everything that it is as if he
had lived there all his life. He names his trees, gives
them identities, and holds conversations with them in
his mind. Sometimes he feels the trees talk to him with
their thoughts.

The red ball has gone under again. He has reached
the place he imagined he would find there on the
road. Perfect. He will set up in the trees, at the apex
of a footpath and what appears to be an overgrown
supply pipeline.

He will run his plan tonight if they come. He has a
plan that could work for up to eight, perhaps even ten
of the little people if he takes care and thinks the thing
out carefully, and of course if luck is with him. He
thinks he can kill even a dozen dinks using his well-
researched and carefully constructed ambush.

This is Chaingang's grenade ambush. First, he un-
loads his M-60, ammo bandoliers and his frags, setting
everything down carefully beside his spool of wire.
Next he removes his ruck and digs down for the wire-

cutter pliers. The important swivel rings. He pats his pockets down. Now to set it in motion. He picks up the frags and a broken branch and limps a bit as he negotiates the footpath.

A wave sweeps through him again, washing his brain in a red-hot kill lust. He will take many lives before the night is over and he doesn't much care whose. But these are the moments when he realizes he must use the greatest care. It is in the times right before he does the bad things that he must execute his plans with the utmost caution and with great concentration.

It is dark as he finishes putting the grenades in place on either side of the footpath, and in front and back. The frags are "canned" in place, that is, he has jammed them into cans before he loaded up, and the cans are just big enough to hold the 'nades in with the spoons depressed but not so tight that a pull won't jerk them loose. Parallel swivel rings are placed and camouflaged as well as possible.

When they are all wired tightly into position and covered, the wires are all laid and pulled back to the ambush control point, as Chaingang takes up the slack in the wires just enough, but not too much; this is very painstaking and he would prefer to accomplish this with daylight. But the darkness is also to his advantage. He can tell just what is visible and what is not here in the last minutes before it is totally black.

Now he hurries back and beginning at the reverse end, covers all signs of the wires with earth and twigs and leaves. He is expert at this. He has done this hundreds of times. Now he pulls the pins on all the frags and, giving the wires and swivel rings a final check, retraces his footing, this time moving backward as he brushes out any sign that he might have left.

He spreads his mosquito netting out beside the ambush position control point, lays his tarps down, quickly scoops up a big pile of leaves, twigs, and other camouflage material, bringing it over from other spots in the darkness and brushing behind him each time. There is no light now.

He goes down the footpath one last time, to the hardball that is completely overgrown in vines and brush. Once he almost trips and falls on his fat ass but he catches his balance in time. Finally he gets the mines set out, after what seems like an eternity. He is using a new system on the claymores this time, a wire pull to detonate the clacker device involving a complex system of parallel rings, but most of this was all rigged in advance. There is no more time now. He leaves it as it is, ready or not, and returns to the ambush spot.

He stands and breathes deeply, thinking. He retraces his movements. He has set out eight fragmentation grenades and two of the claymores. All the slack is out and it all runs back to the two master wires, all running to the swivel rings that will blow the mines back in the hardball trail and the frags along the footpath, which is where he thinks they will come from tonight, if and when they show.

He is a thorough craftsman at his work. It isn't quite right somehow. One thing is missing or incomplete or wrong. Something does not feel quite right. There is no room for error.

Painstakingly, he begins the whole procedure again in his mind, concentrating fiercely, taking each move a step at a time from the moment when he chose the ambush site to the unpacking of his ruck to the placement of the parallel-positioned swivel rings and the wiring of the canned grenades. He rethinks the camouflage, the setting of the claymores, the brushing out of the trail and pathway, the gathering of the foliage and materials. He remembers he has the grenade pins and rings in his pocket and he puts them away.

It is in the master wires. The problem is in the way the master wire to the pathway frags is attached to the wires that lead from the grenades to the swivels and through the rings so that when the master is yanked, the grenades pop out of the cans, thus releasing the spoon levers and blowing. All of the grenades but two are short-fused. The other two, with hacksawed spoons, are just an added insurance variation.

As he settles a bit now he becomes more aware of his surroundings and like a sort of metamorphic dissolve, the real Chaingang emerges from within the surface one. Danny is a lethargic presence. Inert. Not even peering any longer into the blackened gloom. Not seeing at all, in fact. Eyes half closed in a heavy-lidded relaxed state, calm as a rock, listening.

The night symphony has begun. Insects. Animals. Birds. Everything from frogs to cricket noises begins to add layer upon layer to the nonhuman din. There are big cats out here. He likes them and bears them no ill will, although he likes to sometimes think about the few he has had to kill. He is listening patiently, still standing on his tired and sore feet. He is no longer aware of his physical being. He will soon become weightless. He will listen to the trees very soon.

He realizes that he has a leech on him. He is not oblivious to pain or to the sting and itch, but it is a factor so totally under control as to be insignificant, much as you might be aware of a very slight pain in the back. He is aware he is being bitten by mosquitoes, but where you or I might be slapping at them, going nuts from their attack, itching, being driven crazy by it, it is meaningless to him. Less than meaningless. He will sometimes put a bit of repellent on but it will not be tonight. He takes no chances. He will be sniffing for nuoc mam and the little people smells.

His inward composure is nearly complete. He sees himself as untroubled, at peace, and at one with the night. His ankle has ceased to concern him in the joy and prospect of the night ahead. In that way he becomes tireless and his alertness increases. He is aware that a thick, sticky mist has swirled in around him. Soon it will become fog. He loves it. He fucking loves it, wallows in it. He is not stupid. He has read of Jack the Ripper. In his mind he of course *is* Jack the Ripper, alone and safe in the swirling fog. Come now, little people, and let me kill you kill youkilllyoukillyou-killllllllll. He fights the hot surge. Not yet.

The tide recedes once again. Not for long now, with any luck. He lets his body drink in the timeless rhythms of the trees and the fog and the night. He listens out beyond his hearing, as all nocturnal creatures do. He sees far beyond his visibility, which at the moment is near zero. All of no consequence.

He pats his chain and nonchalantly pulls it out and recoils it, returning it to the special canvas-and-leather pocket he wears. He *X*'s two bandoliers of ammo, then changes his mind and removes them. He places his M-60 with a loaded bandolier in position. He locates his other two frags. He remembers what he forgot to do, he meant to bring along his silenced pistol. Ah, never mind. Another time. He pats his huge bowie.

For a moment he allows himself to think about grabbing that one from behind and twisting the chin to the left just as you'd pop the top on a drink can, even less energy than that, then pulling the head back and stabbing up with the sharp steel blade, feeling the blood gush back out on him and twisting, slicing across, severing everything. He had turned that one into a steaming, dripping load of shit in a fat heartbeat. Pleasant memories.

He feels his face pinch slightly and relaxes his muscles, realizing that he has been grinning widely, and he smiles again at this. He lets just a little more of the warm rush begin and then he blocks it.

He sprinkles the piled-up rubbish and cammie material around as he pulls the netting into position. As always, he has positioned himself with unerring confidence. He has all but impenetrable jungle to his back, a thorny impasse that affords him reasonably total security. To his front more of the same. He knows they will come from the left or right if they come at all tonight. Now he lets it begin.

Little Danny turns it on like a faucet. He lets his mind be a vision of purest virgin white. It is blemishless, smooth, hot, a burning incandescence of white heat in a sphere of infinite roundness, and then he punctures it just so, there at the lower left, stabbing it with a tiny needle and puncturing it as you would prick a white balloon and allowing black to slowly fill the sphere, cooling it with its inky liquidity.

He pictures the slow running stream of black as it fills the vision slowly like the ebb of black water rising and falling in a white vase, rising now as the white heat cools the water, letting the center of the curve of the blackness be their rounded, gleaming piano top that his mother played, and in the top of their piano sits a ticking metronome, his mommy's metronome.

Danny breathes in the essence of the black as the metronome ticks back and forth.

Tick . . . Tick . . . Tick . . .

The subtle, imperceptible containment begins. Slower, with each measured tick he slows wills slows his heartbeat slowing it with each tick slowing willing slowing and as he feels his pulse throbbing he slows wills slows the pulsing, throbbing, beating tick of his life force.

Danny takes deeper, longer breaths, stilling his heart and pulse rate, taking in longer, great slow measured inhalations of black essence and force as he watches his mother's ticking metronome slowing almost to a standstill.

Tick . . .

Tick . . .

He is stilled and silent in the deep shadows as the patrol appears a few meters away, to the left, coming down on the high side of the pipeline in the foliage. They will not be in position for the claymores, which rules out his shot at a squad-size ambush. That will have to come another time. The claymores are now virtually worthless as an offensive weapon, unless . . .

His mind comes to life now as the first man is approaching his position. They are very good, quiet. NVA regulars, he quickly realizes. They wear disparate, somewhat ragtag uniforms but Danny admires their quiet. They soldier well, he often observes, as compared with . . .

No time now as they file by him in the darkness. He is quite dissociated from himself and there is only a slight sense of readiness but none of urgency. The men, and so far he can only see four of them, are carrying tiny jungle lanterns, giving the procession a surreal glow as the lights and shadows interplay. They wear pith helmets, which he regards as incongruous. Sneakers.

His inner clock advises him they are walking a bit too fast and he may have to gunfight one or two, this isn't quite working out and oh another one, come on hurry that's five and then yes he sees a sixth man coming slowing for a second he prays that he will not urinate but he continues it is taking way too long the time element was what he had forgotten about this has to be timed precisely with the wires he thinks and then he senses that someone has seen the wire but the sixth NVA soldier is past him and he raises up his blunt, thick, huge cigar fingers lashing out with the links of lethal chain using that thick, muscled wrist with just the perfect snapping motion he's practiced until it is part of him making the chain uncoil and strike like a giant steel snake whipping out of his pocket to split his skull with a near silent strike as you might split a grapefruit and even before he involuntarily screams a deathscream and pitches forward Danny is hurling the chain out throwing it with all his force hearing a scream in Vietnamese as in a blur the black tractor chain snakewhips into the fifth man blinding him in a powerful, fierce, smacking wet bloodsmear of a steel bolo knocking him over on his back as Danny squeezes the trigger of the M-60 blasting a searing, exploding stream of jacketed slugs into the fourth and then the third soldier and missing the others as he falls backward in his carefully timed drop pulling that huge left hand with the tautly drawn wires wrapped around his leather glove in a massive jerk of arm and body weight just as the soldiers raise their weapons to fire and a huge, battering ram of blasts so closely in sync they sound like a bomb going off rips apart the night booming through the quiet of the jungle in a hot blinding storm of razor shrapnel and human offal and bone chip and viscera flying apart and painting the trees with another invisible layer of black, sticky wetness all in a deafening roar of exploding charges that leaves Danny on the ground still holding the master wires and an empty M-60 and he shakes off the concussion like a big Newfoundland shaking off water and struggles to pull himself up to his feet his ears stinging his head full of cobwebs and flashing stars.

He lets go of the wires and the machine gun, dropping them without knowing it moving faster than anyone alive has ever seen him move with the bowie fighting knife out and in his hand hoping that one of them will still be breathing so he can take the heart then, oh, yes—still live don't die yet—all wild and insane with his surging red pressure cooker of a kill hunger blowing and overflowing and hungering for the taste of live human hearts again.

There was once a time when Danny hated messy kills, nor would he even use a blade. But times lie. And now, unseen by human eyes, fresh hot blood drips from the trees like teardrops.

"I'm winning hearts and minds," he mutters out loud, and he slashes with the massive fighting bowie, "but I'm leaving the minds and taking the hearts, leaving the minds, taking the hearts."

As the dripping trees witness the act of madness Danny Boy hears the delicious, nourishing nurturing screams of the snake man echoing there in the darkness and the

"AAAAAAAAAAHHHHHHHHHHHHHHHH" of the blinded snake man resounds and the thing grins and feasts.

When he awoke in RY7/INLET 20 he was ravenously hungry and wolfed down the four cold tacos remaining from the two dozen he'd picked up the night before. He crammed the food into his mouth, devouring the congealed, greasy meat and cheese, bits of lettuce and broken shell and juice dripping from his whiskery chin, and washed it all down with tepid water from a half-gallon milk jug. His huge, obvoluted gut made a gurgling noise as it accepted the appetizer and he promised himself a big breakfast soon. But first he had the cold feeling inside and there was work he must do.

He checked his arsenal and supplies methodically but somewhere inside his head he was still inside the dream. The ambush was as vivid in his mind as if it had actually taken place last night and he could still taste the salty, mouth-watering richness of the hearts, and smell the smoky, hot copper aroma of cordite, pepsin, freshly spilled intestines, the tastes and the smells of unspeakable carnage so pleasurable to him now.

But it was more than sweet memories for Daniel. The ambush had been dreamed for a reason. And as he checked the arsenal it was with a sense of urgency and a perception of shadows drawing near. There were only five of the stolen claymores left. No matter. He would make do with four, he needed one for another plan he was about to spring, but with the dynamite he'd taken from a construction site it would suffice for what he wanted to do. Between the firecrackers and the pies he'd be able to arrange a suitable surprise party for the guests he was expecting.

Chaingang
and the
Flames

It was not that Daniel was consciously aware of intruders coming. There was no isolated warning that flashed inside his head saying enemy approaching. It was only a sudden necessity for preparedness. An inner signal of some kind that prodded his bulk to move and do it quickly. On some level he sensed the proximity of danger.

As a physical precognate, that rarest of the presentient beings, these paranormal warning signals did something else. They forced him onto a plateau of concentration unknown to normal humans. The fierceness and single-mindedness of his powers of directed attention were beyond the level of understanding. They allowed him to compartmentalize his vision, isolate focus, refine scent, sound, vista. They sharpened his intuition and perception, honed his skills and abilities and tactile senses. The closest thing might be the ninja who would sit with his master in a closed and darkened room, sitting silently for hours waiting for sensei to drop a pin, listening to hear the fall of the tiny pin, concentrating so fiercely on that one sound, eyes closed, waiting for that jarring crashing metallic loudness amplified by sheer will.

As he prepared his ambush for whatever was coming Chaingang concentrated in a scary effluence of laserlike will and awesome power. No human creature on earth was so self-centered, in the true definition of the term, than Daniel was when the warning signals tingled. A doctor in the program at Marion had identified it but mislabeled the phenomenon.

He half jokingly told a colleague, "When you're that fat, your girth becomes the physical center of the earth and all decisions radiate out geocentrically." They laughed because it sounded humorous in the context of their discussion but even as an exaggeration the identification of the core element glittered. The gift of the physical precognate was beyond ordinary identifications. Whatever name you applied to the supernormal power behind Daniel Bunkowski's presentience, you knew there was no joking about the frightening acuteness or the absolute pernicious resolve that guided him on a level where science had only begun to probe.

He was truly his own center. He was a human data-processing tool eating raw fact and observation, storehousing experiences, however deleterious, as a kind of pilot survey for future action, relating all movement and change and occurrence to the position of his own person in that part of the universe that touched his existence, measuring the changing data by an assessment of threat, time and space variables, and factoring all possible predictables. Noxious, hateful, even evil—yes. But brilliantly centered and incandescently deadly.

He sensed the necessity for speed now and he moved with surprising speed and agility. Laying out the rough elements first, propelling his great bulk through the pipes and making sure that his earlier work had been concealed from any prying eyes. Working only with the light of a powerful lantern's beam, he rigged his grenade ambush, a variation from "field expedient" materials . . . wire, cable, det cord, cannon fuse, stolen blasters, leads, igniters, tucking his traps out of sight in the manner of the best professional hunters. Then, coming down to the crucial time, carefully connecting the detonation devices to the various charges. Hand movements steady, precise, astonishingly sure, the huge cigarlike fingers connecting the explosive with a jeweler's delicacy.

And when the triple trap is in place, after a last quick check of his procedures, a final enumeration of his mental checklist, he is up and gone. But the huge man does not come up out of RY7/INLET 20, he comes up far away from the access catch basin that is his secret escape route because he knows there is danger nearby and he is nothing if not a survivor.

When he comes back, working his way through the alleyway in between an empty storefront and Flawless Laundry and Dry Cleaners, he sees people and he freezes, turns, slowly and carefully eases his way back down the alley and he is gone even as the one called Retard says to Billy:

"Hey, bro, tell Deuce I got the things," and he goes over to the saddlebags of a huge Hog.

"Deuce."

"Yo."

"Retard's got the stuff. You want a piece?"

"I'll get it," Deuce says moving down the street. "Don't—hey, hold it," he yells at the one called Retard. "Leave 'em in there a minute."

"Jew get the mother fuckers?"

"Yeah. I got six. That twenty-two ain't worth jack shit but I brought it. Fucking piece of shit."

"Give it to Larry, he can't hit shit anyway with the sonofabitch."

"I ain't got a piece," one of the bikers says, coming up to the men.

"Here." Deuce picks a revolver out of the bag and puts it in the man's hand.

"Fucker's loaded?"

"Yeah."

"Who else ain't got a piece? Find out."

"Huh?"

"Fuck it—never mind," the busy general. "Hey, Billy." The biker approached him. "Go ask around to see who ain't carrying somethin'. Tell Nitro and Jim come here."

"*Hey, Nitro!*" the man starts yelling.

"Shaddup you fuck," Deuce stage-whispers, "go *tell* the son of a bitch, goddammit, don't yell it. Shit, if I wanted that shit I could yell the fucking shit myself. Jesus." He shook his head as the large, bearded man shrugged and moved off.

"Deuce, Earl ain't got nothin' but a knife."

"Here." He handed a small foreign automatic to the man and stuck a western-style double-action piece in his belt. Then changed his mind and handed it to the man. "Give one to Earl and see who else ain't packin'."

"Earl ain't gonna' be packin' even after I give the motherfucker a piece," and everyone around close enough to hear began laughing hysterically, Earl having been notoriously short-changed in the masculine-equipment department.

"Where the fuck's Nitro and Jimbo?"

"They're comin. Jim's movin' the ten-wheeler like you wanted."

"Oh, yeah?"

"You need sum'pin, pard?" a hideously scarred face whispered in Deuce's ear, causing him to flinch, which made them both laugh. "Sorry about that."

"That's cool. Soon as Jim comes over we'll go over the shit. Everybody here?"

"Damn straight. Let's go get the motherfucker."

"Deuce," a young, long-haired biker said as he came running across the street. "I got the old Ford loaded with shit and it's up on top of the middle manhole."

"Let's go, Jimbo." Deuce gathered his lieutenants around him and traced a large cross in the dust of a car hood. "Nitro, you take Billy and them dudes and you start here." He pointed to one end of the line he'd drawn. From the air, if you could see through the street, you would know that the holes did not run straight at each other, parallel to the street itself, but were angled in a *Y* shape, but they saw it as a straight line from their street-level point of view. "Over there where the parking lot starts."

"Hey, Deuce. It's on down there. That manhole is on down over in the next block, way ov—"

"Who's fuckin' this goddamn chicken anyway, goddammit, you want to run this motherfucker?"

"Fuck no, I just—"

"Hey! Larry." A tall man yelled yo, and Deuce said, "Where's that old—what's his fuckin' name, Bugs Bunny or whatever. *Woody,* yeah—Woody, where's that fucker?"

"I'm right here, Mr. Younger," the wino said pleasantly, visions of three hundred dollars dancing in his head, with the promise of an elusive and coveted boner not far behind.

"Where'd jew say that big cocksuck comes up?"

"Right here." Albert Sharma pointed to their right, and down the block over there. "That manhole there. I'll betcha' he's down there right—"

"Yeah. Right. Cool, later. Goddammit, take 'em on down there, go ahead, when you get there start in toward this way, making sure it ain't one of us, goddammit. You see some shadows or some shit, don't just start fucking blastin' or some of us'll get hit in the cross fire. We'll start here—and we'll come toward you—and if his ass is in there, we'll catch him in the middle. Right, Jim, you've worked down in those whores—can he get out?"

"Naw. We'll box the motherfucking cocksucker up good and whack his fat ass out, man. He can't come up the hole here so he's gotta' go one way or the fucking other—right?"

"Yeah, okay, let's *go!*"

Someone shouts as he starts moving, *"Deuce! Hold it!"*

"Now what?"

"Wouldn't it be better if we'd blow some fuckin' smoke or somethin' down in there, start fires at either end and burn his ass out."

"Yeah, we can SMOKE the motherfuck out."

"SMOKE the cunt out," somebody else offers. They're less than anxious to go down after him in the dark sewers and water mains but the fearless leader screams:

"Fuck that shit, take it to his ass!" And the Flames shout back to a man, chains, clubs, handguns ready, Nitro and Jim pry hooks under their respective covers, and nineteen men, the Flames MotorCycle Club of Oldtown, nineteen experienced, veteran street fighters, lanterns and flashlights casting spooky beams down into the inky black, lower themselves below the streets of Chicago to do battle and seek revenge.

And Dr. Geronimo and Woody Woodpecker, standing "safely" away from the action, are suddenly blown off their feet in a horrible, indescribable explosion that is really many explosions but so closely timed that they sound like one fantastic sublevel blast ripping through feet of concrete like an awful earthquake, cracking the city street beneath them in booming and deafening explosion and a violent shower of broken concrete and twisted steel pipe and ball bearings and cement and metal and blood and guts and all in a screaming cataclysm that is all the more terrifying because it comes out of nowhere, comes from silent tripwires that trigger U.S. military waterproof/weatherproof ring-release fuse igniter that drives firing pin against primer which ignites a five component powder-core sparking cannon fuse, and comes from nonelectric chemical pyrotechnic ignition matches tripwired by a battery that causes the detonation of blasting caps, and comes from command-detonated claymores synched into a perimeter-attack mode, and imagine two loaded 12-gauge shotguns . . . Rack a shell into each weapon . . . Now drop nine cockroaches into one barrel . . . ten in the other . . . Put the guns in workbench vises facing each other and

weld the two barrels pointing into each other's bore
. . . Using a trigger-wired remote firing device, simultaneously pull the two triggers firing the weapons into themselves at the same precise millisecond. *BBBBBB-BBBBBLLLLLLLLLLLLLLLLLLLLLAAAAAAAA-AAAAAAMMMMMMMMMMMMMMMM!*

This is how you make nineteen cockroaches *all* fucked up.

Chaingang,
Edie, and
Lee Anne

He knows nothing of biker gangs or bearded, leather-jacketed, chopper-riding Flames. To him they belong in the same shit pile with all those other slam-dancing pogoing spike-haired punks. Just another punk. If his trap takes nineteen bikers, nineteen undercover cops, nineteen rock-and-rollers, nineteen midget flute players, he has no interest. Just let the little death pies claim punks.

He drives through strange, unfamiliar, hostile streets now, and he knows that each time he takes a vehicle he comes closer to the red line. He can only go to the well so many times. Of no consequence. His red-hot kill hunger has fastened on the newspaper story. The grainy photo and the words the lies the absurd and maddening shit is burned into his head, engraved on his twisted thoughts, branded into the soul of a thing that lives only to punish and destroy.

His plan is to take the cop. You . . . I will take you . . . He concentrates on this thorn in his side. This lying and arrogant implement of those castrated, suited punks he so abominates. He will show this spineless, posturing liar what it is to taste pure terror. He will bait his trap with the punk's squeeze and make him beg for her.

Cigar-thick killer's fingers squeeze the high-impact

plastic of the steering wheel so hard that he suddenly realizes what he is doing and relaxes his grip before he cracks the wheel into pieces. He would like to make the man watch him with the woman and then take those fingers and pull the rib cage loose so that he could rip the skin and penetrate the cavity where the life source pumps the liar's bodily fluids and the hot, surging thing suffuses him washing over him and he wills the control back. He will find a place and wait for the cloak of darkness to conceal his initial recon probe.

He comes first in the night. His one-man ambush. Stalking. Isolating his prey. Surveilling. Looking for sign. Movement. The telltale signature of another watcher. The parked van or truck or passenger car. The out-of-place thing. The lay of the land. The way it tasted. The exit routes. The means of infiltration exfiltration. The emergency options. The heartbeat stilled, slowed, breathing great inhalations of air in deep, slow, measured, easy, ominous risings and fallings of the barrel chest and enormous gut. Holding the oxygen in there for a long time then releasing it. Contained. Quiet. Motionless. Impervious. Invulnerable. Sniffing the night smells. Scanning for sign. Feeling for the pulse beat of humans. Listening for voices, vehicles, man-made sounds, intrusions upon the night chorus of crickets singing counterpoint to the suburban, batrachian murmur of vertebrate amphibians. Tick . . . Tick . . .

Satisfied, he returns to the stolen vehicle and heaves his bulk into the seat with a groan and crash of mashed springs. He grinds the car to life and heads for a motel with VACANCY neon. He finds a small suitable motel where they probably won't ask too many questions and rings the night bell. The man in his bathrobe fortunately doesn't look before he pushes the buzzer and Chaingang enters the office lobby in a swirl of sewer stink.

"Aw, Jeezus!" the man says aloud before he can catch himself. "You musta jus' got off work."

"Yeah. Want a room just for tonight," he rumbles.

"Pay in advance," and he throws down some twenty dollar bills on the counter.

"Umm." The man eyes the crumpled, filthy bills and forces himself to pick up the money. He wonders how long it will take to get the smell out of the room. But he is afraid to tell the fat man he is full up. Besides there are only two cars out front. He pushes the register over for Chaingang to sign, which he does carefully, printing his newly acquired license-plate number and some other fictitious identification.

The man slides a room key toward him and says, "Checkout time is eleven sharp."

"Yeah." He thinks how easily he could waste the man, grabbing his head by the jug-handle ears and slamming it down onto the counter, how pleasant it would be to see the face bloody the glass countertop and to bang it into the glass again, and again, and then to snap his neck the way you would break a rotten broom handle, snapping it over your leg, hearing the satisfying bonebreak and the scream of pain, and then putting his lights out for good.

But he is here on important killing business. And he will save this filth for another time, not letting himself think about the way the man looked at him when he first came in so that the red tide will not wash over him and force him to do bad things now.

He goes into the room and removes his filthy coveralls, which he pitches into a wastebasket and heads for the bathroom. He pisses into the sink, letting his smelly urine splash down the sides and onto the bathroom floor and lets a trickle of pee strafe the tissue dispenser for no particular reason.

He turns on the hot water and steps into the shower stall, soaping as much of the gigantic body as he can reach, and letting the thick coating of sewer filth wash off of him and turn the floor of the stall a poisonous-looking gray as he luxuriates in the soapy, unfamiliar warmth.

He will sleep well tonight. And either early in the morning or tomorrow afternoon he will take the woman and the girl. It will hinge on vibes, the extra sense he depends upon for his own survival. But—whenever—he will take them. They are less than two miles from the beast now and he sleeps dreamlessly, his inner clock wound to go off at six, only a few hours away.

And his mental clock is no joke but a very real thing that is inexplicable and so dead-on accurate it sometimes surprises even him with the precision of it. And he sits up at one minute before six, fully refreshed and ready. He can smell himself now for the first time in a long while, and he clomps into the shower again, allowing himself to drench the dirty carpeting in urine as he walks, a dimpled grin plastered across his face in joyous anticipation.

Twenty-seven minutes later he is waiting, parked down the street, and he sees the child emerge but the woman is silhouetted there in the door and then simultaneously another child next door and it doesn't feel right. He is only mildly disappointed. This afternoon will be the time. He knows that. He checks out of the motel to the clerk's silent prayer of gratitude and immediately checks into another one where he will rest and wait for this afternoon.

In the stolen vehicle parked a short distance from the Lynches he is waiting for the child when she returns from school. He appears to be reading a newspaper, a workman, no doubt, waiting for someone, but he is letting his currents flow into the trees around him. He has a strange and acute sense of being in harmony with nature. The life cycle of deciduousness, self-renewal, and virescence is a never-ending source of intense fascination for him. He prefers plant life to animals and animals to people. Humans are far, far down the evolutionary list for him.

Suddenly his senses are boring in on the little girl who is walking along the sidewalk toward where he is parked. She is with two other children, a boy and a girl, all talking at more or less the same time in loud, grating voices that annoy him. His sense of timing is sheer perfection. The little boy walks on past, the two girls say good-bye to each other, and as his target heads for the house he booms out at her in his deep voice:

"Hey? Excuse me," beckoning her over toward the car with the most radiant and endearing smile on his face. He knows precisely how others see him and he uses his appearance, when he wants to, with the actor's unerring command of kinematics and illusion. None but the most brainwashed and careful person would resist Daniel Bunkowski when he beckoned to them, smiling that dimpled, open, guileless, baby's beaming grin of a trustworthy uncle. And Lee Anne Lynch is a sweet child who has never met a stranger, as the saying goes, and a hundred warnings are forgotten in the urgent beckoning and sincere, warm smile, and she moves back toward the vehicle to hear what he's saying.

It comes out in a jumble of words, an avalanche of persuasion designed to befriend and bewitch, and she draws closer still, something about how you must be the Lynch girl, about how he's a good friend of Jack's, good ol' Jack, and how it is real important something something and she can't quite make out what he's saying and Lee Anne comes closer to the open window where he grins out at her, speaking so warmly, rapidly, and urgently about Jack and her Mom.

"What?" she ·asks, straining to hear as she moves closer.

"I said, Jack wants you to take this message to your mom. It's real important." His big paw holds a folded piece of paper but it is not stretched out as far as he can reach, it only appears that way. And when she reaches out to take the note from his hand, two things happen. His semicircular vision and 180-degree precognition observe and sense the absence of unwanted watchers and his mighty paw fastens around her tiny arm like a workbench vise, jerking her in through the open window as deftly as you'd lift a sack of potatoes, the heel of the other hand, which is a callused, steel-hard, fearsome thing smashing against her small chin with an almost dainty precision, knocking her unconscious.

And she is down on the floorboard and inert and in one sure movement he rips the thin material of her dress and is moving, out of the vehicle and heading in the direction of the house. The killer is moving fast. Moving through the yard quickly, surprisingly fast and quiet, big blimp body propelled forward on the huge, splayed feet, the rapid flat-footed sliding steps swiftly pulling the bulk like tugs leading a giant ship, guiding the vastness of the torso.

The impression is that of an unexpectedly graceful clown bear, agile fat man, dainty jumbo dancer, XXX-L shirt billowed like a sail or a moving tent, suggestions of agility and power, balance and an odd buoyancy, as the treetrunk legs move the great weight of body toward the house in a massive, unstoppable effort, the big man's compass needle drawn by the magnetic pull of a human heartbeat.

He will take the woman and the child down into the special place he's made for them in a water main. And that is where he will summon the know-it-all cop, and we'll see how he likes it when he comes down to get his whore and the brat, see how he likes it down in the secret subworld. He moves across the yard toward the house where the woman is, already tasting them and grinning with the pleasure of the moment.

Hemo-craving and insatiable, he moves toward the woman, who is unknowingly pulling him to her. And the pulsing, steady throb of a heart is the beat that makes his bloodlust dance.

Jack Eichord
and
Chaingang

What the CIA is to the Girl Scouts of America, what NSA is to CIA, what Lee Iacocca was to Mad Man Cal's Used Cars, that is roughly what director of special intelligence/Illinois Public Utilities, is to a subway cop. This individual, nicknamed Captain Sewer by his senior staff members, was the head of the intelligence division of the Chicagoland utilities oligopoly.

For many years each of the big utilities companies has maintained an extremely secret, highly sensitive office. The purpose of each office is the gathering of raw intelligence, threat assessment, and—for want of a better umbrella name—countermeasures. Countermeasures for the "phone company," for example, have become quite aggressive out there on the sharp, cutting edge. No one speaks of these special departments and in fact many of the employees of these vast, conglomerate corporations remain ignorant of their respective existence. But exist they do.

The intelligence divisions all mesh in a central office called Special Intelligence/Illinois Public Utilities, and the director of this top-secret outfit was briefing Eichord when Jack took the call.

"So what you're looking at here," he was saying as they studied an unfathomably complex map of interweaving lines, "would be the location of the laterals for Site Y Branch Line. And this where you see the catch basins marked is where—" when he was interrupted by his aide, who motioned that the call was for Jack.

"Jack Eichord?" Jack said tentatively, picking up the telephone on the other man's desk, surprised to be getting a call in the director's office.

"Yeah, it's me," Arlen told him. "Jack, you've got an emergency personal. You need to go out to the car and take this on two."

"Affirmative. Lou, who is it? D'ya know?"

"No. They've got it downstairs. I just found you for 'em. They'll be putting you through on a special patch."

"Thanks." He turned to the man. "Sorry, I'll have to get back to you." He was moving. "Some sort of an emergency thing, I apologize"—in motion and out the door even as he spoke, the words thrown like a handful of coins crashing out into the room behind him as he sprinted out of there, saying "sorry" and hearing the one they called Captain Sewer mumbling something to him but he was already gone and down on the pavement and running to the car.

Waiting now, as a patch-plugged call on the switchboard landline was laboriously (in seconds) rerouted through his tactical command radio and knowing then it was bad when he said "hello" hearing Edie breathe his name into the other end of a line somewhere.

"Jack . . ." A word that she sobbed, cried out, crying literally, crying as if in pain and he knew it was bad and he was afraid then. Afraid of what the next words would be and he could feel his inner demons gloating as they grabbed his guts and squeezed them and twisted.

He felt time compress in that awful way time sometimes can. Felt one second become an hour in an hour that would last an eternity, felt time wrap itself into a fetal ball and freeze in that position. Felt it crawl to a standstill as he heard her sob his name. Heard the demons roaring in stop-time.

Do you believe in black magic? Had she called him

up from the dark place—conjured him, it almost seemed—made this happen by seeing the grainy photo of his ugliness for the first time. Forced Jack to show it to her, the thing that had taken Ed and turned his life source into a bloody mess of gristle and torn meat. And when she had seen the picture, it was almost as if she'd made it happen. Because within hours he had Lee and he had her. He had them both to *use*.

She had been so easy. She had seen one of her familiar shadows at the window and knew exactly who it was out there, lurking in the darkness of the shaded yard as the kids trudged home from school—it was Weirdo—her old friend back to pay her a social call. And she had felt no fear, only anger and a bit of remorse but then more anger as she stomped out of the back door and around the house to confront the old pervert and he had taken her in midthought, catching her in the air as she was moving, that is, with a huge paw over her mouth, her body suddenly propelled backward through the air as if by dark magic.

He was pulling her back inside as easily as if he had been carrying a fifty-pound feed sack, effortlessly, and she felt like her neck was going to snap as he carried her right back in, back toward the center of the house and then holding her, with her hands tearing at him, whispering awful things to her, telling her how it would be, telling Edie the terrible things about her daughter, the evil that would befall them if Mommy didn't come with him quietly, a big smile for the neighbors to see.

The horror that she'd summoned up with no more than a stare into an old and grainy photo, the horror had come to take her away. And it had her lovely little child as well, and then it showed her something that was so ugly she couldn't believe the sordid, ugly, nastiness of an ordinary object. He fished a little torn scrap of cloth out of his pocket and held it under her nose and she saw immediately that it was part of Lee Anne's pink skirt that she'd had on at school today and she knew that the horror had the child and she nodded a grim compliance.

And instantly she was moving and a smile forced itself across her face as he whispered S M I L E roughly to her through fierce, gritted teeth, guiding her by the arms with just the proprietary helpfulness you'd expect of a friend, nothing to arouse suspicions from a casual onlooker, and suddenly she was in with Lee and being forced down to the floor and feeling a rope biting into her flesh, and a filthy gag going into her mouth and hearing the engine come to life beside her and feeling them pull away from the safety of her world.

"Jack," she cried, and sobbed out a sentence to him and he couldn't make out a single word of it. "Jack, Jack . . ." She was crying and for a few seconds he let her cry, the thing that was holding her beside a phone somewhere and then he did something to her to make her scream out in pain and he heard her fighting to regain control of herself and she sobbed out "I—oh, I, uh, Jack . . . Oh God . . . Ah—ahhhhhhh —he haaaaaa—he has *Lee,* ahhhhh, I had to . . . *AHHHHHH* help me I . . . Oh, Jack help me PLLLEEEEEEASE I'm sorry oh, I'm sorry"—and then losing it again and hearing her being pulled away and struck and the phone crashing down and a sharp, metallic noise and her sobbing again, and then a quiet, and the thing speaks to Eichord.

"You there?"

"Yes," he replied to the surprisingly deep voice. "I can hear you," he added inanely, his mind freezing from the shock of the moment.

"Listen. Don't bring more police. You come alone or they die, and I let your whore suck me while I eat the rat's heart." That's what Jack thought he'd said for a second then realized he had called Lee Anne a brat. He would eat the brat's heart. Is that what he said? Why would he want to do that? He was fighting to get his brain working. He felt paralyzed. Drunk. He felt as if he was absolutely paralyzed with booze. He couldn't think, move. He strained against the phone, crushing the receiver to his ear before he realized he was holding a two-way radio mike in his hand as the call sizzled on the speaker of the police radio.

"What?"

"You heard me. Don't bother tracing this. And don't be stupid. If I see others, these bitches die bad." The horror gave a location and Jack laid the mike on the seat and started the car, grinding into the ignition having forgotten it was already running, slamming the gear shift down as he screeched out into the traffic, telling himself to breathe deeply and take in some oxygen and get that brain going. Brain dead. That was the only phrase that occurred to him. The patient is brain dead.

The genius cop, Jack Eichord, the crime crusher of all time. Bulldog fucking Drummond and nothing was working up there. Total zero. A cipher between the ears. Come *on*, for Christ's sake. He was staring at the windshield wipers whipping ridiculously across the windshield, mesmerized by the blades, and then shaking it off like water as he became aware he'd somehow managed to turn on the wipers and headlights and correcting that as he sped through the traffic without his redball on. He could hear the voice all deep and bloodchilling, an accentless rumble of words that still resonated in his head as he drove.

"Mommy . . ." he heard somehow, on a wavelength man has yet to discover, imagining he could hear Lee saying to her mother, "It's wet here," and the horror of it was beyond him and miraculously it all just passed over him and he had shrugged off the paralysis and personal fear and just stood on the brakes, a Charger slamming into him and a potential whiplash case trying to see his license to report him to the police even as he Brodie'd and swung into a hard U-turn against the honking, furious traffic, the wildly angry Chicago motorists—as he started back toward where he should have headed all along to get what he needed to make the horror do as he would wish.

The thoughts he had in the interminable six or seven minutes before he finally got to the place where the monster was waiting for him were all business thoughts. He had his main weapon now and it was loaded in a box with a handle that sat on the seat beside him. And in the backseat was a crudely hacksawed riot gun which he was debating about shoving down into his belt. And in the seat he had a box of twelve-gauge 00 buck "maggies" open and he had his speedloaders out and even as he was pulling the car over to the curb he was putting a speedloader in each pocket and pulling the shotgun over to him and getting out.

And he took the shotgun, which wasn't even a Remington, just some old pawnshop Winchester Defender that he'd taken a hacksaw to, and pulled his belt as tight as it would go and shoved it down in back, pointing down. It was nothing more than the grip, trigger assembly, and the hot loads. Two ugly mags in between his fingers like cigars, five of the hot twelve-pellet loads inside, and he racked it back, fingering the safety off and dropping both the extras he had in his left hand in the street in his nervousness. Easing the piece out of his nice leather holster and letting it slide in gently as it could, wondering if the S.W.A.T. boys and a tac unit would be coming up smoking and ruining everything any second as he removed the carrying case from the front seat. It was heavier than he had expected and the movement inside made it even harder to carry the weight.

"Hey!" the deep voice shouted to him. "Get over here." And it was all happening in broad daylight and it wasn't a monster at all, but a regular human being he had just seen, and the head disappeared back down into the manhole. How the hell had he crammed his bulk through that tiny hole? Eichord wondered. And he sat his box down by the side of the open manhole and gently eased the shotgun out, knowing now that it would be useless, and he placed it beside the box. Then the man called up to him from the darkness below, the voice like a peal of thunder, a deep, strong, metallic clapping boom.

"I don't know what you have in there but don't

touch it again. Climb down the ladder unless you want me to twist the head off this skinny cunt," he shouted up savagely to Jack.

"I can't see, please! Wait!" Jack shone a flashlight down into the hole, shouting, "You want me to climb down there?"

"*Get that light out of my eyes and get down here!*" the man bellowed at him. But he'd already spotted the woman was behind him and still alive. "*Don't mess with me or I'll kill her—NOW!*" he warned, and he did something to Edie and she screamed and Jack reached into the box and grabbed the first soft thing he touched and flung it into the hole.

"See that. I've got a whole *box* of them. Do you understand me, you big, fat *tub of shit—a whole box of them.*" He was shaking now and reached down into the box and grabbed another one of the little, furry things and flung it, wiggling down into the hole. He was gambling with lives now and it had to be just right. Just believable enough so that the man would buy it and come for him. The second one was enough and he heard a bull roar of anger.

"*I'll KILL these bitches if you throw another one of them down here!*"

"*Listen, you mountain of blubber, for every fucking second you keep them down there I'll break a paw on one of these mutts and send it down to you do you hear me? Every second you sonofabitch I'm counting to ten now and if I don't see the little girl and the woman up here I start breaking paws. You want proof? Listen.*"

He reached in and did something and one of the little puppies in the box screamed in pain and Chaingang bellowed:

"ALL RIGHT GODDAMN YOU COCKSUCK DON'T HURT THE DOGS HERE THEY COME UP NOW DON'T HURT"—and his head was in the opening and his chain boloing out at Eichord like a silver lightning bolt him coming up that ladder faster than any living person had ever seen him move before, churning and charging upward on those great tree trunks of legs, the links of the chain catching on the lip of the manhole as he tried to fling it out and Jack shooting him three times as fast as he could pull the trigger, hitting him in the face with the first shot and two more times and Jack making himself move now as the man fell back down into the darkness with a loud, resounding splash and first trying to climb down the ladder facing forward and not being able to and half turning, going down with his flashlight beaming down into the stench and seeing Lee bound and gagged and the woman all right then, and saying to them:

"Oh! Okay baby, we'll get you out of here now." Going to her with the gun and light on the monster and taking her and starting to work on Lee's rope as he came up out of the puddle of slime again, rising up and charging a roaring rhino-sized freight train of death screaming down on them in the close foulness of the hole, one cheek blown away, tough Kevlar body armor taking the other two rounds, and Jack icy, calm, shooting him at point blank range, the mad monstrosity roaring, steaming, bellowing, reaching for Jack even as he missed with his fifth shot, his fingers grabbing Eichord in that powerful and deadly vise grip as Jack squeezed off the top last round into this human beast.

And, oblivious to Lee Anne, who had curled into a tight, frightened ball, and to her mother's screams, snapping a speedloader into the piece and his hands shaking so badly missing and letting the precious live shells splash down into the stinking goo, and then forcing himself to move precisely and taking out the last speedloader, like a blind man fitting the shells down into the cylinder with his fingers and releasing the device, closing the cylinder tightly, feeling it click and then move that millimeter more and stop, and placing the barrel in what was left of the mouth of Daniel Bunkowski and firing blindly, not able to see or wanting to, firing, holstering the piece and working on getting them out of there, the loudness of the reports like cannon shots exploding and echoing in their pummeled, deafened eardrums.

Then he had Edie moving up the ladder and climbing out onto the pavement where she lay right beside the open manhole and the box of puppies from the Humane Society, sobbing, cars going by. And Jack brought Lee Anne out, carrying her like a rolled-up rug, and helping Edie up, and all of them blinking in the bright sunlight as they moved toward the curb and Jack got them inside and called it in. He had to force himself to keep moving. He knew if he stopped he wouldn't be able to make himself go back down and he had to get the two pups.

He had to breathe very deeply to keep from getting sick, and he started back down the ladder. He felt a swirl of water eddying around his feet as he quickly gathered up the small dogs and started back up to the street. The water was rushing through now, coming from a nearby pumping station through the branch lines and into the submains. But Eichord was back up and the puppies were safe. They appeared to be okay.

Below, the water level continued rising as the dark swirl washed over the huge carcass and then it gave the body more buoyancy and the eddying force pulled the motionless shape farther down, sucking it into the inky darkness of the water main.

"Where's the DB?" the first evidence technician asked.

"Down there." Eichord gestured toward the manhole.

"If that main connects into the storm drains and all, no telling where he'll end up."

"Probably turn up as a floater," Eichord told him, "out in the lake."

"Could be," the tech said, looking down into the darkly swirling water. "Probably end up down in the sewer system with the rest of the giant alligators and shit."

"I hear that all right," Jack said, tilting his head.

"Oh well."

"Right. Good luck," he said as he headed for the car where the woman and child sat huddled in blankets.

"You too," the man said.